The Fina

Jenny Blackhurst lives in Shropshire where she grew up dreaming that one day she would get paid for making up stories. She is an avid reader and can mostly be found with her head in a book or hunting Pokemon with her son, otherwise you can get her on Twitter @JennyBlackhurst or Facebook. Her favourite film is Fried Green Tomatoes at the Whistle Stop Cafe, but if her children ask it's definitely Moana.

Also by Jenny Blackhurst

How I Lost You
The Foster Child
Before I Let You In
The Night She Died
The Perfect Guests
The Girl Who Left
The Hiking Trip
The Summer Girl
The Final Wife

THE FINAL WIFE

JENNY BLACKHURST

CANELO

First published in the United Kingdom in 2025 by

Canelo, an imprint of
Canelo Digital Publishing Limited,
20 Vauxhall Bridge Road,
London SW1V 2SA
United Kingdom

A Penguin Random House Company

The authorised representative in the EEA is Dorling Kindersley Verlag GmbH. Arnulfstr. 124, 80636 Munich, Germany

Copyright © Jenny Blackhurst 2025

The moral right of Jenny Blackhurst to be identified as the creator of this work has been asserted in accordance with the Copyright, Designs and Patents Act, 1988.

All rights reserved. No part of this publication may be reproduced or transmitted in any form or by any means, electronic or mechanical, including photocopy, recording, or any information storage and retrieval system, without permission in writing from the publisher.

No part of this book may be used or reproduced in any manner for the purpose of training artificial intelligence technologies or systems. In accordance with Article 4(3) of the DSM Directive 2019/790, Canelo expressly reserves this work from the text and data mining exception.

A CIP catalogue record for this book is available from the British Library.

Print ISBN 978 1 80436 511 3
Ebook ISBN 978 1 80436 512 0

This book is a work of fiction. Names, characters, businesses, organizations, places and events are either the product of the author's imagination or are used fictitiously. Any resemblance to actual persons, living or dead, events or locales is entirely coincidental.

Cover design by Lisa Brewster

Cover images © Depositphotos and Shutterstock

Printed and bound in Great Britain by Clays Ltd, Elcograf S.p.A.

Look for more great books at
www.canelo.co
www.dk.com

To my eternal first reader, Laetitia. Let's do it all again, shall we?

Chapter One

Present

There was *so much* blood. It pumped through my fingers, warm and slick as I pressed down on the gaping wound in his stomach, trying to undo what had already been set in motion. But it was too late, he was going to die. That had been the plan all along, of course, but it had never really hit me before just what that meant, what that would look like, what it would feel like to watch as the life slipped from his eyes. How could you be so intimate with someone and not hurt at the thought of them not being in the world anymore? I wondered who I would be now, without my love for him, and without my hatred of him, both tethering me to life like an anchor.

He did this to us, I forced myself to think, before I could allow myself to feel any regret. Regret was useless now, it wouldn't save his life, or mine. *It was his choices that led us here, not mine.*

A sound gurgled in his throat, like he was choking on his own saliva. Oh God, I couldn't bear it if he spat blood at me. This was too raw, too much.

'Luke?' I leaned in close to hear him speak. 'What is it?'

The flagstone floor was cold and hard underneath my knees. I had loved this floor. I'd loved everything about the holiday cottage in the Cotswolds, from the country style kitchen with its navy Farrow and Ball cupboards and thick oak worktops, to the black AGA that we'd used to dry our socks after muddy walks in the hills, and the copper pans that hung from the ceiling. It had all been so perfectly styled, like everything in Luke's life – from the outside. Even the indoor plants were fake, although they looked real until you got very, very close and realised they didn't smell, didn't rip if you crumpled them between your fingers.

'What is it?' I stroked his forehead and leaned in closer. 'Luke?'

His lips were next to my ear now and I expected to hear him say that he would always love me, no matter what I had done. I knew that he loved me, despite all that we had been through. He was mine and I was his, he had promised me that in the hills surrounding this very house more than once. There was only me, he'd said. Only me who'd mattered, anyway. But he'd been lying then like he lied every time, to all of us. He'd told all of us the same. One after the other we had been wound into his web of deceit. One of us had had to break the spell.

My silent tears rolled into his dark hair. *What have I done?*

'Game.' Luke's voice was hoarse, barely above a whisper. He coughed, a spray of blood hitting my cheek. 'Game over.'

Yes, it was almost over, but not quite. As his eyes closed I laid his head down on the cold floor. I had work to do.

Chapter Two

Rebecca

I'm already awake before my phone even rings, the high-pitched tone piercing the early morning silence. As I fumble around in the darkness to lay my fingers on it Jimmy lets out a vulgar snort and rolls over without opening his eyes.

'Dance,' I answer, not bothering to keep my voice down. Jimmy is near impossible to wake, especially given the amount he drank last night.

'You asking?' is the predictable reply. Like most things, the joke is even less funny at – I check the clock – 2.45 am. Eurgh, no wonder it's so dark.

'Well?'

'Domestic stabbing. Matthews is going straight to the crime scene, wants you to meet him there.'

'Suspect in custody?'

'On the way.'

'Fine.'

He reels off an address and I hang up the call without saying goodbye. Rolling myself up off the bed I give Jimmy a poke. 'Oi. *Oi*.'

I've tied back my unruly dark brown curls, washed and dressed and am pulling on my boots before Jimmy opens his left eye in response to my incessant poking.

'Eh?'

'Get dressed,' I tell him. 'I have to go to work.'

'What time is it?' Jimmy rubs his eyes, his expression confused. Side note: Jimmy's expression is rarely anything but confused. 'Can't I just stay here until morning?'

'No. Get up.' I finish lacing my boot and start on the other one. 'You've got until the kettle boils, then I'm gone and you're on the doorstep with or without your pants.'

I'm stirring the third sugar into my coffee when Jimmy appears in the doorway looking dishevelled and half asleep – but at least he's dressed.

'I don't understand why I can't stay in bed and let myself out,' he complains. I hand him a mug of coffee, strong enough for a spoon to stand up straight. 'It's not like I'm going to nick your TV.'

'You really don't know, Jimmy?' I narrow my eyes at him. 'I'm a police officer. I can't have you flogging your gear from my flat. Don't bother denying it—' I cut him off before he can protest. 'I don't give a shit if you move a bit of weed in your spare time, do I? I just don't want you doing it from my humble abode, okay?'

Jimmy grins. His smile is one of the reasons I end up in bed with the feckless idiot time and time again. He ruffles his dark hair. 'Yeah, sure. Can I at least get a lift home? Pretty little thing like me shouldn't be walking the streets at this hour alone.'

'You won't be alone,' I say, grabbing my keys and gesturing my head towards the door. 'You've got your massive ego to keep you company. Do you think you can get a move on though? I don't really want to risk my neighbours seeing us together.'

Chapter Three

Rebecca

We turn up at the cottage in the Cotswolds before the sun has bothered to make an appearance. On a regular autumn day it would be another few hours before I'd even be thinking about getting up, either warm in my bed or on the sofa, depending on whether I'd managed to sleep at all, dreaming about how at nearly thirty years old I could be DCI by now, or some entrepreneur business mogul, if only I had the willpower to struggle my ass out of bed right this minute and go for a run, mumble some affirmationy type shit about my perfect day being just a manifestation away and then take a sadistic cold shower. Instead – and we're talking every morning without fail – I manage to convince myself that after the week I've had I deserve that extra ten minutes under the covers. Who knows what I might have to deal with today? Best I'm fully rested.

Not today, though. Because Mrs and Mrs Whitney didn't have the good grace to keep their row within a nine to five window, so as Matthews and I pull up at their Cotswolds holiday home after a forty-minute drive, I'm giving a massive yawn. At least I didn't fall asleep on the way here and drool on his window.

'Just getting it out now,' I say as my DCI 'call me Derek' Matthews raises his eyebrows at me. 'Don't want to look unprofessional, do we?'

'Heaven forbid,' he says, abandoning the car haphazardly across the driveway. Hopefully none of the forensic team have emergencies to attend before we get done.

Bushes grow wild around the stone-fronted house, ivy creeping up around the front door, but the lawns are immaculate – even the unkempt plants here are by design. It's too late for lots of colour and despite this being a second home someone has already put out some autumnal decorations, an orange, green and brown wreath on the sage green front door with a small heart-shaped window embedded in the grooves of the wood, ripped straight from the pages of *Country Home* magazine. There are fake pumpkins dotted around and a pile of logs stacked up by the front door. From the outside it looks like the perfect holiday home, not even the smallest hint of what may have happened within.

A uniformed officer is walking to meet us, the gravel crunching under his heavy boots. He looks fairly young but confident.

'Sir,' he says, shaking hands with Derek and nodding at me. 'PC Mason Hinds.'

'What do we have?' Matthews looks surprisingly bright and chipper given that he isn't usually a morning person, let alone a middle of the night one. He's even managed to find time to brush his thick grey hair and tuck his shirt into his trousers, covering the paunch that has got gradually more noticeable over the last year. Judging from the flask he's gripping in his hand like the Holy Grail he'd managed to wake his wife Rita up to see him off with a coffee. I think of Jimmy getting up to make me a cup of coffee to take to work. As if. I check my watch again. It's four forty, he'll have gone back to his pit and won't emerge until the time is in double figures. If you hadn't guessed by now, Jimmy is not the next Tony Robbins, or whoever the kids are watching on TikTok these days. Hell, he's not even the next Walter White. Jimmy is like comfy slippers, you're reluctant to chuck them out despite the numerous holes – but you know there is going to come a time when you have no choice but to replace them.

The PC reads from his notebook as though it's a takeout menu. 'Forty-three-year-old male, Luke Whitney, DOA following a domestic stabbing. The wife, Anna Whitney, is in custody. It's an open and shut one this, this is the couple's holiday home, Mrs Whitney called police here saying that she had stabbed her husband. When we arrived he was already in the ambulance and she was sat on the floor covered in his blood. She didn't deny that she'd done it and she was arrested on the spot. She's said nothing since but there was no one else in the property.'

Matthews almost groans – domestics are the bane of his life and obviously not what he'd been hoping for. I wonder what kind of homicide would have been acceptable to him. Maybe he only gets out of bed for a gruesome serial killer these days. He takes a sip of his drink and asks, 'What did she stab him with?'

'Wait,' I cut in, the perpetual frown I seem to wear like an accessory these days deepening. 'We're presuming it was her who stabbed him then? What happened to "assume nothing", guv?'

I can tell he's trying not to sigh. See, around here, I'm that annoying kid in class who puts their hand up and reminds the teacher they've forgotten to set homework. I see an open and shut case and I have to wedge the hinge. I am the perpetual fly in the orange juice.

'Fine, I'm assuming nothing. Why don't we see what Jack has to say?'

'Two cars on the drive,' I note, writing down the licence plates. 'Think they travelled here separately?'

'Maybe she planned to do a runner after she offed him,' Matthews grunted.

'But she chose to ring the police and turn herself in.'

We are signed in at the front door, decked out in our babygros and met almost immediately by Jack Brady, one of the best crime scene managers I've ever worked with. There isn't a new technology, test or thesis released without Jack having known about it for months already.

'Jack, you've already solved our case, I take it?' Derek says, giving the other man a friendly nod.

Jack frowns. 'Got a strange one here. You're going to love it.' He turns to me and lowers his voice. 'He isn't really. But *you* probably are.'

'Weird in what way?' Derek glares at me as if it's my fault the evidence I haven't seen yet is causing our star CSM problems.

'Don't tell us yet,' I say quickly. 'I need to go through it from the start.'

We step into the hallway, more glossy perfection. A dark wood dresser sits to the left, three photographs of Luke and Anna Whitney framed on top. In all three photos they are laughing and smiling at the cameras or each other, set against stunning backdrops, the beach, the mountains, the very house we are standing in. Anna is beautiful, and Luke picture perfect – if I didn't know who these people were I'd think they were the photos that came in the frame.

On the wall to my right are four coat hooks, although only one wax jacket and two scarves hang from them. An umbrella rests against the wall next to two pairs of clean wellies.

'So I come in,' I say to Matthews, stepping forward as though to demonstrate 'coming in'. 'And I hang up my coat on the hook. Except Anna's coat isn't there.'

'Maybe she's not as neat as you,' Matthews replies.

If he'd seen my flat he would realise how ridiculous that statement is, but okay, perhaps Anna didn't take off her coat as soon as she walked through the door, maybe it's hanging over the kitchen chairs or there's a special coat wardrobe that posh people have. People don't always behave in the way you would expect them to, I'll take that.

'Okay, so she still has her coat on. It's been freezing this week – she's got to have had a coat on.'

We don't know yet the exact sequence of events of last night, whether Anna and Luke went straight through to the kitchen, or whether they went upstairs to have sex. They might have watched TV until fifteen minutes before she stabbed him. Derek had wanted to get to the scene as soon as we got word that forensics were there, before we spoke to Anna. We only have twenty-four hours to release or charge her and a crucial part of that will be making sure the evidence at the crime scene fits what she's telling us.

The bulk of the activity is in the kitchen, where Luke was found, and Matthews gestures there now.

'Can I tell you now?' Brady sounds like an eager child waiting to open their Christmas presents.

'Okay fine,' I say. 'But don't go rushing around all over the place, you'll only confuse the gaffer.'

'Spoilsport,' he mutters. 'Right, fine. Can I start with the murder weapon?'

He leads us over to a pile of broken glass on the floor, the neck of a broken bottle of Budweiser bagged up on the kitchen island. He picks it up by the corner and holds it up for us to examine.

'What am I looking at?' Matthews says. 'And don't say a broken Bud bottle – I can figure that much myself.'

'I can tell you what you're not looking at,' Brady replies. 'Fingerprints. Not a one. We'll take it back for further analysis, obviously, but I know a cleaned murder weapon when I see one.'

'But the broken end is covered in blood.'

'Ding ding!' It's a testament to how the rest of the team are used to Jack, no one even looks up from what they're doing when he makes his stupid noise. 'So they just cleaned the prints off it. They weren't trying to hide the weapon, just their identification. Same with the phone.'

'The phone?'

'House phone was wiped clean.'

I raise my eyebrows and say, 'Ooh, interesting.'

'Interesting, my arse,' Matthews snaps. 'So she called 999 to confess to murder then wipes her fingerprints off the phone and the murder weapon? What is she playing at?'

'Maybe she knew that a confession wasn't enough to convict her?' Brady suggests.

'Then why confess in the first place? She was covered in his blood and there wasn't anyone else here,' Matthews sighs. 'Go on, what else?'

'Go and look in the sink.'

Matthews practically storms over to the Belfast sink and peers in. 'What about the sink?'

'Fucking hell, sir, it smells like a winery,' I practically choke. 'Someone's emptied a bottle of wine down there at least.'

'Maybe posh wine tastes like shit.'

'Or maybe someone was trying to make out more had been drunk than actually was,' Brady offers.

'I think he knows that,' I whisper before Matthews can start on any kind of tirade. He barely puts up with me being obtuse – two of us is really going to piss him off.

I look down to step on the silver floor plates that have been placed around the crime scene markers, and that's when I spot the bloody footprint.

'Um, Jack?'

I point down at the footprint and he nods.

'I was just getting to that. UK size ten from the measurements. The only footwear we've found for the victim is a pair of wellies by the door in a size twelve.'

'No other footwear for the victim?' I ask. 'That's weird. So you think we have an unidentified male at the scene?'

Jack nods. He was right, the scene is interesting. Unfortunately it seems to be throwing up more questions than answers and Matthews is hating it. He detests anything not adding up neatly, and currently not a single thing about this scene makes sense. Except to me. It all makes perfect sense to me, because I knew the minute I walked in that this crime scene was staged.

Chapter Four

Anna

When I'd watched *The Bill* in the past I'd always thought how uncomfortable police cells looked, wondered how the prisoners could sleep on those flat hard beds and sit for hours staring at the same bare stone walls. I know now. I mean of course you don't have a choice about being there, the police don't care that you've never stayed anywhere less comfortable than the Marriott, or that a hard mattress gives you a pain in your neck that's impossible to shift – but none of that matters, really. If you're in that cell your world is already falling apart. What difference would a comfortable mattress make to the fact that my husband is dead because of me? Would a continental breakfast and a robe make up for spending the rest of my life alone?

And yet I feel surprisingly numb. I'm not even afraid, which is the strangest part. If you'd ever asked me, at any point in my life, how scared I would be to be locked in a cell accused of murder the answer would be full-scale panic attack, trembling and vomiting terrified. Yet here I am, staring at the grubby, puke-coloured wall, and I feel nothing. Perhaps it's the shock. Can you think in full sentences when you're in shock? Or perhaps I'm just glad it's all over. I no longer have to second guess my husband's every move, analysing his every word, just waiting for him to pull the rug out from under me, the way he did to Rose. I thought I was so clever, so much better than she was. Isn't that a laugh? I'd always just had her down as some brain-dead bimbo who didn't have the foresight, didn't have the mental smarts to hold on to a man like Luke. The thing is, men like Luke will always have the upper hand, because whether we like it or not, everything always comes back to the money. You marry well, you think you have financial security, but financial safety doesn't exist when you have to rely on someone else for it. The dynamics change when one of you holds all of the earning potential. You, the pauper holding out your hand for scraps, you see every spat, every disagreement differently to them. It's a bigger deal to you, and in the end you stop disagreeing, because even though *they* might not realise it, in the back of your mind there is always the knowledge of how easily you could be cast aside, how easily they discarded their last marriage without so much as a glance in the rear-view. I think, looking back, that's why Luke never wanted children. Everyone knows that it's the children who give the women power – fathers have to provide for their offspring, of course. But without a child a stay-at-home-wife is dispensable; agree a decent settlement, sure, but a one-off payment to someone who has been out of work to cook your dinner and iron your clothes for years doesn't exactly cut it, does it? Anyway, I'm rambling. Maybe it's the shock. Or maybe they're right about me, maybe I really have gone mad.

But for the first time in a long time, it feels like I can breathe. I'm not plotting my next move, or anticipating Luke's. Of course now I'm fighting for my freedom, but there is a not-so-small part of me that wants them to take it from me. Lock me up, take away my responsibility. The rest of my life not having to care about what those stuck-up assholes at the golf club think about me anymore. I would be forgotten in no time, an after-dinner anecdote for a while but eventually, no one. A ghost. The very idea sounds quite appealing.

How did I get here? If you could have seen us six months ago you would have thought we had the world. I've got the time, I could tell you the whole story. A story of betrayal, murder and the games we play with the people we love. But be warned, you're only getting one side of the story. And everyone knows there are three sides to a story. His side, my side, and the truth.

—

The first time I saw Luke and Rose Whitney was a Friday night in early October, seven years ago. A twenty-eight-year-old admin assistant by day, my evenings were spent working the night shift at Benicio's, an upmarket restaurant in Faringdon, to get enough money together for a deposit on a place of my own. After my dad died his landlord had been pretty good about letting me take over his tenancy, and every morning I'd wake up and make myself breakfast in the kitchen where my father had taken his own life. It was a miserable existence so I worked to avoid being at home, and the flipside of that was that I was slowly getting the money together to leave behind the place I'd grown up in and all its shitty memories. Besides, I quite liked waiting on people. I treated it as less of a job and more of a game, like I was six years old and just playing at having to wear a uniform and serve from the left, clear from the right. I was good at basically being invisible to the patrons, who wanted their dinner served to them quickly and without interrupting their conversation. I always remembered who had ordered what and so I slipped the plates onto the tables and poured the wine and they never had to call me back to complain. The chefs liked me, they would let me plate up the desserts sometimes and always plated me up a meal to take home. They didn't do that for everyone.

I don't suppose I'm painting quite the picture of wealth and privilege one would expect from a woman with a holiday home in the Cotswolds, even one who stands accused of murder. The fact is that until I met Luke I was a girl going nowhere, on a hiding to nothing, my dad would say. I often wondered, afterwards, what Dad would have thought of Luke. Would he be as taken in by him as everyone else was? Would he congratulate me on how well I'd done, as if it had taken blood, sweat and tears to bag myself a wealthy surgeon to secure my financial future, instead of being in the right place at the right time?

The truth is, there were no bolts of lightning, no sting of Cupid's arrow when I first saw Luke Whitney. No love at first sight, well, not for me at least, but I realised afterwards that something in me sparked something in him, and I was never fully sure what it was. He decided that first night, I think, that he was going to have me, and much like everything in his life he believed he would get what he wanted. Maybe if I'd been a little more worldly-wise I could have spotted upfront what he was planning, and if I had I'm certain things would have been different. My whole life would have been different, because one thing's for certain – and Rose will say different but I don't care – I never, not for one second, set out to steal her husband. Or anyone's husband. If she knew me she'd know why, not that I think it would make much difference to how she feels about me. She is always going to hate my guts, and I can't exactly blame her.

So on that Friday Benicio's was *tabled out*, as we used to say – which basically meant that all of the tables were full. The kitchen was especially hot and noisy and the chef was in a foul mood, even with me who he was usually quite sweet with. I was dying to slip outside for a cigarette but there were only four of us working the floor that night, me, Abby, Ellen and Tom and no chance I would be getting off the floor anytime soon. Two people had just not bothered to turn up and no one else had wanted to cover at last minute on a Friday night, the bastards hadn't even answered their phones. So the four of us were doing the best we could – or three of us were, and Abby was just being her usual incompetent self, mixing up the table numbers, using her own brand of shorthand on the order slip rather than our agreed language, sending bread rolls flying across the room like mini bowling balls. So the first time I saw the man who was to become my future husband was when I handed his wife a meal that could have killed her.

'Erm, is there soy sauce in here?'

I'd already turned to leave the table, so I looked back at the woman who had spoken, seeing her properly for the first time, and instantly I was struck by how unnatural she looked. Not that she was unattractive – on the contrary, I was sure plenty of men would have thought her incredibly attractive; it was just that there wasn't a bit of her beauty that hadn't been purchased over the counter. Her poker-straight platinum blonde hair was the most noticeable thing about her, chemically coloured and straightened, framing a line-free face, and eyebrows plucked into perfect arches that made her look perpetually pissed off – though admittedly she was actually pissed off now. I mentally ticked off the procedures I was certain she'd undergone as her voice rose an octave with every sentence that she spoke.

Botox, tick…

'I told that dippy cow who took our orders that I am allergic to soy.'

Lip fillers, tick…

'I *knew* she wasn't listening when I was saying it. That's why I told her twice…'

Breast implants? Probably, but surely it would be rude to sneak a look when the poor woman was so close to death. Listening to her now I was almost certain that Abby had left the soy in on purpose.

'I'm so, so sorry,' I cut in when she'd had enough airtime, and picked up the plate. 'I'll get both meals redone and a full refund. Please accept our sincerest apologies.'

'I'm not sure your sincerest apologies are good enough to be honest—'

'Rose, please,' her husband cut her off before she could get into her stride again. I hadn't even looked at him while I was pricing up his wife, but I did now and noticed that he was far more naturally attractive. The kind of 'ages like a fine wine' who makes a not even middle-aged wife feel ancient and frumpy. He looked to be around his late thirties, which meant she probably was too, only the work she had had done had unfortunately added about six or seven years to that. By contrast his dark hair starting to grey at the temples and laughter lines just made him hotter. 'I'm not sure she can do much more than apologise and give us free meals,' he told her. 'You didn't eat it, you're not dying, there's no harm done.'

He flashed me a warm smile that seemed to apologise and convey that he knew exactly what his wife could be like at the same time. I got the impression it wasn't the first time he'd had to smooth over one of her rants. Poor guy.

'I'm sorry again.' I whisked the meals away before she could start her motor up again.

'These are no good.' I held up the two spoiled meals to the chef and slid the food into the bin. 'Order 464. She's allergic to soy.'

'Why didn't the dozy bitch say that when she ordered it? This isn't fucking McDonald's, this shit doesn't come off a production line.'

I tried not to wince and shrugged. 'No idea. She must have forgotten.'

An hour later, when things were quietening down slightly, I pulled Abby to one side. 'You nearly killed one of our customers,' I hissed. 'Try listening when someone says the word "allergic" in future, eh?'

Abby looked crestfallen, as she always did. 'Shit, sorry, Anna. What do you want me to do?'

I shook my head. 'Don't worry, I've sorted it this time. Just be more careful, eh, Abs? And cover me for ten minutes while I have a ciggy.'

Abby nodded. 'No problem.'

As I passed the till point I upended the tip jar and totted up the notes and coins. There was nearly four hundred and fifty quid. That was the upside of working somewhere like this, people expected higher quality service but when they got it they tipped generously. And despite Abby's occasional cock-ups, they did get it. I split off my share of the money and shoved it into the till with a heavy heart, cancelling the bill for order 464 before shedding my black apron and slipping out of the fire exit for a cigarette. Shit, that was over a hundred quid less towards my escape fund, but this was Abby's only job and she needed the money way more than I did.

As I pulled the smoke into my lungs I closed my eyes, imagining the scalding hot shower I was going to get in a few hours' time, washing the smell of food and relaxing my muscles tight from physical work. And tomorrow was Saturday, I could get a lie-in, maybe even—

'Excuse me?'

My eyes snapped open at the unfamiliar voice. It wasn't exactly forbidden to pop out for a fag break – most of the managers smoked so they turned a blind eye for fear of ruling out their own breaks if they banned them – but the unexpected company made guilt flare in my chest. It took me a few seconds to recognise him as the super-hot husband of allergy woman.

'Sorry, is something else wrong?' I tried not to sound too irritated but it was blatantly obvious by the fact that I was wedged between two recycling bins that I was on a break. Had he followed me out here to complain about something else?

'No, not at all.' He held out some money folded in half, twenty-pound notes by the look of it, and more than necessary. 'When I thanked your manager for dealing so effectively with our misunderstanding he had no idea what I was talking about, seemed to think we'd settled the bill ourselves.'

Oh God. If Pete found out Abby had fucked up again he might actually fire her this time. Especially with allergies, that was the cardinal sin in waitressing, and for good reason. I sighed. 'What did you say to him?'

'I apologised and said my wife must have paid when I was at the gents.'

I breathed out in relief. 'Abby's on her last warning,' I told him. 'She doesn't mean to be so dopey, she's harmless. Well, apart from almost killing your wife. I am really so sorry about that.'

I pushed myself away from the wall, dusted myself down, suddenly keenly aware of how attractive Mr Soy Allergy was and hoping I didn't smell of bin.

He grinned. 'Don't worry about it. She is slightly allergic but it's not as bad as she makes out. She just goes a bit blotchy for a day or two. Doesn't lose her voice unfortunately.'

I smiled politely, not wanting to get in the middle of a domestic. He was still holding the wad of twenty-pound notes and he pushed them forward at me.

'Here. I'd feel terrible you paying for our meals – they tasted amazing and it wasn't even your mistake to begin with. You don't want to give me sleepless nights, do you?'

I was only human. I took the money, all the while thinking how I wouldn't mind giving Mr Allergy a few sleepless nights at all.

I forgot him almost instantly. Sure, he was good looking, but we got a lot of attractive older men through the restaurant. Of course afterwards, when we regaled each other with stories of our courtship, I always told him that I hadn't been able to stop thinking about him for weeks, because who wants to hear that they'd barely been given a second thought? It was nothing against him anyway, I had two jobs to occupy myself with and any casual sex I needed – which really wasn't that often – I got from Dan, the-ex-who-wouldn't-go-away. I know I keep saying this but I swear I never set out to steal him away from Rose – I never even knew I wanted a better life until Luke gave me a taste of his. And that kind of existence, one full of 'yes, ma'am's and 'how can I be of service?', that life is like a drug. One taste and I was hooked. I never stood a chance.

That's not what the papers will say though. I know the light I'll be painted in and it is scarlet. To everyone else I will be the 'other woman', who stole Rose Whitney's husband and then killed him. I can already picture Rose milking the hell out of the photo opportunities – 'Attempted murder suspect killed our marriage'. The thought of her painted face and bleached white hair makes me want to puke, but my cell is small and the smell will be unbearable. How the hell did I got here? How have I let things get this far? Have I made the biggest mistake of my life?

Chapter Five

Rebecca

I'm aware that I'm being unusually quiet on the journey back from the Cotswolds to Oxford Police Station. I know better by now than to start spouting my theories off at Matthews before he's had his fourth cup of coffee, and at the moment I haven't got anything strong to back any of my suspicions up with anyway. At least I could tell Jack had agreed with me – there was something not right about that crime scene. Now I just have to try and make Matthews come to the same conclusion.

'Mrs Whitney is in cell three,' the officer on the front desk tells us as we walk in. 'Her lawyer is on the way, coming from central London.'

I glance at the clock. He'll be an hour at least. 'Can you get us a transcript of the 999 call while we wait please?'

The officer looks at DCI Matthews, who just nods in a vaguely 'humour her' kind of way. I bite my lip, realising once again too late that I'm supposed to let the boss bark the orders.

Curious about our suspect, I take a look through the slot into the cell of Anna Whitney as we pass. The woman looks like she's dressed for Halloween, the ends of her long ash blonde hair clumped together into bloody strings, the front of her cashmere jumper barely showing any sign that it had once been pastel blue thanks to the amount of blood that has soaked into the fabric. She sits straight backed, staring at the wall in front of her, eyes not moving even when I draw the cover back on the observation grate. Shock, I suppose. Well, if she's in shock now she isn't going to like what comes next. Her clothes will be taken, her body swabbed and examined for defensive wounds. Then the questioning will begin. Mrs Whitney is in for a shock indeed.

We head to the canteen to top up on coffee while we wait for the lawyer to arrive. It's only just seven am, Mrs Whitney's lawyer will have been dragged out of bed, probably had to shower, do his morning routine… They do this, lawyers, keep you waiting, shave a bit off the timer. It's an old foxtrot and it matters little in the grand scheme of things, we'll get an extension easily. So you can imagine my surprise when we've barely finished filling our cups and the young, eager face of PC Fellows appears beside us. PC Tim Fellows is a nice guy, soon-to-be family man, and used to fence fake designer gear from his nan's front room until his sister was caught up a gang shooting that was nothing to do with her and he decided he wanted to be a police officer. Obviously I've never mentioned the knockoff gear to anyone else at the station, or how much of it I used to buy from him. 'Sorry to interrupt. Mrs Whitney's lawyer is here.'

I flick a look at Derek, who raises his eyebrows. 'Come on then, Dance, and do try to let me get a word in edgeways, won't you?'

Anna looks up as Derek and I enter the interview room together. Her face is ashen grey and her green eyes are red-rimmed. Her hair sticks to her face where her husband's blood has dried onto it. Now she's wearing a pale pink jumper and a pair of black leggings – she obviously has the kind of lawyer expensive enough to rush to her aid, bringing designer clothes for their client at seven am. I've only ever seen one suspect get that kind of treatment before, and he'd run an entire drug cartel. Her nice clothes don't do much to improve her appearance today, however. Even without the streaks of blood she's pallid and puffy. I shove a stray lock of my own dark brown hair behind my ear and feel positively glamorous next to Mrs Whitney right now – although I know that wouldn't have been the case just yesterday. She looks desperately young and vulnerable, and I notice that for the wife of a plastic surgeon she also looks incredibly natural. Even now, with her husband dead and herself under arrest for his murder and looking like death, Anna Whitney still seems composed, one of those women who is always put together, my mum would have said. It could be the shock, I suppose, but for some reason I just can't picture this woman having a violent outburst, or any other kind of outburst for that matter, in her life.

'Hello, Anna.' I sit down facing the woman; Derek takes a seat to my left. He looks at Anna Whitney as though she has already been convicted. 'I believe you've been made aware of your rights?'

An almost imperceptible nod from the other woman, her head now bowed.

Anna's lawyer, an incredibly tall thin man with a voice too deep for his stature, speaks first. I haven't come across him before – most of our usual suspects can't afford the firm he works for. His name is Patrick Tate. 'I should inform you that I've advised my client not to comment until her emotional state improves.'

'Or until you can coach her better on what to say,' Matthews mutters.

'It's not necessary. To stay silent. I mean,' Anna says quietly, looking at Derek and avoiding my gaze. It's almost as though she is appealing to him to believe her. Maybe she thinks she'll have better luck with a man. 'I've told your colleagues, I did it. It was me.'

'She made that statement before she'd had correct legal counsel, and before she had been made aware of her rights. I'll be moving to have it struck from any evidence,' Tate says in a monotone voice.

'And are you making that statement again now, Anna? After receiving legal counsel and being fully aware of your rights?' Derek looks at Tate the entire time he is talking. Anna doesn't even look at her lawyer, who is clearing his throat like it's the first day of winter.

'Yes,' she says quickly, before Tate can comment. His poker face gives nothing away but I know he will be furious. *No comment* is the usual route of choice. 'Yes, I am. I've told you already, I stabbed Luke. I killed him. It was me.'

'Then who was the man at the scene, Anna?' I ask. Whoever owned those size ten shoes, we need to find him as a matter of urgency.

'Man?' Anna looks confused. 'It was just me and Luke there. No one else. I don't know what you're talking about.'

They call me the Truth Wizard in the station. It's a reference to the something like five per cent of people who can tell when another person is lying almost instinctively. I'm not saying I'm infallible – I'd be sitting here as the SIO if I was, and anyway, just knowing when someone is lying isn't enough, more's the pity. As police officers we have this pesky rule of having to be able to prove things with evidence and the such. I also don't know why a person is lying – I just have a pretty good idea that they are. Anna Whitney is lying right now, I just don't know which part she's lying about.

'Tell me, Mrs Whitney,' Derek interrupts. 'How does a nice woman from a background like yours stab a man by accident?'

'We were arguing,' Anna says, looking at Matthews and avoiding my gaze. Can she tell that I know she's lying? Why won't she look at me? 'I thought he was going to attack me.'

'Has you husband ever attacked you before?'

'No.' Anna directs her answer to Matthews, even though I'm the one who has asked the question. It's getting on my wick. 'Never.'

Tate is looking more and more furious. There goes his domestic abuse case. She's going to leave herself without any defence before long, sitting there talking herself into a corner. I imagine Matthews is over the moon.

'Then why would you suspect he was going to attack you this time?' I press. 'Presumably you've argued before?'

'Of course we've argued before.' She turns her eyes on me now for the first time, and I can see that she's angry at me. Did she expect that we'd just accept her story and that would be that? That we wouldn't ask any further questions?

'And he never hurt you when you've argued before?' Matthews takes up the line of questioning. 'Yet this time you are so scared for your life that you stab him with—'

'What did you stab him with?' I interrupt quickly. Matthews looks furious at my interjection, but only so that I can tell. He's good at that, he has a look that only people he works with can tell means 'what the fuck do you think you're playing at?' To Anna and his lawyer I'm sure he looks the picture of serenity.

'A broken wine bottle,' Anna says. I try not to give Derek my own version of a 'look'. I'm not sure how I'd pull off a 'how do you explain the fact that she doesn't know he was stabbed with a beer bottle' look anyhow.

'What were you arguing about?' I ask instead.

'I can't remember.'

'A bad enough argument that you thought your husband was going to attack you and you can't remember what it was about?'

Tate clears his throat. 'My client has had a traumatic experience where she feared for her life. You could measure your tone in light of that, Detective. She's answered this question several times.'

I smile at him. 'Thanks for the advice.'

'Yes, right.' Matthews doesn't even look at Tate. 'Anna, we were wondering if you could start by telling us everything that happened yesterday, from the time you arrived at the house? In your own time, I recognise you have been through a traumatic experience.' At least he stops short of making air quotes around the words 'traumatic experience'. Anna stares at her nails some more and doesn't say a word.

'We can't help you unless you speak to us,' I say as gently as possible, trying to convey in my words that I know there's something she's not telling us. 'We just want to get to the bottom of what really happened.'

She looks up at me and nods slightly. 'I arrived at around four pm,' she says, her voice barely above a whisper. 'Luke had driven over before me – I had things to do in town and I told him to go on ahead, get everywhere opened up and start a fire going. It's a forty-minute drive from our Oxford house to the Cotswold house.'

I make a note to ask her what she was doing in town later. In a case like this sometimes it's the little details that matter.

'What did you do when you first got there?' Matthews asks. Despite it being him who asked the question, Anna directs her answer at me. It's like she's suddenly decided that I might be her best bet.

'We went for a walk. There are some nice hills and you can be completely alone. Well, alone together – you know what I mean.' She hesitates. 'Wait, first I put the stew on – in the slow cooker so it would be ready when we got back.'

'Who bought the ingredients for the stew?' I ask suddenly. Anna looks confused.

'What?'

'The stew. If you came separately, who bought the ingredients? Did you go to the supermarket on the way, or had Luke already picked them up?'

'Oh, um.' She scratches absently at her left eyebrow. 'They were already at the cottage when I got there.'

'So Luke must have gone shopping for them? Does Luke ever do the cooking?'

Anna looks sideswiped. 'No, I do the cooking. He works quite late...'

'Did he get everything you needed, for the stew?'

Anna looks at me and for a second I see something in her eyes, something like anger, or maybe fear? What is she afraid of letting slip when she hasn't even got to the fight yet?

'Yes, Detective, my grown husband knows how to shop for stew ingredients. I told you, they were at the house when I got there, so Luke must have bought them, hadn't he?'

'Well, unless someone else was at the cottage before you. Was there someone else at the cottage with you both? Did someone turn up while you were there? We have an unidentified male shoe print in a size ten in your husband's blood, Anna.'

'There wasn't anyone else there,' she insists. 'Maybe the print belongs to one of the paramedics? Luke got the shopping on the way, there was no one else there.'

'Okay,' Matthews says before I can ask any more about the stew. 'So you put the stew on and go out for a walk. Did anyone see you?'

Anna shrugs. 'I don't know. Maybe. I don't remember seeing anyone, but that doesn't mean no one saw us.'

There's a hint of cleverness behind her answer. She's right, of course, it's a stupid question. She has no idea what anyone else saw – only what she saw.

'What time did you get back?'

'Um, about six, I'd say. The stew was about an hour off being done so Luke stoked up the fire and I went and had a shower, my feet were freezing. When I got back down we ate dinner, then Luke showered while I flicked through the TV for a film for us to watch.'

'Did you find anything?'

Anna answers immediately. '*Shutter Island*.'

I make a mental note to check if *Shutter Island* is on the cottage's fancy Sky Q planner, but I have a feeling it will be. With all the details she's been shaky on, this one came to her far too easily. So what does that mean? That the rest of her story is true? How would she know what Luke had watched that evening if she hadn't been there with him? And not forgetting she was in the house when the paramedics and police arrived – just the two of them.

'So tell me,' I ask. 'How did things go from a nice walk, a meal, a film, to your husband lying on the floor of the kitchen, a broken bottle in his stomach?'

If it's possible, Anna whitens further. 'We had been drinking all evening. We started arguing. He was getting angrier and angrier and then he came forward, like just lurched at me. I don't know how I even had the bottle in my hand, I can't remember picking it up.' Her voice has taken on a monotone quality; it reminds me of someone reading a script, badly. It sounds like something you might say if you'd been watching one too many bad crime shows. And it's a lie.

'What were you arguing about?' It's futile – I know, but I try again.

The 'no comment' comes almost instantly.

I don't press it. 'Did you call 999 straight away?'

'I think so. No, wait, I sat down next to him and put my hands on his stomach to try to stop the bleeding, like this.' She puts her hands together and mimics pressing down. 'But it wasn't working. I knew he was going to die if I didn't get help so I left him for a minute to get the phone.'

'Where was your mobile?' I ask. She frowns.

'What?'

'You used the landline to call for an ambulance, not a mobile. When you were arrested your mobile was in your pocket. Why not use that? It would have been quicker.'

'It wasn't in my pocket then,' Anna replies, her eyebrows knitting into a frown. 'I must have picked it up afterwards, when the police were on the way, or after they got there.'

Derek gives me a 'where are you going with this' look. We all know that look too.

'There's no blood on the phone,' I tell her, watching her face drop as she comprehends what I'm saying. 'Your hands were covered in blood. So your mobile was in your pocket while you went into the hallway to get the house phone to call 999.'

Anna begins to cry, but her head is in her hands to conveniently disguise whether there are actually any tears. 'I don't know.' Her muffled voice comes from between her fingers. 'I don't know why I didn't use my mobile, I just panicked. What difference does that make?' She looks at Matthews beseechingly. 'I've admitted I did it. What difference does it make which phone I used?'

'DS Dance usually has her reasons,' Derek says, putting a little too much emphasis on the word 'usually' for my liking.

'Do you need a break?' her lawyer asks. Anna shakes her head.

'I just want this over with.'

'You don't have to answer anything you don't remember exactly, Anna. If you're not sure, remember it's best to say "no comment".'

It's a familiar line I've heard from defence lawyers a million times but it makes me dislike this one intensely. Something about the way he says it, as if she's the victim.

'Why don't you want to tell us what the argument was about?' I try again. 'What are you hiding, Anna? Why come in here and admit to stabbing your husband but refuse to say what you were arguing over?'

'No comment,' Anna mutters, her eyes dropping to the table in front of her. This, Tate looks comfortable with.

Say nothing, don't incriminate yourself further. Give him something to work with.

'Has Luke ever hurt you before?'

'I already told you, no.' Anna looks at Tate again, who gives a small shake of his head. 'I mean no comment.'

'Why would you pick up a broken bottle to defend yourself against a man who'd never hurt you in the past?'

Anna shakes her head. *No comment.*

'How did the wine bottle get broken?'

'I dropped it. I mean, I knocked it over. Maybe Luke knocked it over, I don't know.'

'During the argument?' I asked. 'Before?'

Anna sighs. Her fingers turn her wedding ring around and around. I wonder if she even knows she's doing it. 'No comment.'

'Okay.' Matthews puts his hand down on the table in front of me, time's up for now. 'I think we should take a break. Mrs Whitney, take this time to speak to your lawyer – you will have time to prepare a statement, after which you will be charged or released.'

'Released?' Anna looks between us, confusion on her pretty face. 'But I did it. I'm guilty. I *told* you.'

'Unfortunately, Mrs Whitney, that's not your decision to make.'

Chapter Six

Rebecca

'You don't think she did it.'

It's not a question from Matthews, it's a statement, and it's a pissed-off one.

'As a matter of fact, no,' I reply, setting my notes down on my desk and reaching over a sea of detritus to grab my coffee mug. 'But it doesn't matter what I think, does it? You're the boss.'

DCI Matthews aims a scowl at me. I bet he wasn't bad looking, once. He's got that look about him that says he thought he was going to stay twenty forever, then woke up one day to find he was pushing fifty and had wrinkles you could wedge your fountain pen in.

'Sometimes I seriously doubt anyone around here remembers that,' he practically growls. 'But believe it or not I do actually value your opinion. Unless I disagree with it. So go on, get it over with.'

'She didn't know what he was stabbed with.' I start with the obvious because it sounds more convincing than 'I've got one of my "feelings"'. We make our way through to the canteen, which is deserted at this time in the morning. The coffee machine is up all hours though, thankfully. I stick my mug underneath and press the button for a latte. 'She thought it was a wine bottle.'

'So she's hazy on the details,' Matthews replies as my mug fills with steaming coffee. He practically shoves me out of the way the minute it stops. He's obviously out of Rita's magic flask. 'You've done this job long enough to know that the details don't always match one hundred per cent. What else?'

'She says she can't remember what they were arguing about, but that's bullshit. It was important enough for him to allegedly attack her, even though he's never laid a finger on her before. So either they weren't arguing at all or she doesn't want to tell us why. And she couldn't find anything to stop the bleeding? Not a single tea towel or jumper?'

'So she didn't want to save his life. That makes her more guilty, not less.' He's now pouring his bodyweight in sugar into his coffee. 'She was the only one at the scene. She's covered in his blood and – I hardly need to remind you – she's admitted it. I think you're trying to overcomplicate things.' I'm grateful he doesn't add *as usual*.

'Maybe,' I admit, but not because I agree. He's my superior and a man. A combination of facts that means he doesn't enjoy being argued with. 'But we've got to put this case to the CPS, and if she did do it we don't want her getting away with it because the case against her is full of holes. I'm not saying she didn't do it,' I add quickly before he can argue. 'But you're the one who taught me that we don't take everything a suspect says as true unless the evidence backs it up.'

The flattery does the job I intend it to do. He nods, obviously mollified for now, and I don't feel the need to push my point any further by insisting that Anna Whitney is innocent, and she's covering for somebody.

Chapter Seven

Anna

DS Dance is an interesting character. She looks straight into my eyes, like she can see every guilty thought that is running through my mind. She is the woman I would have been, I think, if I'd pursued an actual dream instead of letting life pull me along in its slipstream. And yet just a week ago, if you'd seen me sipping on my matcha latte and having my highlights done with a bag full of designer clothes at my feet, you would look at us and think that I had made the better choices in life. Funny how your fortunes can change with just a little shift in perspective.

She is arrogant, though, DS Dance. I suppose that's sexist of me to say, because on a man it would be called confidence, or even the baseline for competence, the courage of one's convictions. On a woman though, it comes across as just a little bit smug. Her clear good instincts have probably steered her right in the past, led her to know that she's good at what she does, and that has given her an inflated sense of importance. She's the junior officer in the interview and even I can feel how her boss bristles when she interrupts him, but he doesn't reprimand her or cut in, so for all I know this could be their version of good cop bad cop. I have never been inside a police station in my life – even when my father took his own life the police conducted my interview in the hospital. I wonder, actually, if they will look at his death again now, given that his daughter is under arrest for murder. I hadn't considered that but now, as I look at DS Dance and her bitten-down fingernails, it's all I can think about. Poor Dad. He really did take his own life – there's no need to worry that I'm some kind of serial killer – but I am concerned that the manner of his death might complicate things now.

'No comment,' I say, because I wasn't listening to the question, I was too busy picturing my father's swollen purple face the last time I saw him. It doesn't matter that I've refused to answer, I'm allowed to say 'no comment' as often as I like, my fancy lawyer says, in fact he encourages it. As a child I hadn't realised this, and just as well, because if I'd known I could get away without answering questions from the police I can't imagine I'd have put up with my English teacher as long as I did.

DS Dance looks disappointed in me and that gives me the tiniest bit of satisfaction. I could tell as soon as she walked into the interview room that she grew up like me, hand to mouth, in and out of houses on the estate, down to the shop to get your mum bread, milk and twenty B&H with a note. I wonder if she hated it as much as me. The whole interview so far I've wanted to ask her if she can still smell the barbecues, but that would have been far too Hannibal Lecter, and I didn't want to go over the top and risk my poor lawyer thinking he has an insanity plea.

Urgh, I could have done without thinking about the estate right now, least of all the barbecues. Most kids love when the sun comes out but I used to dread pulling the curtains open in the morning and being hit by the warmth of the British summer. At the first sign of any sun the phones would start ringing, then all the kids would be sent to the local shops with a tenner to get sausages, burgers and buns – you could hear the hiss of the cans of Stella being opened for miles. We all knew that it was just the adults' excuse to start drinking at midday but no one cared because it meant extra freedoms as the air turned thick with smoke and the smell of burning meat and the rules around childcare got even more lax than usual, which was saying something. We would all take it in turns to go to different people's houses and usually I would prefer when everyone came to ours. As my mum drank more and more, and got louder and louder, she would forget I even existed, and at least if we were hosting I could sneak off to my bedroom until I was summoned loudly to corroborate one of my mother's tall tales or to demonstrate a point she was trying to make – usually how thin I was or how I bit my nails to the quick or something else derogatory about my appearance – and then I'd be summarily dismissed. When someone else hosted I had to pretend to be interested in the stupid games the estate kids played or find a quiet corner of the tiny rectangular garden – behind the sheds usually worked – to hide from the adults who would constantly try to get me to go and play with the others so they could talk about grown-up stuff they didn't want me to hear. Not that I was interested in anything they had to say.

If you can't tell, I hated barbecues. I hated them a long time before the day I overheard Tanya and Denise and their poisonous gossip, but even more afterwards.

It was one of our turns to host; I'd managed to sneak up to my bedroom and was sitting on the stacked-up pile of pillows that constituted the reading corner behind my door when I heard them coming up the stairs. As an only child I had the second biggest room in the house, which felt absolutely ginormous compared to most of the kids my age on the estate who had two or three older siblings and were either sharing the second bedroom or had been stuck in the small room with the box over the stairs. My reading corner was usually in the back right-hand side of the room, but I had moved it to behind the door for today's barbecue because if anyone pushed open the door to glance inside they wouldn't see me and would think the room was empty. A plan which worked a bit too well, unfortunately, because either Tanya and Denise thought I was outside playing with the other kids or they were too drunk to care that I might be curled up behind the door.

It was Tanya I heard first – I knew that because she had a nasally kind of voice that always sounded as if she had a cold. Mum said it was because of some stuff she put up her nose – I never really understood what she meant until I was much older when I realised that most of the parents on the estate had had a coke habit. As much as I came to loathe the presence of my mother, I don't believe she was one of them, but maybe I'm just naive. Anyway, Tanya and Denise both had the exact same colour hair – as if there had been a two for one sale on bleach at the offie or they had gone halves on a jumbo bottle at the cash n carry – but that was where the similarities ended. In fact, when they stood together, side by side, they looked like a normal person had gone into a house of mirrors. One reflection had distorted them fatter and the other much thinner. The fat mirror, that was Tanya, was soft and doughy with enormous breasts and droopy arms, while Denise was the thin mirror, all sharp angles. Even her black eyebrows were spiked in the middle, making her look like she was always shocked at something. They looked like they have been drawn on with thick black marker, but at aged eight I didn't think they could have been because why would anyone draw something so stupid-looking on their face? When I read *James and the Giant Peach* a couple of years later I pictured Tanya and Denise as Aunt Sponge and Aunt Spiker and being flattened by a huge peach rolling over the pair of them. That was my favourite daydream for months.

'Do you think he knows, then?' Tanya was saying. She was leaning up against the wall right outside my room and I could hear her as clearly as if she was in the room with me, even with her stupid snot-filled voice.

'How could he not?' Denise replied. 'Everyone else does. She's not exactly subtle about it, is she? Did you see her draping herself all over Martin before?'

I knew who they were talking about instantly and my face burned with shame. Even at eight years old I'd seen the way my mum was different to the other mums on the estate, how she would fawn over the men, laughing louder at their jokes than she ever did when my dad said something funny, rubbing their arms and pressing herself against them. I had seen too the scowls of the other women when she acted that way – it was so strange to me how my mum didn't see them. Or maybe she did and she didn't care. She didn't care that her voice was always louder when she spoke to men, or that she stuck her boobs out more when they were around, or that she always looked so very bored if there were only women in the conversation. I never could understand why she came alive much more around men, what it was about them that lit her up like it was Christmas. Even the ugly ones, she was like it with all of them. It was humiliating.

'God, that's so sad. Why does he put up with it? My Dave would have chucked my stuff out the window and kicked seven bells of shite out of any bloke who touched me. What makes her so special that he doesn't just chuck her?'

'It must be her magical vagina.'

They both cackled at this and I wished in that moment they would both choke on their cans of cheap lager. How dare they talk about my parents like that in our house, and then go downstairs and stuff their faces with our food and drink?

But they were right, weren't they? I mean, even if it was mean, they had a point. Why *did* my dad let Mum treat him like that? I'd seen her sitting on Martin's knee too – everyone had – so why didn't Dad tell her to get up and to stop making a show of herself and of him? What was he afraid of?

'Seriously though.' Tanya's voice dropped and I hated myself for moving closer to the door to listen. 'I feel so sorry for the poor bloke. It's pathetic the way he puts up with her putting it about all over the place. *Pathetic.*'

And in that moment I wanted to burst into tears and to scream all at once. I wished for a meteor like the ones in my space books to come down and crash into the house, killing Tanya and Denise with their stupid cackling and my mum and Martin, but mainly my dad for being sad and pathetic and letting my mum treat him like a pathetic idiot in front of everyone.

God, I've completely zoned out again. Both officers are looking at me like I've missed a cue.

'No comment,' I say.

Chapter Eight

Rebecca

We enter the briefing room at nine, to the irritated faces of the rest of the team, pissed off to be pulled in on a Sunday. They don't look surprised to see me here first – I signed up to be on call more than everyone else because I have less to be at home for.

'What's going on?' DI Tom Kerrigan asks, nodding at the murder board full of my scribblings.

'Possible domestic homicide, which you'd know if you read my text messages,' I say, trying for a pissed-off tone. Tom is my partner in crime, or I should say I'm his, as he's my superior. I've been a DS for three years now and he's been going on at me to take my inspector's exam for the last twelve months. 'Suspect in custody. Matthews has just been checking on the status of the ninety-six.'

'CPS are being cagey,' Derek says, walking straight to the front of the room. He looks at me and the four other faces looking back at him. There's me, Tom, DS Kim Beckford, DS Andy Moss and DC Rob Stone. They all look intensely relieved that they hadn't been on call last night. 'As it stands we still only have seventeen hours to question our suspect, one Anna Whitney.' He checks his watch. 'Actually, sixteen and a half.'

He turns to the board, where a crime scene photo of Luke Whitney has been pinned at the top.

'Our victim, Luke Whitney, was stabbed in his holiday home in the Cotswolds at one thirty this morning. The emergency call was made by his second wife, Anna Whitney.' He points at the booking photograph of Anna. 'She confessed to stabbing her husband with a broken bottle following a row at the property.'

'Self-defence?' Kim asks. Matthews shrugs.

'She says she was afraid at the time, but she's hardly making the best case if she intends to claim self-defence,' he replies. 'She admits he has no history of violence and can't tell us why she was so scared of him at this particular time. Kim, I need you to check if there have ever been any reports pertaining to either suspect or victim.'

Kim nods and makes a note on her pad. She's only been a sergeant a few months and is desperate to prove herself – which makes her a good member of the team but is frustrating to try and keep up with. I'd wager she gets a full night's sleep and does those irritating morning rituals I keep meaning to do like meditating and visualising myself as a fully functioning member of society. Her desk is always tidy too. And although she's a good copper she never manages to piss the DCI off by insisting that someone is lying without being able to tell him why or what about.

'So if it's an open and shut, what's Dance looking so constipated about?' Tom asks. I stick up my middle finger as the rest of the team snigger.

'I'll let you tell them the good news, shall I, DS Dance?'

'Cheers, boss.' I stand up and face the team. 'I don't think she did it.'

Everyone groans on cue, it's like working in a bloody panto.

'Wait a minute, before you all start chucking tomatoes at me.' I point at the board where I've written down all the reasons this case isn't what it seems. The entire team squint and pull faces like they're trying to work out a strenuous multiplication problem.

'Nope,' Andy says after a minute. 'Not got a scooby what that's supposed to say.'

'Wait, is that word "cunt"?' Tom asks, feigning complete ignorance. Wow, what a bunch of funny fuckers.

'Alright, you've made your point, Dance's handwriting looks like she should have gone into the medical profession,' Matthews says. 'Believe me, her bedside manner suggests otherwise. Why don't you read it to the team, Rebecca, before we have to call for an interpreter?'

I make a face at the rest of my team, who are all grinning. 'Fine, you bunch of bastards. That word your mother would wash your mouth out for using, Tom, is "*coat*". We found Anna Whitney's coat in her car but I'll get to that in a minute. First.' I hold up one finger. 'Her story is full of holes so big you could get DI Kerrigan's ego through cleanly and still have space for Andy's porn collection. Two.' I move on quickly before either can object. 'She's refusing to tell us what they were arguing about. Three, Anna Whitney says they went for a walk as soon as she arrived at the cottage that afternoon but her coat – yes, *coat*, Tom – was in the car. Which means for her story to be true, they went for a walk and when they got back Luke hung his coat up on the peg and Anna went outside and put hers on the passenger seat of her car. But four – and this is the biggie – according to forensics she phoned for an ambulance and the police, confessed to stabbing her husband, then wiped all of her prints off the phone and the bottle used to stab him.'

When I take a huge theatrical breath to show I've finished, three blank faces stare back at me. Only three because Kim is scribbling down everything I've said in her bloody notebook.

'Was there anyone else on the scene?' Andy asks, clearly having taken no offence whatsoever at the porn collection remark.

'Not when the police turned up.'

'How long did it take them to get there?'

'Ten minutes. Easily enough time for someone to get away.'

Kim holds up a hand, her face full of confusion.

'You don't have to put your hand up, DS Beckford,' Matthews tells her for the millionth time.

'Sorry, yeah. Um, so are we thinking that Anna Whitney was there when he was stabbed and is taking the blame for someone else, or that someone else did it, left the scene and she just happened to turn up once they had gone?'

'Yes, one of those,' I say. She opens her mouth and closes it again like a fish.

'Soooo,' Matthews says, motioning for me to sit back down. 'Someone needs to talk to the neighbours. There's only one house within screaming distance, separated by a bloody massive garden and a hedge, but they might have heard or seen something. There's a village five minutes' walk west and hills on the other side. Rob, Andy, can you two get down there and get statements from next door, then go on to the village and question everyone you can get your hands on. See if anyone saw them arrive, or can corroborate their story at all. See if there's a B and B, that's where you're most likely to find the hill walkers, they might have seen this little jaunt the Whitneys went on. Do not order lunch.'

DS Reynolds and DC Stone give a nod each and go to pick up their coats. Tenner says they order lunch.

'Oooh.' I jump back up. 'And the only footwear at the scene was a size twelve pair of wellies presumed to belong to the victim. There's a size ten footprint in the victim's blood in the cottage.'

DS Beckford starts to put her hand up again but catches herself at the last minute. 'Shall I send an action to uniform to check the victim's shoes at his home address?'

'That would be great, thank you. They are probably on their way there actually – I think the uniform's details are—'

'I have them.' Beckford smiles. Of course she does, bless her.

'Beckford, when you've done that I need you to find as much info as you can on the Whitneys,' Matthews says. 'Mrs Whitney is a yoga teacher at a posh gym, and Luke was a plastic surgeon. I want a list of people to talk to as soon as possible.'

'Yes, sir.' Kim spins around to her computer and I know full well that she will have enough information on the Whitneys to write their biographies by the end of the day, complete with that glossy picture section in the middle.

Matthews turns to me and Tom.

'You two are going to run this show. Dance, because you were unlucky enough to be on call in the middle of the night, and Kerrigan, because you are the only one who can understand what she's chomping on about half the time. Let's get this straight – I still think Anna Whitney is guilty, and we are not part of her defence team. But I actually agree with you on some of the points you've raised, DS Dance, and if we're going to make charges stick I don't want anything thrown back at us at trial, so I want this done thoroughly.'

I might have made Derek sound like he's a bad DI, but he's not. True, he prefers an easy life – he doesn't enjoy the thrill of piecing together evidence the way I do, moving around each piece until it makes part of the bigger picture – but I get the impression he did, once. He's been in this job so long that it's lost its shine; he likes the uncomplicated nature of a robbery or a gang killing, one where the motive is clear from the start. That's why he dislikes domestics, I think, because there's so many different motives – greed, jealousy or just pure rage. And so many emotions involved. Often in a domestic case, not homicide of course but GBH or assault, we'll put all the work in and the charges will be dropped anyway. Then the offender will go home and repeat the pattern until sometimes we really are investigating a homicide. But in this case, something is different. Is Anna Whitney an abused wife who finally snapped? Or is she the volatile one? Wives abusing their husbands isn't as uncommon as you might think, and if that's what we are dealing with here then none of us want to watch her sail through on a self-defence plea.

As if he'd heard me almost complimenting him, Derek moves towards the door.

'If you need me I'll have my phone with me.'

'Where are you going, sir?' I ask, knowing the answer already.

'To get some bloody breakfast.'

Chapter Nine

Anna

They take me back to my tiny cell where I've been sitting now for an hour and a half, staring at an ant who has somehow had the misfortune to navigate into my humble abode. I always thought ants travelled together, I don't think I've ever seen one on its own before. I think the words 'what're you in for, mate?' but I don't say them out loud because that would be me officially talking to an ant, and I've got to try and stay sane. Going all Dr Dolittle won't help my cause whatsoever.

The boss man, I've forgotten his name, asked me if I wanted anything to eat, but the thought of ever eating again makes me want to vomit. I didn't tell him that, I just said no thank you and hung my head. I would have thought that if they only have twenty-four hours to question me then it's counterproductive to leave me here for ninety minutes of that, but far be it from me to tell them how to do their jobs.

I wonder if Rose knows yet that Luke is dead. I imagine her face on finding out and it makes me feel a little better about my predicament. Will she feel like he got what he deserved in the end? Or has she always held out hope that one day he would leave me and go back to her, announce that he'd made a terrible mistake? That was never going to happen, so at least now she's out of her purgatory of waiting around for him to come running back. She should thank me, everything I've done for her, but after all of this I can't see us becoming friends, somehow.

—

I'd never noticed Luke and Rose at the restaurant before that first night Abby nearly killed her, but after that they were regular Friday night customers and I came to look forward to seeing him. Her, not so much. She would eye me suspiciously as I took their order, touch his arm and try to order for him – like she was a kid who'd latched on to the popular girl on the first day of school and was refusing to give up her position as BFF. I understood later, of course, and after all, Rose had been right, hadn't she? So maybe she had a sixth sense about the way Luke acted when he was hunting, and she'd seen it in the way he was with me. She always looked immaculate, her blonde hair shining in the candlelight – although I did worry about how close she was to an open flame with all that plastic. He had thick dark hair, blue eyes that always looked amused and a boyish smile that I was sure allowed him to get away with almost anything. It almost seemed unnatural for a man that attractive to be tied down – it didn't surprise me that his wife would feel like she had to play defence even while ordering seafood.

And then one Friday night I noticed him sitting at the table on his own. After he'd been there twenty minutes or so I went over.

'Can I get you a drink while you wait?'

He barely looked up at me. 'A beer, please.'

'Do you want to order a drink for your wife? I can bring it over when she arrives.'

Luke – I knew his name was Luke by then, although I still thought of them as Mr and Mrs Soy Allergy – shook his head. 'To be honest I'm not even sure she's going to turn up.' He looked up, his face miserable. 'We had a fight. She said she wasn't coming but I kind of thought she might anyway. I didn't think even she would humiliate me like this.'

I had no idea what to say to that so I mumbled something about being sure she'd turn up and I'd come back when she did and scuttled off. But I watched him more that night than any other. I guess that was the night I *really* noticed the man who would become my husband. I saw him checking his phone every few minutes and his beautiful face looking more dejected each time. After another half an hour I went back over feeling stupidly awkward.

'Another drink?'

He'd given me an embarrassed smile that was somehow more attractive than his confident one. 'I think we both know my wife isn't coming and I look like a total idiot.'

'No, of course you don't.' I smiled. 'Every couple has fights.'

I half expected him to try and carry the conversation on but he gave a thin smile and nodded at his empty beer glass. 'Can I get another please?'

'Sure. Do you want to order some food?'

'I can't eat on my own – I look pathetic enough as it is. Why don't you join me? My treat.'

I thought he was joking, you get used to a bit of banter even when you work in an upmarket place like Benicio's. Besides, I'd pulled pints in some of the biggest dives in the UK during my college days. I gestured around and tried to look apologetic. 'I'm a bit busy here.'

'I can sort that out for you if you say you'll save me from eating alone.'

Wait, was he serious? Did he honestly think I could just take off my apron and sit down to eat with him? What in the cheesy rom com was this behaviour? I gave a small embarrassed laugh because telling him to get real seemed a bit mean, given that he'd been stood up already tonight. 'Unless you want to serve these tables while I eat in peace, sorry. I'll bring you your beer.'

I wasn't annoyed by his arrogance as much as amused by it at that point. Fifteen minutes later, however, when I was approached by Pete, the shift runner for the evening, I was furious.

'Paul says you can go.' Paul was our manager and there was no reason whatsoever for him to let me go home in the middle of a shift.

'What? Why? We're not overstaffed and I need the money. Tell him to send Tim home if he doesn't have the payroll, he's been moaning about some game he's missing out on all night.'

I turned to walk away but Pete caught my arm and pulled me back. 'I don't think it's an issue with the payroll, Anna. Some customer spoke to him and then he came over and told me to tell you you can go on your date but not to think you can make it a regular thing. And you should have told us it was your birthday. I thought your birthday was June?'

I didn't bother to answer him. I could feel my blood boiling in my veins as I stormed towards where Luke was sitting. Could he not take no for an answer? He looked up and gave me a huge smile. 'You're welcome.'

'I'm welcome?' I hissed, trying not to make a show of us.

'I spoke to your boss.' He gave me a sheepish look, like a schoolboy who'd been naughty and got away with it. 'I told him it was your birthday and you hadn't wanted to let him down. Now you can come to dinner with me. Problem solved.'

'No, my problem is not solved,' I told him, my voice sharp but still quiet – he was still a customer, even if he was being a presumptuous prick of one. 'Because my problem is that I have a customer who doesn't know what "no thank you" means. And now I have to explain to my boss that it isn't my birthday and I don't want to lose three hours' pay.'

'I'm so sorry,' he said, holding up his hands. 'You're completely right. I shouldn't have spoken to your boss, it was presumptuous and rude of me, completely out of line. I honestly thought the reason you didn't want to join me was because you couldn't get off work and I felt like such an idiot sitting here on my own. I thought… well never mind.' He pushed his chair back and stood up. 'I really am very sorry.'

He grabbed his coat from the back of his seat and went to walk off, and despite my fury I felt terrible. He was just trying to get some company – his wife had humiliated him by standing him up and by the looks of it he needed someone to talk to.

'Wait.' And in that instant, with that one word, I'd changed my future irreparably. I could have let him walk out of the door and he would have been gone. I'd still be Anna Chapman, Rose would still be Mrs Whitney and I wouldn't be sitting in this cell on a murder charge. But instead I looked around me to check no one was watching and I nodded. 'I'll get some food with you, but not here, I'd never hear the end of it. Meet me out the front when

you've paid for your drinks. And this is not a date, okay?
I don't date married men.'

Chapter Ten

Rebecca

Tom looks at me pointedly as soon as Matthews has left the briefing room.

'So you really don't think she did it?' he asks me like I'm some kid who's going to confess to winding Dad up when he's out of the room.

'The crime scene is clearly staged, Tom. As soon as you see the pictures you'll agree.'

Tom looks at his watch. 'Who was lead?'

'Jack.'

Tom nods. 'I bet photos will be on already, he's good. I'll get Kim running the room so you can stick with me.'

'So what's the plan?'

I see Tom glance at my whiteboard – hmmm, so he can read it then.

'Anna Whitney says she arrived at four o clock,' he says. 'Why didn't they travel to the cottage together? What was she doing until then?'

'She says she had things to do in town. But she also said Luke bought the ingredients for the stew. Now I know I have a dim view of men…'

Tom raises his eyebrows.

'Sorrynotsorry. But I wouldn't be trusting Luke to get the ingredients for the stew when I was in town anyway.

Anna said he never cooks. Why didn't she get the shopping?'

'Maybe Luke Whitney has a bit more about him than Jimmy Douglas,' Tom says, without any eye contact whatsoever. I feign being shot in the chest, clutching my breast and staggering backwards.

'Wow, low blow,' I say. 'Who told you about Jimmy?'

I'm trying to sound casual but a ream of curse words is running through my head. I hadn't wanted anyone to know I was sleeping with Jimmy – not least because everyone around the station knows he's a dealer, even if he doesn't have a record. Don't get me wrong, Jimmy isn't some kind of scumbag hanging around the school gates, he just sells to his mates, and their mates, but still, dealing is dealing and it doesn't exactly make me look like a professional. I'd be surprised if Matthews knows and hasn't said anything though.

'Tarryn's mum saw him coming out of your place last week,' Tom says. He still hasn't looked at me. 'Don't worry, I haven't told anyone.'

I realise that the person I least want to know about Jimmy is Tom. I don't want Tom to think less of me because I respect him, and I can't help thinking that he'll respect me a bit less, being mixed up with the likes of Jimmy.

'Nothing to tell,' I lie a bit. There isn't, really. Jimmy and I won't ever be anything more than benefits – we're not even the friends bit really. We're not having deep and meaningful conversations late into the night, or even early in the evening. Jimmy's most meaningful relationship is with his guitar. Yes, I'm a cliché. 'Jimmy came to, um, he was… fixing my pipes.'

Tom does look at me now, with a 'don't fucking insult my intelligence' expression on his face. He shakes his head. 'Well, I hope your pipes are sorted now. Anyway – back to the Whitneys. I'm not grasping the relevance of the stew ingredients.'

'Neither am I,' I admit. 'It just seemed quite strange, that she'd be out shopping but let him buy the food for dinner. It might not mean anything.'

Tom glances again at my board. He takes in a breath. 'Do you think we've fannied around in here long enough for Kim to have set up the incident room?'

'Oh yes,' I say, wiping everything off the board. 'She'll have solved the whole thing by now.'

–

Kim, unfortunately, hasn't solved the curious case of Anna Whitney, but she has – as expected – set us up quite nicely in incident room three. Matthews likes to do all of his briefings in the big room on the next floor up because the incident rooms are fairly cluttered with desks and he doesn't like having to get too close to us. He blames the pandemic but his intense need for personal space predates COVID by at least a decade and I'm all for it. The less I have to smell his coffee breath the better.

My car crash of a whiteboard has been replicated from Kim's notes in her perfect handwriting, the word 'coat' clear as day. She has also fixed the crime scene photos to the side of the board, a flip chart has a list of the jobs everyone has been allocated in one column and a blank column so we can all write our updates. As a team we can be like ships in the night, and we've found these simple ways to keep everyone updated with every aspect of a case until the next briefing. Kim runs our incident room and, as you can see, is bloody excellent at it.

'We've got just under sixteen hours to hold Anna Whitney before we charge her,' Tom tells us. 'As it stands, if I had to make a choice now, I'd be charging her with manslaughter at the least. I think Matthews would too. But I trust your instincts, Becky, and so does the guv, so we'll look at other suspects.'

'Thanks, Tom,' I say. 'Why don't we—'

The door to the incident room opens and PC Fellows sticks his head through. 'Thought you should know there's a woman downstairs causing a bit of a scene. Name's Rose Whitney. Think it's the ex-wife.'

I look at Tom. 'I suppose we can't just send uniform to talk to her?'

'You suppose correctly, DS Dance. Come on, any luck she had her ex-husband's holiday home under surveillance and you can be back warming Jimmy's bed in no time.'

Dickhead.

—

'Mrs Whitney?'

The woman is pacing the reception of the police station and looks up at the sound of her name. Her eyes are red and bloodshot but even in considerable distress she is one of the most well turned out women I've ever seen. It's true that with her perfectly straight peroxide blonde hair, her carefully drawn eyebrows and the benefit of Botox she doesn't have the natural beauty of Anna Whitney, but she is undeniably a head turner. Her nails are manicured, her outfit is impeccable. Even the tracks of her tears in her make-up look perfectly parallel. She looks like one of the mean girls in a teen high school film.

Tom steps forward. 'My name is—'

'Is it true?' Rose Whitney cuts Tom off, her eyes wild. 'Please say it isn't true. Luke's not dead. He can't be dead.'

'Mrs Whitney, who told you—'

She flaps her hands in a gesture that looks both dismissive and a little unhinged. 'Why does it even matter who told me?' she snaps. 'Luke's mother called me, obviously. She was beside herself. She said…' Rose collapses into tears before she can finish her sentence. I rush forward and catch her as her knees crumple and I guide her onto a hard plastic waiting room seat.

'I'm so sorry, Mrs Whitney. Luke passed away in the early hours of this morning. He was the victim of a stabbing.' I watch her intently, trying to figure out how Luke went from this woman to Anna Whitney. They couldn't be more different, Rose with her emotions on her sleeve and Anna so packed away. Rose an unnatural parody of the younger, unprocessed new wife. Is this who Anna would have become if Luke had still been alive in ten years? 'Would you like to go somewhere more private so that we can talk?'

'She did this, didn't she? Anna.' Rose rounds on me and spits out the word as though Anna's name is laced with poison. I don't know if her flair for theatrics is for our benefit or if she's always like this, but geesh. She's gone from sobbing to scowling in the blink of an eye, I'm half expecting her to throw herself onto her knees and beg for mercy in the next scene.

'Why would you assume that, Rose? Why wouldn't you assume that Luke was attacked by an intruder?'

Rose looks at me as if I'm a complete idiot. 'Because she's crazy! Surely you know that? Fucking crazy. I'm telling you, I warned him about her. I said to him – that

57

woman will ruin you, and when she does don't think you can come back to me. I gave him everything I had and she comes along and flutters her eyelashes and he's gone. It was literally as fast as that. I'm sure he told people that things hadn't been right between us for a while or some other bullshit to justify him running off with that crazy slut. He's been telling people that *I'm* the crazy one, if you can believe it. Bitter, I think the word he used was. And yet here we are.' She falls silent, as though realising she's made herself sound as bitter as her husband had made her out to be. 'You're not looking for some intruder are you? You'd be wasting your time, I'm telling you.'

I can't help thinking that Rose Whitney seems to have a habit of 'telling us' without actually telling us much at all.

'Mrs Whitney, I realise that this is extremely difficult for you,' Tom says, trying to gain some sort of control back over the conversation. 'We're very keen to find out what happened to Luke, to make sure that justice is done for him. So while you're here I'm going to have to ask you a few questions if that's okay?'

Rose Whitney sniffs in reply. She must be entering her grieving ex-wife era.

'Okay, Mrs—'

'Please, can you call me Rose? Is that okay?'

'Of course, Rose.' Tom smiles at her and I see her soften. I don't like stereotypes – it's why I refuse to become an alcoholic or eat donuts – but in this case I'd have to say that I could have predicted that Rose Whitney would warm more to Tom than to me. He can be incredibly charming with women who are not me. 'I realise this isn't easy for you to talk about,' he continues, smile, head tilt, 'but can you tell me anything about Anna and

58

Luke's relationship that might help us understand why this happened?'

Rose looks confused. 'Why don't you just ask her why she did it?' she asks. 'What's she saying? She's denying it, I suppose? Or... oh God, was it a murder–suicide? Is she dead too?'

'I'm afraid I can't tell you anything about the incident at the moment,' Tom replies. 'But any information you can give me would be a real help. When you say she's crazy, what do you mean by that? Has she ever been violent to Luke before?'

Rose shakes her head, her peroxide blonde hair barely moving under the weight of all the hairspray. 'Not to Luke. Not that I know of, anyway.'

'What do you mean, not to Luke? To someone else?' I realise my voice is too eager and I temper it slightly. Wouldn't hurt to give the old Tom tactics a try. 'Did Anna ever hurt you, Rose?'

She looks at me and gives a small nod. I reach out and rub her arm.

'It's okay, you can tell us.'

Encouraged by my sympathy, I like to think, Rose begins to speak.

'I went round to see them once not long after he – after we broke up. I had some papers for Luke to sign,' she says. '*She* was there. Anna. In *my* house, acting as though it was already hers even though they had barely been together five minutes. She was all simperingly nice while he was around, "Lovely to see you, Rose, you look well, Rose, can I get you anything, Rose?" Then Luke went upstairs to fetch some post that had come for me and that's when she did it.'

'Did what?' I try to keep my voice soft and we exchange another woman-to-woman look. See? I can be good at the people side of the job too.

'She was holding a cup of tea. She walked towards me and I just thought she was reaching for something behind in one of the cupboards next to me. Then I felt this searing pain on my legs, she'd flung the tea all over the front of my dress. I screamed and Luke came running in – she made up some story about me going for her but it was clear to Luke that I'd been sitting down when she'd thrown it. He yelled at her to get a wet towel and covered my legs with it – he always was good at first aid.' She gives a small smile at this, then bursts into tears.

'I'm so sorry, Rose,' I say, reaching out to pat her arm again while at the same time trying to think of a tactful way to ask what needs to be asked. There isn't one. I try and wait a reasonable amount of time – at least until she stops sobbing and gives a huge sniff – before I say, 'Can I ask where you were last night?'

Rose raises her eyebrows at this abrupt change in sympathy level but she doesn't go off the way I'd expected her to.

'At home,' she replies. 'Alone.'

'Do you have any way we could verify that? Just to be thorough? Ring doorbell, or any visitors? Takeaway delivery perhaps?'

Rose starts to shake her head, then stops. 'I was on the phone to a… a friend.' She looks defiant. 'A *male* friend. It was my mobile not landline though, is that any help?'

It would be, if it came to the need to track her phone records, but we wouldn't be doing that at this stage and I tell her as much.

'Is there anything else you can tell me about Luke and Anna's relationship?' Tom asks, already getting up to leave.

Rose lets out a noise somewhere between a sob and a sigh. 'I don't know. How do I know anything about their relationship? I was hardly invited to dinner. I *told* him it would come to this. I told him! I said that when he left me he made the biggest mistake *of his life*. And now he's dead and I'm never going to see him again. I hope she rots in prison.'

Chapter Eleven

Rose

Anna and Luke's first date was on 7 October. It probably sounds shocking to hear that I know exactly when their affair started down to the very date – I'm not sure even they could tell you that themselves, although Luke always was very good with anniversaries so maybe *he* could. I don't know, maybe they marked their duplicity every year with a huge white cake iced with the words HAPPY CHEATIVERSARY!! At this point, nothing about my ex-husband would surprise me.

I know the date because I followed him.

We'd made a habit of going to Benicio's every Friday night – something that Luke had engineered. I hated the place, from the incompetent, judgemental children who waited tables to the dark and dreary 'ambiance', as they would say, but Luke wanted us to have a 'place', and he'd decided that Benicio's was it. I realised afterwards that I'd taken my eye off the ball slightly – of course he'd been going back for Anna, I saw that eventually, once it was too late. But like everything in his life, it was calculated. He would sometimes ask to be seated in a window table away from her section, so we weren't always served by her. I didn't catch him looking at her, or paying too much attention to her, he didn't change his tone of voice or try and have anything other than normal customer/waitress interactions. He didn't try to be witty, or confident. There wasn't one single sign I could look back at and say I should have spotted, except the fact that he knew I hated it there and still insisted that we go every Friday night. The food wasn't great, it wasn't a Michelin-starred restaurant, our friends didn't all rave about the place. He had no reason to choose Benicio's as our weekly date. That's how I should have known. I was usually so good at spotting those types of things but the one time it mattered I had been too enthralled by my husband's attention to realise that I was losing him, and to a *waitress*.

That Friday, 7 October, I received twelve red roses at the house. I knew Luke well enough to know that bad news was to follow, and to be honest when it was just a dinner cancellation I was slightly relieved. I often wondered afterwards if he'd realised that he'd gone slightly overboard, because when he came home from work and told me that he had to go and meet some colleagues to discuss a complaint he was curt, almost unapologetic. You could go mad overthinking it. Well, some would say I did go mad overthinking it.

What made me follow him, then, that night? I hadn't had the usual alarm bells sounding, he hadn't been getting text messages that he was concealing from me, or staying at work late – none of the usual clues. Call it women's intuition, I suppose, and although mine had been woefully inadequate around that time, it went off the minute Luke left the house, huge terrifying sirens that brought me to my knees in the exact same way as they had done on a wet and miserable evening four years before. And the same as before I grabbed my coat and I followed my husband.

I wasn't surprised when I saw Luke park in town and make the short walk to the restaurant, and neither was I particularly concerned. If he really was meeting colleagues then this was as good a place as any. And as I watched… nothing. No other woman showed up, and no colleague either. He glanced at his phone often as he waited there alone, and eventually the pretty blonde waitress stopped to talk to him. She smiled, and my interest was piqued. Had my gorgeous, charming husband been stood up? But by the time the evening was over I realised that the target of my husband's affection had been there all along – and when I saw the pretty blonde waitress grab her coat and leave with him it struck me just how devious Luke could be when he'd decided he wanted something. It hadn't worked last time, I thought, and this time would be the same. I'd put a stop to his affair once before by being one step ahead, I could do it again. Luke wasn't going to get away with this, and neither was the waitress.

Chapter Twelve

Anna

After the barbecue – the one where I'd overheard Tanya and Denise discussing my loose-moralled mother and weak-willed father – things were not the same for me at home. I resented them both but probably – completely unfairly – my dad the most. I used to wonder what he'd done to make her cheat on him – in my world it was always the man who cheated on the woman, it didn't really make sense for my mum to want to be unfaithful to my dad so I assumed it was his fault, he must have cheated first, or maybe he was just too controlling or overbearing. Of course now I feel terrible for putting the blame all on Dad. Even though I only ever did it in my head I still wonder if it showed in the way I treated him, if somehow he knew. If that was part of the reason he took his own life. I'll never know, of course, can't ask him and he didn't leave us a note. That's the kind of thing that can drive you insane, not in the cold light of day when you can be reasonable and rational and empathise with the young girl you used to be, but in the deepest small pockets of the night, when there is nothing to chase away the monsters inside your head. Because of you… because you didn't love him enough… because you blamed him for your mother's failings… because he knew you were never going to make anything of yourself. Because you're weak, small, pathetic, not enough for anyone.

My last memory of my mother is just before my thirteenth birthday. It's funny, because she didn't leave us until I was over fourteen, and yet now, looking back over twenty years, I can't summon up one single memory of her after this one. I'd gone into town with two girls off the estate – not friends exactly, because I didn't much like the other girls on the estate, they were loud and brash and had more confidence than I could ever have hoped to have, or maybe their insecurities were just louder and swearier. Christina and Becky, that's what they were called, and they weren't horrible girls, not really, and I wonder now if I disliked them before this day or because of it.

We were walking up the high street, having already been to Pilot, Tammy Girl and the Body Shop, when one of the girls nudged me hard in the ribs. I was chewing strawberry Hubba Bubba and I remember that I almost swallowed it, which everyone knew was the leading cause of death in twelve-year-olds.

'What was that for?' I asked loud enough for people around us to turn and look, and it was then that I saw her.

She was draped all over some bloke and it took me a minute to recognise who I was looking at. She looked like a teenager, in low-slung white jeans, a crystal G-string sticking out of the top and a bright red halter top. She didn't have very big breasts and you could tell she wasn't wearing a bra. My thirty-seven-year-old mother was sitting on the lap of some strange man I'd never seen before, her arms wrapped around his neck. She was giggling and it was clear she hadn't seen me, or heard my dramatic outburst.

'Oh my God, Anna, is that your mum?'

'Jesus fucking Christ,' I remember saying, because I nearly never swore out loud, and both girls looked more shocked to hear me say the eff word than to see my whore of a mother hanging off some bloke who wasn't my dad with her unsupported tits practically in his face.

They never said anything to me at school about it, Christina or Becky, and I don't think they told the other girls at school either because no one ever mentioned it to me. I should have been grateful to them for that, I suppose, it would have been an easy bit of gossip for them to use to elevate their status for a day or so, but they never did. But I grew to hate them because they were there – what is it they say, to bear witness? – and I've never been able to think of them since without thinking of that day and my mum in her white jeans and red halter top and the grinning pink face of the man who wasn't my father.

Chapter Thirteen

Rebecca

'Am I the only one who thinks Luke Whitney is lucky he lasted as long as he did?' Tom asks me when Rose Whitney has been picked up from the station by a friend. He doesn't expect me to play along, and I don't. 'He's got a pretty batshit taste in women,' he adds. I still ignore him. He wants me to go on a feminist rant about the way women are played against one another by men et cetera – get all riled up. He likes lighting my touchpaper then standing well back, but today I'm too busy thinking. So shove that in your pipe, Tommo.

'Do you think we need to subpoena phone records to verify her alibi?' I say eventually.

Tom shrugs. 'That'll be up to Matthews. I suppose it depends if we can find enough evidence to prove it was wife number two.' He pulls out his phone and scrolls down the notes app. Tom does everything on his phone – I still use pen and paper. Not because I hate technology, but having my head in my phone every time I want to check something makes me feel a bit rude.

'We should go and do Whitney's place of work this morning,' he says. 'It's a private practice, looks nice.' He holds up his phone and I take in the bright white interior, navy suede chaise longue.

'Better wipe your feet before we go in,' I say.

The 'private practice' Tom refers to is a cosmetic surgery clinic in Oxford. According to the clinic website Luke Whitney works here three days a week and does two days with the local NHS hospital, or at least he did until yesterday. The outside of the surgery looks like your average Victorian terraced house, only a discreet W interlocked with an O by the buzzer denoting what the building is actually used for.

A woman opens the door to us and it's clear from the look on her face that the news about Luke's death has made it this far already. Either that or she's taking 'before' pictures for the clinic's website. Her face is puffy and blotchy and she clutches a torn soggy tissue like a safety blanket. She opens her mouth, presumably to tell us that they are closed, and then sees Tom's warrant card and steps aside.

'Donald is in his office,' she says, indicating a door slightly ajar.

I smell the 'O' of the W&O Cosmetic Clinic, Donald Osbourne, moments before I see him. As the door to his office opens we're hit by a dark, spicy scent, followed by the strong smell of coffee, followed by the man himself. Tom had called ahead to make sure he was expecting us so there is no surprise on his face, just a sadness.

'Detectives, please come in.'

The man in the doorway looks to be in his late forties – although given where we are he could be a hundred and three for all I know. He's tall, trim and groomed, in an expensive, well-fitting suit. He has a kind face, a face that would definitely put you at ease before he shoved a ruddy great needle full of toxins into your forehead. His smile is incredibly white but it doesn't reach his eyes, which are red and bloodshot. He's been crying, presumably over his partner.

'I didn't know if I should just go home,' he says as we follow him inside. There are only two chairs – his behind the desk and one in front. I take the chair in front, leaving Tom to stand. 'I can't get my head around anything. I don't have surgery today but I have four consultations and people travel here from all over…' His words tail off. He doesn't look the type of man who is easily rattled, but right now he can't finish a thought. 'I can't believe it. Is it true then?'

'I'm afraid so,' Tom says. Donald closes his eyes and rests his head on his hands.

'Who told you?' Tom asks him.

'Rose called,' Donald replies. 'She was hyperventilating over the phone – it was all I could do to understand a word she was saying.'

Tom nods. 'Mrs Whitney was particularly upset at the station.'

'Of course she was, she was devastated, poor bean. Rose has always been, and will always be, completely in love with Luke. Ever since way back at university.'

'Which was?'

'Oxford.' Donald turns around and picks up a framed photo from a shelf behind him, hands it to me. It's a group of fresh-faced Etonian-looking teenagers, mostly boys but there are two girls in the photo too. In my head I hear a guffawing laugh and an RP accent saying '*naturally*'. An image of a room full of politicians all saying 'yah' and 'tot-ah-ly' fills my head and—

'…as I'm sure you can imagine. God, this is all so horrific.'

Oh shit, I've missed something. I'm usually pretty good at remembering to maintain focus, not let my mind wander off thinking about how a man as busy as Donald Osbourne manages to keep his shoes so shiny, and does he have a housekeeper who does that for him and what does a housekeeper actually do anyway, and I've done it again.

'Sorry,' I interrupt, and I can feel Tom glaring at the back of my head. 'What can we imagine?'

Donald frowns, as if he's not sure what I'm not understanding. I silently berate myself for not being stricter about paying attention. 'Well, a medical student dating a philosophy student, the kinds of arguments they would have. Okay, so it was politics and philosophy that Rose studied, but still, she gave him a run for his money. He always used to say that she stimulated him, intellectually. That's why we were all surprised when he... when they...'

'When he cheated on her with Anna,' Tom finishes. I am still processing what he said. Rose Whitney, the Rose Whitney we saw this morning, is a philosophy and politics graduate? Talk about not judging a book by its cover.

'I was going to say when they broke up, but yes, of course, it did start as an affair, with Anna. I knew he was having a fling with some waitress, and Luke knew that I wasn't happy about it, but what can you do? I don't think any of us expected him to marry her.'

He splays his fingers out on the table in front of him and stretches them in and out. He doesn't feel comfortable talking about this, and that's understandable, he and Luke have been friends since university, they've probably kept plenty of each other's secrets.

'I mean, don't get me wrong, Anna was, is, beautiful, but... well, like I said, Rose worshipped him. It wasn't right.'

'Was Anna the first affair Luke had had?' I ask. Donald purses his lips as if he's trying to hold the information in.

'I'm not really comfortable answering that question,' he says. Neither I nor Tom say anything in reply, the silence growing thick between the three of us. We are incredibly good at this, this awkward long pause. As always, we win.

'Well, look,' he says, lifting up his hands. 'I suppose it's all in the past now, and Luke...' His words tail off but the meaning is clear. Luke can't get in any trouble now, can he? 'There was one other woman, well, one that I know of. Seemed very taken with Luke, got a bit problematic I think. But him and Rose sorted things out that time. Anyway, like I say, it's all in the past. Look, can you tell me what happened? I'm finding this all incredibly surreal, it's like a nightmare.'

Tom clears his throat, an indication for me to say nothing.

'We're investigating all possibilities,' he says instead. 'You say Rose was still in love with Mr Whitney?'

Donald lets out a humourless laugh. 'Love, obsession, whatever. I'm not sure Rose even knows anymore. She gave so much of herself to him... or rather she gave what she thought Luke wanted. The surgery, the Stepford Wife routine – but Luke needed someone he couldn't handle. Rose was... Wait, God, you're not saying... did Rose do this?'

'She's not currently a person of interest,' Tom replies with a shake of his head. Donald looks relieved.

'And Anna? Is she okay?'

Tom smiles so his next words don't come across as a reprimand. 'I was hoping we could ask the questions, Mr Osbourne. Although I can tell you that the current Mrs Whitney hasn't been physically harmed. Now, can you think of anyone who might want to hurt Luke? Anyone at all?'

'Are you asking if Luke was universally liked?' Osbourne asks. 'Because he wasn't. For a start, he was arrogant. He knew that women found him attractive, and that his wealth made him doubly so. His arrogance and his success made him popular with some and unpopular with others. Would those people piss on him if he were on fire? Maybe not. Do I know of any of them who would want to physically cause him harm personally? No.'

He says all this as if he's giving a speech at the Oscars. Almost as if he'd written, planned and rehearsed it. But that isn't possible, is it? Because he said he only heard about what happened to Luke when he arrived at work an hour ago.

'Could he handle Anna?' I ask, impatient to get to the point. I don't look at Tom, even though I know he's looking at me, probably very intently, and doing that annoying throat clearing thing again. I don't really care – he could cough up a lung and I'd still want to get the answers we came for. No more pussyfooting around because this guy smells like his lawyer would be expensive.

Donald looks puzzled.

'You said Luke needed someone he couldn't "handle". Could he handle his new wife?'

'Oh, I see.' Donald rubs his face and sighs. 'Anna is certainly different to Rose. Rose is a clever woman in an academic sense, but Anna went into her marriage in possession of all of the facts. She knew Luke had left his first wife for her and she knew she needed to be different than Rose if she wanted him to stay.'

'Did their arguments ever get heated? Physical?'

Osbourne laughs at this, then his face turns serious. 'You're kidding, right?'

'I don't consider domestic violence a joke, Mr Osbourne.'

'No, sorry.' He looks suitably chastened. 'You're right. The idea is just so ludicrous. I can't imagine Luke hitting any woman, let alone Anna.' He hesitates. 'He might have had a couple of scraps at uni, but with blokes, not women. Then there was a story doing the rounds that one of the guests at a party got a little, let's say, handsy, with Anna. Got the wrong end of the stick, thought she was propositioning him. Luke punched him in the face, broke his nose the rumour was, but when I asked him he played it down. But the idea of him hitting Anna is preposterous.'

'And Anna? Did Luke ever mention any occasion where she was physical with him?'

Osbourne frowns. 'Not to me. And I can't picture that either.' He shakes his head as if having some conversation with himself. 'No. Absolutely not.'

'And what about their relationship? Any problems that you're aware of?'

'I really wouldn't know,' Donald Osbourne lies incredibly smoothly. 'Luke hasn't mentioned anything to me.' He's been telling the truth – I'd bet my job on it – right up until now. So there were problems between Luke and Anna.

Tom has no idea that Osbourne has just lied to him – although I doubt he'll be hugely surprised when I tell him.

'Thanks, Mr Osbourne. One other thing – what size shoe do you wear?'

'Twelve. Why?'

'Standard question,' Tom says unconvincingly. 'Thank you for your time.'

Chapter Fourteen

Anna

The music, the lighting, the ambiance; it had been five years since I'd worked in Benicio's and not a thing had changed except the staff. But even though I didn't recognise any of the faces of the table staff, these teens and twenty-somethings could have been any of us from back then – their plastered-on smiles hiding their exhaustion and desperation to get outside for a cold beer and a fag. The only person we'd seen who had remained unchanged was the front of house, Marco, who had given Luke and me an appraising look, a look that clearly said that he hadn't forgotten where I'd come from.

I was browsing the menu when Luke excused himself to go to the toilet. The menu hadn't changed either, and I still didn't like anything on it – it was all far too fancy. I took the time alone to take in everything around me – despite nothing having changed, everything looked different from the other side of the table. The other patrons looked less like the enemy, ready to complain about the slightest of inconveniences, but rather human beings just enjoying a Friday night out.

Just when I was thinking that Luke seemed to have been taking forever at the loo, I noticed him standing in the foyer – nowhere near the toilets – tucking his phone back into the pocket of his suit trousers. He wasn't alone. Standing next to him was a beautiful leggy brunette, still smiling as though they'd just finished sharing a private joke. I felt a shockwave of jealousy shoot through me. What were they talking about? Had he just taken her number? Luke was watching her with a look I'd seen him direct at me a million times. *Lust.* They stood for a moment, finishing whatever conversation they'd been having. My husband was clearly in no hurry to get back to his wife sitting on her own at the table waiting for him. A slow smile spread across his face, open and genuine, and like a punch to my stomach he reached out a hand and touched the woman's bare arm.

I tried my best to look normal when he came back to the table. I managed not to ask immediately who she was, or what he was playing at – I reminded myself on a daily basis that I was not Rose. I didn't need to be some jealous harpy, I was his wife. I was not going to be replaced by some gurning floozy in a tight dress.

You weren't even wearing a tight dress when he replaced Rose with you, the little voice in my head reminded me helpfully.

We ordered food that I knew would be pretentious and overpriced, because that's who I was now. Back when I worked here I couldn't even justify spending the amount the customers dropped on a tip on a meal, now I didn't even check the price before I ordered. Luke was talking about something that had gone on at the practice that day but I didn't take in a word, just got steadily more and more irritated by the fact that he hadn't mentioned who that woman was. He must have known that I'd seen him, that I'd want to know who he was talking to. Was he withholding the information on purpose, waiting to see if I would ask? Was I being tested to see if I was just as bad as the ex? Was this who I was now? Some jealous wife who couldn't stand her husband saying hello to another woman. From the amount of work she'd had done it was most likely Luke had been responsible for those lips, or worse, those breasts. I'd had to get used to that fact over the years, that Luke's work was almost as intimate as you could get, so why was it bothering me so much this time?

You know what he's capable of... a voice in my head told me. *You know how he pursued you.*

'Excuse me,' I said, getting up from the table a little more sharply than I'd intended. 'Ladies' room.'

I gripped the edges of the cold marbled sink and looked at myself in the mirror. *Get it together*, I told my reflection. *Luke loves you. Just because he tired of Rose... you are not Rose.*

I was still distracted on my walk back to the table, lost in crazy thoughts of returning to my seat to find the leggy brunette sitting there ready to replace me the way I'd replaced the previous Mrs Whitney. So much so that I nearly collided with one of the waiters returning to the kitchen.

'Oh, I'm sorry,' I apologised, looking up into a young face that would be handsome had it not borne the scars of adolescent acne. He couldn't have been more than nineteen, twenty maybe and he looked mortified at our near collision. His name badge said Will.

'My fault.' He motioned to the plate in his right hand, empty but for some dregs of jus. 'I'm just glad you didn't end up with this on that beautiful dress.'

I smiled at the compliment and he continued, 'It's only my third shift and I dread doing something stupid like that. The people who eat here are all just so...'

'Stuck up?' I offered. His face reddened even deeper.

'I was going to say well dressed.'

My smile widened to a grin. 'I used to work here,' I confided. I snuck a look over to where Luke was waiting at the table for me. I wasn't a hundred per cent sure but I could have sworn I saw his head snap back down. Had he been watching me talking to this boy? I put a hand on his arm. 'I'm well aware of what the staff think of the guests.'

His eyes widened. 'You worked here? Wow, I wouldn't have guessed. You've obviously moved on to somewhere better now.'

I smiled, flattered that he hadn't assumed that I could only afford to eat in a place like this now because I was with Luke, although of course it was the truth. Dinner for two at Benicio's cost at least a day's salary in my teaching job, more if you had dessert and coffee.

'Well, we all have to start somewhere. I'm sure you're heading for better things too.'

He looked sheepish. 'I'm saving so I can go travelling, I want to do some volunteer work abroad. No idea what I'm going to do after that.'

A feeling I couldn't quite identify, the sensation that I'd swallowed something stodgy and unpleasant that was lodged somewhere in my chest, materialised at his words. *I wanted to do that once*, I wanted to say. *I was going to volunteer abroad, or head up a charity. I was going to make a difference.* But I didn't say any of that out loud. Sometimes life doesn't work out the way you've planned, but that doesn't mean it's better or worse than you'd hoped for it to be. How do you plan for a man like Luke sweeping you off your feet? I couldn't say I'd sacrificed a dream when it had never felt like a sacrifice to me. If you dreamed of winning fifty grand on a scratchcard would you call it a sacrifice if you won a hundred instead?

Instead I gave the top of his arm a slow rub, hoping my husband was watching once again. 'That's a good enough plan as any,' I told him, suddenly feeling every one of my thirty-two years, worldly and wise. 'You should always follow your dreams, and do whatever it takes to get there.'

When I arrived back at the table Luke's face was a picture of hard lines.

'What, you didn't invite your new friend to join us?' He motioned his head towards the waiter I'd been speaking to.

'My new friend?' I smiled, trying for innocent confusion. It pleased me that I could provoke this kind of reaction in him, the same reaction he'd provoked in me when I saw him talking to the gorgeous brunette. Served him right. Did he think I was going to go down without a fight?

'Oh, you mean Will?' I raised my eyebrows and Luke inclined his head. 'What a sweet kid. He's saving to do volunteer work abroad. Very noble, don't you think?'

A tight smile crossed his lips. 'Very.'

'I wonder if *your* new friend does charity work?' I said pointedly. 'Or maybe her only hobby is flirting with married men?'

Luke followed my gaze to where the woman was still sitting, one leg crossed over the other, laying bare an expanse of creamy tanned thigh, her manicured fingers grasping the stem of the champagne flute she was holding as comfortably as I nursed my half pint of cider. Luke didn't even have the good grace to look embarrassed, in fact his mood seemed to improve.

'Oh yes.' He grinned. 'The lovely Jemma. Don't sulk, sweetheart, it doesn't suit you. Jemma doesn't hold a candle to you as far as I'm concerned.' He leaned over and kissed me lightly on the mouth. 'Shall we call it one all, my darling? We'll have to forget the food – you understand I can't sit and eat somewhere where my wife has intentionally tried to humiliate me. Now shall we go home and you can tell me what I'm going to get from you that your toy-boy waiter isn't?'

That was the night that we both discovered that jealousy turned Luke on. He cancelled our meals and dragged me home to 'punish' me, where we had the hottest sex of our lives, me telling him in a helpless, frightened voice how sorry I was, and how I'd never look at another man again. I'll admit, I liked it too, that feeling of being dominated, taught a lesson. We both thought then that it was a bit of harmless fun. No one needed to get hurt. How foolish.

It was obvious that me pouting over his 'harmless banter' with another woman wasn't about to stop him flirting with women, and I knew that I would have to give him a reason to keep coming back to me – a reason Rose had failed to discover. To do that I knew I was going to have to play a game that Rose had clearly not known the rules of. So play I would. But I wasn't like Rose, and I wasn't like my father. In this marriage this was my game, and I would be the one to make the rules.

Chapter Fifteen

Rose

Everyone saw her as such an innocent young girl – even though at twenty-eight she was only five years younger than me. I suppose she's got one of those faces that men fall in love with – they want to protect her, and they nearly never realise it's them who need protecting from women like her until it's too late. Well, now it's too late for Luke.

Luke was my everything from the moment we met, and I thought that because he treated me to nice restaurants and gifts, told me that I was the only woman he'd ever loved and showered me with compliments, it was forever. And it was forever… until it wasn't. Looking back that's the way it had always been with Luke: you could literally be the centre his universe, rotated around until the next shiny object moved into his field of vision. I knew that about him, I knew him better than he thought I did – why do you think I ended up the way I was? Always made up like a shop mannequin, always striving for perfection. Luke spends too long talking to the big-breasted sales assistant? Rose gets her boobs done. Luke shows more than a passing interest in the bleach blonde hairdresser? I reach for the bottle. Now you're thinking that I'm some kind of insecure nutcase, but that wasn't how it was, I promise.

Let me try to explain to you about life with Luke Whitney. When he first sets his sights on you, when he decides you are the one, it is the most wonderful feeling in the world. It's like you've lived the rest of your life in darkness and he has come along and turned a spotlight on you. You'd do anything to stay there, basking in the warmth of his attentive gaze. He is as addictive as any drug; once you've had a hit of him, the idea of not having him in your life, of being shut off from his love and attention, is terrifying. You would do anything to keep that life, change anything about yourself that he finds lacking, destroy anyone who threatens your perfect existence. It's not rational – you become like a stranger to yourself. So how does he do it? He never once asked me to change a thing about myself. He never once told me that he preferred that girl's hair, or that my breasts weren't as pert as they once were. It's way more subtle than that. Luke just slowly withdraws his attention, a slight shift in his axis from you to, well, anyone or anything else. If you've made him happy he only has eyes for you, you will spend the day bathed in his love and affection. He will link his fingers through yours as you walk down the street, place his hand on the small of your back and rub his thumb against your skin, you'll spend afternoons feeding ducks in the park and lunching in rooftop restaurants. Once he hired a camper van and drove us out to a clifftop, opened the side and we watched the sun setting, snuggled under a blanket with glasses of champagne in our hands. You might think it doesn't sound that special, sitting in a car drinking and talking about the future, but it was all planned to perfection – maximum effect, that's Luke. With him there were none of those never-ending conversations, 'what-do-you-want-to-do, I-don't-mind-what-do-you-want-to-do' – he always had a suggestion, always a plan to make your day more special than regular people's. Life with him – on the good days – was like living inside the pages of a novel.

And that's what made Luke so dangerous. Because try explaining to someone that you know your husband is disappointed in you because he let you choose what you wanted to do this weekend, or because he didn't make some elaborate plan to picnic on top of some mountain somewhere. And how you know he'd prefer you had bigger boobs because he bought you new lingerie two cup sizes too big. You'd sound paranoid, crazy. Because normal men get things like that wrong all the time. But not Luke. Luke knew my dress size, what colours, shapes and styles suited me the best, where I got my hair cut and the name of the woman who cut it.

Like when I put on a few pounds and Luke had a work party coming up. He insisted on treating me to a new dress, only he purposely bought a size smaller than I usually took, knowing I wouldn't want to admit that it didn't even do up. I barely ate for three weeks, more of a fast than a diet, drank nothing but water and did sit-ups until I thought I was going to throw up. And on the evening of the party, when I slid into the dress, almost crying with relief, he looked so proud that I instantly forgot that he'd manipulated me into losing twelve pounds in three weeks. He'd done me a favour, I thought, I'd never have found the motivation to shed those extra pounds if he hadn't given me an incentive. Clever Luke. And he was so concerned, so loving and caring when I collapsed at the party – it wasn't his fault that I hadn't eaten more than vegetable soup for three days.

I knew, by the end, that he was being unfaithful to me. I knew about Laura, watched the situation, and when it seemed as though things were getting too serious with her – he was spending more time with her than at home, he was taking bigger risks – I dropped the bomb that I was pregnant. He never admitted to the affair but I knew when it was over. He came back to me, and was so supportive, so attentive. And he was devastated at the 'miscarriage'. But Laura was out of the picture by then and he was mine again.

Until Anna.

Chapter Sixteen

Anna

'What are you playing at, Anna?'

My very expensive brief's face has turned so pink that he looks like he's been on a two-week holiday too close to the equator. I almost feel sorry for him – a client who admits her guilt minutes into the interview is hardly ideal, but with the amount he charges it wouldn't kill him to work a bit harder for his exorbitant fee. My head pounds and bright lights begin to seep into the corner of my vision. Stress migraine. I've suffered from them for years, the only surprise really is that it's taken this long to come on.

I sigh, and try to put on my best 'little girl lost' face, but the throbbing gets too much and I have to cover my eyes with my hands. When I take them down Tate hands me a cup of water, his face softening slightly. 'I just want it all over with, Mr Tate, I can't stand all of this, it's horrible.'

Patrick leans over and rubs my arm. He doesn't know me well enough to touch me – I could hardly use Luke's lawyer and I've never needed one of my own – but he does it anyway. If I was a man he wouldn't dream of rubbing my arms, but now isn't the time to start spouting feminism at the man who is trying to secure my release from prison. I've been awkward enough, I'll let him off his pitiful, misogynistic attempt to make me feel better about my husband's murder. 'I know it feels like you should be answering all of the police's questions,' he says, 'but you're not under any obligation to say anything – especially if it's going to incriminate you in a murder. I would strongly advise that you answer "no comment" to all further questions. Or at the very least stop professing your guilt to anyone who will listen.'

'I don't see how—'

'No, Anna, it's me who doesn't see,' Tate cuts me off, his voice back to migraine-inducing sharp. 'I don't understand why, if you didn't kill Luke, you are insisting that you did?'

Hearing him say Luke's name in that offhanded way, as if he's just another dead husband, a number on the call sheet, feels like a stab in the chest, and I have to force myself not to cry. Crying is good for my case, of course – I need to look like I'm an emotional mess after all, but it's also almost guaranteed to set off the threatening migraine, and I need to be thinking straight when the officers come back in to interview me again. 'I don't see what difference it makes,' I say, hearing the weary tone of my voice. 'Even if I said I was innocent they wouldn't believe me, would they? They're predisposed to think everyone they take into that room is a liar. At least if they think I'm a liar then that means they think I'm innocent.'

I am fully aware of how ridiculous this sounds as I hear myself say it, but it's the best reason I can give for why an innocent woman would plead guilty to murder, other than the truth, and I can't exactly hand that to Patrick Tate, he'd have a bloody embolism. I have to count on DS Dance doing what she is good at – questioning the obvious.

'Is that some kind of joke?' Predictably, Tate is furious, and I can hardly blame him. I hope he doesn't resign as my lawyer but it doesn't much matter if he does, I suppose. Nothing much matters anymore – the wheels are in motion and what will be, will be. 'This isn't some TV programme, Anna, you can't mess about giving false confessions to the police. Juries have been known to convict on confessions alone. Do you want to go to prison for murder?'

I shake my head, doubts creeping in that he might be right. What if the police ignore everything else and the CPS decide to convict me based on my confession alone? I suddenly feel incredibly stupid, and naive. Have I been a complete idiot? Am I going to prison?

No, I've got to stick to the plan. But I need DS Dance to keep questioning the validity of my confession, my freedom depends on it. I've just got to hope she's as good at her job as she thinks she is. Well, maybe not quite as good. I don't want her finding out the *whole* truth, after all.

Chapter Seventeen

Rebecca

Anna looks worse the second time we meet, and it reminds me that even though twenty-four hours feels like a ridiculously short time for us to gather enough evidence to charge or release, it's a long old time for someone sitting in a cell staring at the same four walls. It's twelve thirty pm, less than twelve hours since she arrived, but already she looks like she's spent six months behind bars – this woman is not cut out for jail. Skin that would have been described as 'alabaster' yesterday would be called pallid today, and under her eyes is a livid purple. Now she's picking at the loose skin around her thumb and avoiding looking at either of us. She looks almost broken.

Tom starts the tape – he's not messing around. He does all of the usual spiel and looks at Anna.

'Mrs Whitney, we have some follow-up questions.'

Anna nods, not looking at either of us. I wonder what she's thinking. Has it dawned on her, the consequences of what she's admitting to? If I'm right and she is lying about stabbing her husband, who would she be protecting? I could easily believe that a mother would take the blame for her son or daughter but they don't have children; a sibling, perhaps, yet Anna is an only child and Luke's only brother lives in Australia, which is a pretty watertight alibi.

Rose? Anna stole Rose's husband, her home, her life – is this some kind of atonement? Or is Anna a murderer and I've read the whole situation wrong?

'We've spoken to Luke's ex-wife,' Tom starts. I see Anna sit up a little straighter.

'What did she say?' It's the first time I've seen her show any real interest in something we've told her. Tom repeats the story Rose told us about the scalding tea. I can see Anna's jaw tighten – she's furious.

'Is what Rose told us true?' Tom asks her.

Anna hesitates. Eventually she mutters, 'If that's what she says,' and looks back down at her fingernails.

'Why don't you tell us *your* version?'

'Is this relevant to the situation with Mr Whitney?' Anna's lawyer cuts in.

'Yes,' Tom says, his voice showing his irritation. We aren't in court and he doesn't have a judge to answer to, the lawyer is just trying to assert some dominance.

'I would remind you that you have been advised to answer "no comment",' he says. She shakes her head and he lets out a sigh that indicates just how fed up he is with his client.

'It's fine.' Anna sighs. 'Rose came to the house, still furious after all that time, which was strange because Luke had always told me that she was the one who wanted things to end and that they were basically over before we ever got together.'

I almost roll my eyes. Surely she knows that's cheating husband 101? She doesn't meet my eyes as she carries on.

'I know what you're thinking, every married man says that. Probably they do, but I'd never been with a married man before and I wasn't exactly worldly-wise. Anyway, so Rose comes round, furious about something. I was in the kitchen and she just came at me. I was nursing the cup of coffee I'd just made when all of a sudden she was in my face as I turned around, flying at me with her fake hair and a face as blood red as the nails she always wore. I didn't have time to react, my coffee flew from my hands, landing all over the beautiful yellow sundress she was wearing and turning her leg the same shade of red as her face. She froze in shock for a second then started to scream. Luke rushed in just as I'd regained my senses enough to hurl a tea towel under the running faucet. He snatched it out of my hands, the healthcare professional inside him jumping into action. He doused the burns with cold water and made her take off the dress. I fetched her one of my dressing gowns – admittedly the oldest and most unflattering I could find – and as I returned to the kitchen I was just in time to hear her telling Luke how we'd been arguing when I'd flung my scalding hot coffee in the direction of her legs.'

Almost the exact opposite of what Rose had told us. 'Did Luke believe her?' I ask.

'I just sort of spluttered that it wasn't true. I was so shocked at such a blatant lie told right to my face I was practically incapable of normal speech. He told me to wait upstairs and his voice was like ice. Then Rose... she smiled.'

Interesting.

'Why would Luke believe what she said over his wife?' Tom asks.

'Rose can be incredibly convincing,' Anna says with a shrug.

'Donald Osbourne seems to think that it would be very out of character for Luke to become physically violent with you.'

'You've been busy,' Anna says, and I see a spark of the woman she might be outside of all of this. So far she's done little more than stare at her thumbnail and squeak out the odd answer, but hearing that we've been speaking to people that Luke and Anna know has lit a bit of a fire under Mrs Whitney. Did she honestly think that by confessing to the crime we would close the case and not speak to anyone else she knew?

'It's our job,' I reply. 'He also said that the only time Luke has ever shown any sign of violence was when someone was inappropriate with you.'

Anna frowns slightly, then comprehension dawns. 'Oh yes, the party. Well, again, that was another misunderstanding.'

'You have a lot of those, do you? Misunderstandings?'

'Luke was very protective of me,' Anna says. 'That's really all there was to it.'

And there's another lie.

Chapter Eighteen

Anna

The driveway wound around the perfectly manicured lawn and was littered with dozens of cars which combined cost more than the house I grew up in. The grand front entrance was lit by uplighters either side and conifers flanked the doorway like sentries. Luke placed a hand on my knee as the Bentley we were in rolled to a stop and the front door opened. Our driver, Bill, walked around to Luke's side first – as he always did – so that when I was helped out of the car with a chivalrous hand my husband was waiting for me to join his side. This was another thing about this lifestyle I had had to get used to, waiting for my door to be opened rather than throwing it wide myself the minute the car stopped like I did the first time Bill took us out. He'd smiled, embarrassed for me when I'd nearly hit him in the face with the car door as I'd hauled myself out. Nowadays I knew better.

'Thank you, Bill,' I said demurely, then gave him a quick grin. I lowered my voice so Luke didn't hear. 'You like my dress?'

Bill smiled and gave me a discreet thumbs up. Of course he liked it – my entire outfit cost his month's wage, it was obscene. I smoothed down the front of the red sequinned gown, fluffed the front of my freshly highlighted hair and adjusted the diamonds at my neck before turning to join my husband.

'You look sensational,' he murmured in my ear, his fingers lacing around the spaghetti straps, twisting them into place, making certain I was presentable for his important friends. 'I'm the luckiest man here.'

'You'd better believe it,' I replied, turning my face so his kiss landed on my cheek. Best not to smudge my lipstick just before we walked in.

Our host tonight was Dr Jeffery Henshaw, and as was evidenced by his impressive home, the doctor was not your average GP. In fact he was a surgeon for a private practice in Cambridge – one of the finest in the country. Luke informed me before we left home that he had recently returned from conducting pioneering heart research in California. That's why Luke had been so antsy all evening – Dr Henshaw was a 'proper' surgeon.

Luke was a proper surgeon as well of course, only he saved people's faces rather than their lives. I was ignorant of most of the politics that surrounded the medical community but despite all Luke's wealth and reputation I knew that he always felt second class to the likes of Henshaw. Which is why it was so important that I made a good impression tonight.

I took my husband's arm and walked as steadily as I could across the gravelled driveway in my heels. We made a stunning pair, there was no doubt about that, and I knew the other wives at the Henshaws' party tonight would be nudging one another, wondering if I had availed myself of my husband's magic hands, a nip here, a tuck there. I have come across them before, stupid jealous women who are threatened by younger, natural-looking women. The fact is I hadn't yet needed to consider plastic surgery. My blonde hair was mostly natural, with some expensive and well placed highlights, I was blessed with good skin and I ate well. Even if I would need the odd procedure as I age I would die before letting someone make me look like I'd been moulded from wax, the way Luke's ex-wife did.

Stop it, Anna, I chided myself. Now wasn't the time to be thinking about Rose Whitney. Tonight we were going to have fun.

—

Two hours later and the idea of fun was a distant memory. Luke had disappeared half an hour ago and I had been stuck in a circle jerk of congratulatory medics ever since. *Oh, I heard about the work you did in Cambodia, isn't it just amazing to be able to give something back? Well that's nothing compared to the money your fundraiser made for *insert charity of the moment*.* I had nodded and laughed in all the right places, even added a witty one-liner here or there – not enough to monopolise the conversation but enough to demonstrate my intellect. Now I was bored.

'Excuse me,' I murmured, well aware that the two men I was talking to (or rather listening to talk) would barely notice I was gone. What was the point of a dress like this if all the men here were too self-absorbed to even notice? And where exactly was Luke?

Approaching the doorway of the vast open-plan kitchen I could see exactly where my husband had disappeared to. He was standing at the far end, next to a sweeping marble breakfast bar, laughing loudly – far too loudly for anywhere except maybe a comedy club – at a woman with ginormous breasts and a dress two sizes too small to contain them. He was propping himself against the breakfast bar with one arm as the fingers of his other hand swept the woman's elbow gently. Ah, so that's how this was going to be. Without making myself known, I turned and left the kitchen, pushing my way to the stairs. I took a jacket – God knows whose – from a peg in the hallway and made my way to the guest bedroom, which I'd noted on the tour of the house Henshaw had given when we first arrived had its own balcony.

Pushing open the door the first thing I noticed was that I wasn't alone. A tall man in a long jacket stood at the far end of the balcony, a cigarette in his fingers. He looked up guiltily when I stepped into the light, but smiled when I held up my own pack.

'Didn't think I'd find anyone else smoking at a doctor's party,' I said, pulling out my phone to check for messages. Nothing. I tapped out my own and clicked send. 'Aren't you supposed to be telling me how many days I'm shaving off my life with one of these things?'

'Insurance broker.' He held up his hands. 'I can tell you how much it will add to the cost of your life insurance, if you'd like?'

'Tell my husband,' I remarked with a shrug. 'He pays for all that.'

'In that case…' The man held up a lighter and I moved in closer to hold my cigarette up to it. Up close I could see that he wasn't completely unfortunate looking – not attractive like Luke, but not ugly, either. He had that monied look about him, the one that screamed private education. His dark hair was thinning slightly – I bet he'd be paying for plugs in the next few years – and his nose was a little too prominent, but he was well groomed and expensively dressed. He'd do.

'This is the part where I ask you if you find these things as tedious as me, and you tell me you're the host's brother or something,' I said, not stepping away once my cigarette was lit. The man smiled, amused.

'Yes, and no,' he replied. 'Henshaw is an old friend of my wife's father. Which means I get dragged along to listen to how much money they've all donated to whichever charity is on the most-worthy list this year.'

My smile was genuine then. 'Oh, same. My husband is a cosmetic surgeon, which inevitably means he'll be in a foul mood after spending the evening in the company of all these life-saving heart surgeons.'

The man's eyes widened and he grinned. 'So even the elite feel inferior to someone. He must be very good, your husband. I would have sworn you'd had no work done at all.'

It was the type of remark that would usually have infuriated me – an insult veiled in a thin compliment. But I thought of Luke flirting with the huge-breasted woman and forced myself to raise my eyebrows good-naturedly.

'You have some cheek. I've never been under the knife and you know it.'

'You certainly don't need it.'

'Oh, I don't know.' I slipped off the stolen jacket and ran my fingers over my chest, watching his eyes follow their journey. 'I've always thought I could use some enhancement in some areas.'

The man swallowed. 'You look perfect to me.'

'You're too kind.' I took his hand in mine. His palms were clammy and I could bet that if I pressed my hand to his chest, his heart would be racing. I lifted his fingers to the thin strap of my dress and hooked them underneath. This would be the moment – when he made the decision about just how much he loved his wife. As always, the answer was *not enough*.

He slid the strap down over my shoulder, exposing the top of my breast. I slid the other strap down myself, hearing his breathing quicken. I reached up to undo the buttons of his pale blue shirt, gently leading him backwards into the warmth of the room behind us. The balcony was too exposed, anyone could be walking the lush green gardens below and look up, get their very own show.

His shirt was on the floor now, and he pushed my dress slowly down to my waist, as though I was some rare animal that might scarper if he made any sudden movements. He took a sharp breath in when he saw that I wasn't wearing a bra. In fact, if I'd planned to let him get much further he would see that I wore no underwear at all – Luke preferred to know I was completely nude underneath whatever expensive dress he'd chosen for me.

'Just as I said,' he whispered, his mouth next to my ear, his hand snaking around the back of my neck. 'Perfect.'

He leaned down to kiss me but I turned subtly away, moving his head instead, downwards. He went where I guided, kissing my neck, then my collarbone, then moving his lips to my taut, rounded nipple. I knew that he wasn't lying when he said my body was perfect. I'd been careful to keep myself in shape, I'd had no children and I was still young enough that everything was where it should be. And if I should begin to sag or wrinkle I would have no problem availing myself of the best my husband's profession had to offer. Luke liked the way I looked and I had every intention of staying like this for as long as I could afford.

The man let out a small moan of pleasure and I wondered when the last time was that he'd had sex. Was his wife the kind of woman who held out, using her sexuality as a weapon or a bargaining tool? I didn't understand women like that. Did they not realise that men were simple beings? If they weren't getting what they needed at home they would eventually go where they could get it. And judging by how easily this one had been broken, and how eagerly he took my nipple into his mouth, he wasn't getting anything at home. I tried not to let him see me checking my watch behind his head.

'I see you've met my wife.'

So consumed had he been with my bare chest that the man hadn't heard the door to the guest room click open. But he heard Luke's voice and his head snapped backwards sharply as my husband grabbed him by the hair and yanked his face from my breasts. I let out a small scream, not loud enough to draw attention to the room from the party below, and grabbed my dress, pulled it up to cover myself.

'Luke, please.' I let out a sob as Luke pulled back his fist and slammed it into the man's face. The man sagged to the floor, but Luke wasn't finished. He dragged him up again and landed a punch to his stomach. 'Luke, stop!'

The man held up his hands in a pathetic attempt to shield himself from Luke's blows. 'I'm sorry,' he gasped. 'I didn't know she was married.'

Luke dropped him to the floor and shoved him with his foot. 'Get out,' he snarled. 'Get the fuck out. And if you tell a single person about this I'll make sure Enid knows all about every woman you've ever fucked behind her back. See how long Daddy's trust fund sustains you after that.'

The man scrabbled to his knees and towards the door. 'I'm sorry. Please, I...'

'I said get. Out.'

The door slammed behind him and Luke turned to me, still holding the front of my dress over my chest.

'What the fuck, Anna?'

I faked another sob. 'Luke, I'm sorry, it was a mistake—'

Luke's face was pure fury. 'A mistake? It didn't look like a mistake to me. From where I was standing it looked like you knew exactly what you were doing. Or should I say, what he was doing to you.'

'What do you want me to say?' I moved towards him and he grabbed the straps of the dress I was still holding against me. Luke grabbed both of my wrists and the dress fell once more to my waist. He released my wrists and yanked it the rest of the way down until I was standing before him completely naked.

'I don't want you to say anything,' he hissed through gritted teeth. His fingers moved to the zipper of his suit fly and he yanked it down, shoving me face down onto the bed and grabbing a handful of my hair.

-

'You took your time,' I said as I fixed my hair back into a chignon. Luke took my hand and turned it over to examine my wrist. There was a small red mark where his fingers had bitten into my skin less than half an hour ago.

'Shit, did I hurt you?'

'A little.' I smiled and moved my arm away. I sometimes wondered if that was his favourite part of the game, the anger, me helpless and pleading forgiveness. He'd actually scared me a little this time, but I wasn't going to let him know that. 'Don't look so worried, you know I like it when you get a little rough. Did you have to hit him so hard though? Won't people ask what happened when he goes back to the party with a shiner?'

'Simon Reynolds? Slimy little bastard deserved it. Did you not tell him you were married? I thought we'd agreed you'd tell them. It's hardly fair not to.'

'Of course I told him.' I clicked open my bag and ran my lipstick over my lips. 'Twice, in fact. What kept you?'

'Funnily enough I was talking to Simon's wife,' Luke said, smoothing down my dress and taking the opportunity to run his hand over my backside at the same time. 'But I'm guessing you already know that, given your little performance. A bit risky trying it here, sweetheart.'

'I didn't realise it was his wife you were flirting with,' I said honestly. 'Blimey, given the size of her chest I'm surprised he almost shot his load when I got mine out.'

Luke snorted back a laugh. 'Yours are perfect. And they're natural. Plus I doubt Simon's seen Enid's tits since their wedding night.'

'Poor bloke. First bit of action he's seen in years and you burst in and almost break his nose.'

'Oh, I'm sorry, should I have let you two get on with it then?' Luke teased. He pulled me in for a kiss and I squirmed away.

'Oh bugger off, I've just fixed my lipstick. Come on, Enid will be wondering where you've got to.'

'Don't tell me you're jealous?'

'Jealous?' I stopped in my tracks and fixed him with a look. I made the room, remember? 'You watch your lip, Mr Whitney, or next time I'll leave it at least five minutes longer before I send the text.'

Chapter Nineteen

Interview with Mr and Mrs Tovey

Present: Moss and Stone

#

Moss: As I'm sure you're both aware, there has been an incident at the cottage next door, in the early hours of this morning. We're talking to everyone in the area but obviously you are the nearest neighbours to Mr and Mrs Whitney and therefore the most important potential witnesses.

Mr Tovey: We didn't see anything.

Stone: People often think that they haven't seen or heard anything useful but often remember something much later. Were you in yesterday?

Mrs Tovey: Yes, all day. Well, I popped down to the butcher's in town, to get some meat for dinner, but Roy was in, weren't you, Roy?

Mr Tovey: I was in the back room, can't see anything of next door from there.

Moss: What time did you go out, Mrs Tovey?

Mrs Tovey: Well, it was about two thirty. She was still there then, anyway, because her car was in the drive.

Moss: Who was there?

Mrs Tovey: Mrs Whitney. When I got back, must have been about three fifteen, she was still there. Well, her car was there. I didn't see either of them, actually, just their cars on the drive. I thought it was odd, didn't I say, Roy? How odd it was.

Mr Tovey: You're always saying things are odd. We keep ourselves to ourselves, mostly. Don't get involved – that's my way. But Janet, she always seems to see something odd.

Moss: And what was odd about Mrs Whitney being at the house? I gather they come here fairly regularly?

Mrs Tovey: Well not her, not anymore. Not since the divorce anyways.

Moss: Divorce?

Mrs Tovey: Oh sorry, love, I've been all confusing. It wasn't Anna's car I saw, it was hers. The other Mrs Whitney. Rose.

Chapter Twenty

Rebecca

'Did uniform get anything useful from the Whitneys' home address?' Tom asks Kim. She promptly pulls a sheet of paper with four different coloured labels on and hands it to him.

'Nothing I could see that would help us,' she says. 'But this is a list of everything they took.'

'What about the shoes?' I ask. 'Did they check his shoe size?'

Kim shakes her head. 'It's not on the list but I've had a PC downstairs send a message to the officers who went for confirmation – they didn't log any shoes into evidence but probably still checked the size.'

I nod, glad that Kim is so on top of these things. 'Postmortem will confirm anyway,' I say just as the phone rings.

'She's sure it was Rose's car?' I'm gesturing frantically at Tom, who comes over, frowning.

'Rose Whitney was at the house,' I mutter. Andy is speaking again.

'Says it was her car she saw. She knows it was Rose's car because she remembers Luke buying it for her, says it's got one of those flashy personalised plates that "her sort" have. She doesn't seem to think a lot of the former Mrs Whitney.'

'And what about the current Mrs Whitney? What did she have to say about her?'

I hear rustling of paper, like Andy is consulting his notes to make sure he gets the wording just right.

'Lovely thing, very pretty and much chattier than that other one. When they had snow last year Anna apparently went round to check if they needed any supplies getting from the village, which means she can't possibly have hurt Luke.'

His voice drips with sarcasm.

'Of course it does,' I say. 'Does she remember seeing Anna at the house last night?'

'No,' Andy confirms. 'But she didn't go out after three fifteen, Mr Tovey lit a fire in the back room and they watched TV. She said she might have heard a car at about four-ish but she couldn't swear to it.'

Anna claims to have arrived at four – was Rose still there when she got there? Had she discovered something going on that she shouldn't have seen? But if Anna had seen Rose there at four, what happened in the eight hours until the stabbing? Did they just go for a nice walk and start arguing about Rose after their film? It doesn't make sense.

'Alright, thanks, Andy. Let me know if you get anything else.'

I hang up the phone and repeat the conversation to Tom, who has taken charge of writing on the whiteboard – so people have a chance at actually reading it, he informs me.

'Maybe she didn't catch them doing anything that was provable,' Tom suggests. 'Perhaps she gets there, and Rose is just leaving, or getting ready to leave. Luke makes some excuse about why his ex-wife is in his shag pad – sorry, holiday home – but as the night goes on Anna can't let it go. After a few drinks she brings it up again and they argue.'

'It's possible,' I agree. 'More plausible than anything we've got so far. And it might explain why Anna doesn't want to tell us why they were arguing – if it looks like she thinks Luke was sleeping with his ex, there goes her self-defence – now she's a woman scorned.'

'And we know hell hath no fury like those,' Tom says. I look at him to see if he's directing that at me but he's already turned back to the board and is filling in the new information.

No, I haven't slept with Tom. But I nearly did, at the Christmas party – and I don't need telling how much of a cliché that is. The thing is, the Christmas party is a cliché for a reason. Spirits are high, emotional and alcoholic, and things that might never usually happen when one is un-Christmassy and sober, well they have a habit of happening. Or nearly happening. We don't talk about it, in fact we pretend neither of us remember it, but every now and then Tom will say something that makes me think he knows exactly what happened. Or didn't happen. The problem is, I think he's convinced himself *he* turned *me* down.

'Okay, so we have a possible motive,' I say, choosing to ignore the barb. 'And we know that not only was Rose Whitney at the cottage yesterday but she chose not to tell us that when we saw her earlier. We need to find out why. Because I'm wondering why, if she dislikes Anna so much, she withheld a possible motive for Anna's attack on Luke.

And there's one other option, which is unlikely but might explain some of the inconsistencies in Anna's story.'

'Anna didn't arrive until much later,' Tom says with a frown. 'But even if she did show up later, she catches them at it or something, stabs Luke in a jealous frenzy – why wipe down the murder weapon and the phone?'

'But what if Anna wiped them down, not because her prints were on them – but because they weren't? What if Anna didn't stab Luke at all? What if it was Rose?'

Chapter Twenty-One

Anna

I don't know what possessed me to call in to Luke's work that day, it's not something I did regularly. Things might have been completely different if I hadn't, who knows, but there's no use dwelling on that now, is there? He was working at his private practice – again, I wouldn't have visited him at the hospital when he did his NHS work, but the private practice was a totally different atmosphere, still sterile and professional but lighter.

Sandra at the front desk smiled and buzzed me through.

'He's got half an hour before the next consultation,' she said, gesturing for me to go on up.

The desk in what used to be a waiting room was the first change I noticed. The chair behind it was empty, and the door to my husband's office was closed. I know, we all know what comes next. I pushed open the door without knocking – Sandra had already told me there was no client in there, hadn't she?

The woman perched on the end of my husband's desk swung around, her face a picture of guilt. I say woman, she was barely more than a girl, although she wouldn't have described herself that way, I'm sure. Luke was standing feet away from her, she was holding a notepad and had clearly been taking notes when I walked in – so why the guilty face? They hadn't jumped apart, they were both fully dressed. Yet I knew. You just know, don't you? It's like women are built with a radar – well, mine was a siren. I suppose you could say it was no less than I deserved, after stealing him right from under Rose's nose the way I did, and you'd be right. But that didn't mean I was going to let it happen to me.

'Anna.' Luke beamed, crossed the room and kissed me. Over his shoulder I could see a sour expression cross the girl's face as she got up to leave us alone. He never uttered a word to her, or about her once she'd left, but I'd seen the way he looked at her, the same way he used to look at me. And he knew I'd seen it, too. That was the way Luke liked to work, he'd let you know in his own little ways that you weren't measuring up, or that you were completely replaceable. Well he wouldn't replace me as easily as he had Rose, I knew that for sure.

The rules of our game had been simple. We only ever played together – no secrets and no lies. And my husband was skirting dangerously close to breaking them.

—

I lay in bed later that night thinking about how I was going to deal with this new threat. Because I had to deal with it, and swiftly. I was smarter than Rose. She'd lost everything when she lost Luke and she'd never recovered from it. She'd grown bitter and obsessive and I wouldn't let that happen to me. And I wouldn't go back to being poor and miserable.

When I was eleven years old my mother used to take me to visit charity shops. She loved to spend a Saturday afternoon browsing through other people's things and I would drag my feet along behind her until one day I moved a dirty moth-holed blanket and unearthed a tower of hardback books, each one small and shiny with gold lettering. *Poirot Investigates*, *Five Little Pigs*, *Death in the Clouds*. The author was someone called Agatha Christie and I fell in love instantly. They were two pounds each and there were fifty in total. I bought one that first Saturday morning, covering the rest back up with the blanket, and devoured it in a week. The next Saturday I went back, praying no one would have found my secret stash, and used my pocket money to buy the next in the series. The man who worked there watched me going in week after week with my money clutched in my hand – I got four pounds a week for doing the jobs my mum needed help with around the house – and I would spend hours stroking the spines and choosing which one to spend half my weekly budget on while my mum left me to do the food shop. Eventually, after four or five weeks I think, he took the entire collection off sale and would carry them out into the shop as soon as I walked in. He and I would talk at length about how I'd liked the one I'd bought the week before and I would talk animatedly about my preference for the great Hercule Poirot – an arrogant but likeable fellow – over the shrew-like Miss Marple. Even at that young age I was vaguely aware of how Poirot was proud, boastful even, of his of his greatness and yet Miss Marple was forced to be humble to retain her likeability. Perhaps even then I was learning about the differences between the way the world viewed my sex compared to the opposite one. I was in awe of the way that Poirot felt no inclination to hide his intelligence, downplay his greatness, claim that it was a fluke or a lucky guess when he unmasked villain after villain and no one ever called him a square or a loser.

It took me an entire year to own every single one of those books, but own them I did. A hundred pounds was a lot of money to me then and I cherished my prize, reading them over and over again, spending hours dusting the spines and reordering them, alphabetically, by favourite, by date. The day I watched my mother pile them up at the end of the garden and set fire to them because I'd been late home for tea, I swear I felt my soul scream.

—

I had to accept that Luke may never be totally faithful to me, and it was possible that I could deal with that. What I wouldn't deal with was having someone else take what was mine away from me. *My* home, *my* husband, *my* life. No, something was going to have to be done to keep Luke under control.

Chapter Twenty-Two

Rose

The main thing I miss about no longer having huge wrought-iron gates on the front of my house is the lack of forewarning when people turn up. With the gates I could pretend not to be in, and there was CCTV to show me who I was avoiding. Unfortunately, when the police show up at my door I have no such luxury, and not only can they see my car on the drive but I'm actually unfortunate enough to be getting out of said car and walking up my path when they pull up.

It's the same two officers I'd spoken to previously, a plain-looking brunette, DS Dance, and a slightly above average-looking man, whose name escapes me. That's not good, I think – details are important, and I should be on top of this. I realise that I'm probably going to be a suspect in my ex-husband's murder at some point, maybe I even am already, and I need to have my wits about me.

'Mrs Whitney?' the man calls out and I turn slowly, as if it's the first time I've noticed them. I'm about to smile when I remember – *murder suspect or grieving ex-wife?* – to plaster on my sad face.

'Detectives, hello.'

I wonder if they might be judging me, then I admonish myself for my naivety. Of course they are judging me –

they have been since the minute I turned up at the police station and perhaps, depending on what that bitch Anna had said about me, before even that. Do they feel pity for me? Scorn? Have they been to Luke and Anna's beautiful home only to find mine seriously lacking in comparison?

I didn't do badly in the divorce, but I was launched out of that marriage with no job and no children — I wasn't fairly compensated for my losses, let's put it that way. After everything I'd slowly given up to support Luke's career, and I walked away with enough money to buy a decent four-bed property and little else. I've even had to get a job, something that once I wanted desperately but now every day only serves as a reminder that I haven't chosen any of this. The life I had chosen was ripped out from under me and replaced with this fairground funhouse mirror of what it used to be.

The slightly disdainful-looking DS Dance probably thinks that she would never give up her career for a man. Maybe she's right, but all that would mean is that she's never met a man like Luke Whitney. It doesn't happen all at once, of course. It starts slowly, imperceptibly unless you have experience in spotting it. Luke and I met at a party in our first year at university, introduced by a girl whose name I don't even remember. He was studying medicine, and I was a politics and philosophy student. If philosophy and medicine sound like oil and water it's because that's what they are, and together we swirled around one another, argued opposite sides of the same coin, butted heads, shouting over the music but also because we were both so full of passion. And oh-so disappointingly predictably we ended the evening in his bed, not emerging for longer than a toilet break or to collect our takeaway meals for nearly two days.

Afterwards I found out that spontaneous hedonism was just the university experience – everyone had a similar story. Not everyone's story ended the way ours did, of course – most people came to their senses after a bedroom lock-in. Donald swears he once stayed in bed with a woman he met at the corner shop for a week. I'm not sure how true that is – whose toothbrush did she use?

Luke always said that that he loved that I challenged him, and I believed him. I took pride in the fact that my boyfriend didn't want a pushover, he wanted an equal. So why did I find myself challenging him less and less over time, and never in company? Why did all of my sentences begin to start with 'Luke says…' or 'Luke thinks…'? He's so clever, I would say, whenever my girlfriends pointed this out. I wasn't losing my own opinions, I was learning to see things differently, to think differently. I don't see those girls anymore but I don't think they'd be surprised to learn how things have unfolded at all.

I lead the detectives through to the lounge and offer them a seat and a cup of tea. DS Dance declines in typical bad cop fashion, but the other one – DI Kerrigan, I remember – accepts.

'What can I do for you both?' I ask, trying to sound casual as I move the pile of proofreading from the coffee table and place one of my best mugs in front of the officer. He thanks me and I take a seat on the silver velvety couch opposite them.

'We just wanted to clear up a few things that have come up since we last saw you,' he says. My eyes narrow and I have to work to force on a neutral expression. DS Dance is glancing over my shoulder at the photo of me standing next to a younger but still recognisable Tony Blair. She looks confused and I feel a smugness that doesn't befit the situation. Let her wonder who it is she's really dealing with. Let her wonder if she's underestimated the bottle blonde Stepford Wife stereotype.

'I heard that Anna confessed,' I say, clearing my throat. 'What else could you need to know from me?'

DI Kerrigan is direct, a tactic I respect. 'I'm wondering, actually, Mrs Whitney,' he says, 'why you didn't mention, when I saw you yesterday, that you had been at your ex-husband's holiday home the afternoon he was attacked?'

I arch my eyebrow. 'And who told you that?' I ask. 'Anna, I suppose?'

'As a matter of fact it was the next-door neighbour, a Mrs Tovey. She saw your car on the driveway at three fifteen. Can you confirm you were there?'

I consider the question and decide against lying. That old busybody knows exactly who I am and I bet she was just wetting herself at the chance to put me at the crime scene. She had always hated me. 'Yes,' I say, lifting my chin upwards slightly in a defensive gesture. 'I was there. But Luke was fine when I left, so I really don't see what difference it makes.'

'Did the current Mrs Whitney know you were there?'

I give a thin smile. 'You'd have to ask her that. I didn't see her, doesn't mean she didn't see me I suppose.'

'Why were you at the Whitneys' holiday cottage, Rose?' DS Dance asks. I wonder if she's switched to 'Rose' on purpose now. 'I was under the impression that your relationship with your ex was what you might call acrimonious.'

'What you call "acrimonious"' – I spit the word back at her – 'I call *complicated*.'

'Funny,' she says. 'That's exactly how Anna described their relationship.'

'Yes, well I expect all of Luke's relationships are complicated.' I put down my mug of tea and fold my legs under myself, trying to look more comfortable than I feel. 'He's never been boring, that much is certain.'

'What exactly do you mean by "complicated", Rose? Were you still sleeping together? Did Anna find out on Friday evening? Is that why you were so upset before, because you felt responsible for what had happened?'

I let out a laugh, thinking of the last time I spoke to Luke. 'I'm not responsible for anything. Luke asked me to come to the cottage on Friday. I got the feeling he needed someone to talk to but he never got round to what he wanted me there for. One minute we were chatting like old friends, taking selfies the next minute he went all weird and flipped out, said I couldn't be there and demanded I leave, so I did. Whatever that mad bitch did to Luke is nothing to do with me.'

Dance shakes her head. 'How do you know it wasn't anything to do with you if you'd already left the cottage? Maybe Luke told her you'd been there and she got angry. If she thought you were still having sex…'

'There's one thing you need to understand about Anna and Luke,' I say, considering every word as I say it. 'And that is that they don't see sex quite the same as normal married people. Luke told me once that their relationship is based on trust, not monogamy.'

'And how do you trust someone who is sleeping with their ex-wife?' Dance asks. I smile. She's more than happy to believe that Luke and I were sleeping together. I suppose it's a neat enough motive. New wife finds out hubby never stopped having feelings for ex-wife. New wife stabs hubby to death. Neat, but not true.

'You'd have to ask them that, wouldn't you?' I ask. 'That's the problem with making your own rules. In your relationships, DS Dance, I assume things are very black and white. You are with me therefore you are not with anyone else. It keeps things simple. That's how *my* marriage was – I was faithful to Luke and I assumed he would be faithful to me. Anna's smarter than that – or so I thought. She realised that Luke wasn't the type to ever be faithful, not unless he found someone who was his sexual equal. So they began to stretch the rules of regular relationships, mould them until the grey began to seep into the black and white and no one knew what was right or wrong anymore. And now he's dead.' I lean forward and pick up my tea, take a sip, allowing a dramatic pause. I'm quite good at this, I think. 'So I'd guess that somewhere along the way, the rules got broken.'

Chapter Twenty-Three

Anna

I sat in the hotel lobby, legs crossed at the knees. I was wearing a tight black pencil skirt, black Louboutins and red silk blouse, and in my hand were two A4 brown manila envelopes. I wondered if the secretary would stay the night at the expensive hotel – I knew Luke would make an excuse not to, but perhaps room service for breakfast would be the ambitious young girl's consolation prize. I almost felt sorry for the girl – yes, she knew Luke was married of course, but so had I. Luke was incredibly handsome, rich and was used to getting what he wanted; it would take a will of steel and the morals of a nun to be able to resist his charms.

I glanced at the expensive watch on my wrist, a fifth anniversary gift. Luke never missed an anniversary. I wondered if the woman currently upstairs, naked under my husband, had chosen it for him. Ten forty. Good Lord, this girl was getting the platinum member treatment.

Just as I was beginning to wonder if I had been wrong, if Luke really was going to stay all night – a worrying thought – I heard a ping, the clunk of steel doors sliding open, and my husband stood framed by the stark lights of the lift. He looked more beautiful than ever, and a sadness slid over me. I'd known he was here, and exactly what he was doing, but I hadn't allowed myself to fully believe it until I saw his face lose all its colour at the sight of his wife waiting for him. Thank goodness *she* hadn't been with him.

He crossed the foyer, regaining his composure with every step. 'Anna,' he said, giving me one of his famous killer smiles. 'What are you doing here, sweetheart?'

'Waiting for you, my love.' I stood and went to move to kiss him, felt a stab of pain when he stepped back. Couldn't risk his wife smelling his mistress. 'I trust you've got everything out of your system?'

He feigned confusion at this, and I rolled my eyes.

'Don't waste your mental energy making up excuses, Luke.' I nodded to the reception desk. 'Go and pay your bill and meet me in the bar. I'll find us somewhere private, somewhere we won't be overheard.'

I saw my husband hesitate. Here was a man who was very much used to being in charge, who, when confronted about his affair with me, had gone upstairs, packed a suitcase and walked out of the door of his home, turning up on my doorstep in the pouring rain. For now, however, he gave a nod and did exactly as he was told.

I entered the bar and asked a waiter to bring over a whiskey and a soda and lime. I found us a table next to the huge glass windows – it was too dark outside to be afforded much of a view but the bar was quiet and we wouldn't be bothered out of the way over here. I shivered, not sure if it was the cold darkness beyond the glass or the subsiding of the adrenaline that had been pumping through me in the foyer. I might have looked the picture of serenity, but inside pieces of my heart felt as though they were slowly perishing.

Had I really thought that our little game would be enough to stop him straying? That by allowing the reins to loosen a little on the traditional setup I would somehow override his need for external gratification? What a fool I'd been.

The question now was could I really go through with what I was about to do? If I did, our entire marriage would be irrevocably changed – although of course it already had been, just by virtue of him being here. *I* still had a choice though. I could still decide to pretend that I believed whatever lame lie my husband made up, pretend I'd come to the hotel because he'd forgotten something, and that would be that. We would both know that the other was lying, and from that moment it would have been presumed that I accepted his infidelities while becoming the talk of the social scene. Like poor Emeline Bancroft, whose husband had been seen out wining and dining his hired help so often he'd been nicknamed the Good Samaritan for all of his outstanding charity work. One of our friends had once asked why Emeline continued to hire such attractive staff, to which she had replied sadly, 'If it weren't them, it might be someone I care about.'

No, that would not be me.

Luke pulled out the chair opposite me and slid onto it. Confusion was etched into his beautiful features.

'What's going on, Anna?'

I placed the two envelopes on the table in front of him, my hand resting on top of them.

'Do you love her?' I asked. Luke looked as though he was about to deny everything, act as though he didn't have a clue what I meant. I held up the hand that wasn't guarding the envelopes. 'I don't want to sit here all night, so let's assume I know everything and I'm not an idiot.

So be honest, Luke, and know that I will know if you are lying. Do you love her?'

Luke sighed, and seemed to deflate in front of my eyes. 'No,' he said, and I knew it was true.

'Did you intend for it to be more than one night?'

He nodded, his expression miserable. I pushed the whiskey towards him and he eyed it suspiciously. 'It's not poisoned,' I said, picking it up and taking a sip for his benefit. He took the glass from me and slugged the rest. I picked up one of the envelopes and handed it to him.

'Divorce papers,' I said. Luke went to protest but I held up a hand. 'I haven't finished.'

I took a sip of my drink. I might have looked cool and collected on the outside but my heart was hammering against my chest and my mouth was like sandpaper. I slid envelope number two towards him.

'Your accounts for the last five years. The ones you submitted, at least. I got these from your tax portal – you shouldn't leave everything logged in by the way, sweetheart, if your laptop gets stolen there's no telling what damage someone could do.' I let this sink in, then slid the last envelope over. 'This is a list of every discrepancy in those accounts. You wouldn't believe how long it took my solicitor to compare the submitted accounts to our statements. And some of those shell companies were really well hidden. I had to pay him a *fortune*. Well, you did, I suppose. There are also details in there of every shell company you own and every tax evasion method you have ever used.'

Luke sagged even further in his chair. I had never seen him quiet for this long, so lacking in control over a situation. It felt good to be in control of my husband for once. I took another sip of my drink and signalled for the waiter to bring Luke another whiskey.

'What's going on, Anna? Are you threatening me?'

I held my answer until the waiter had delivered the whiskey. He set it down in front of Luke, who picked it up and knocked it down in one.

'Yes,' I admitted. There was no point in trying to colour what was happening. 'You are going to sign those divorce papers, agreeing to an abnormal sum of money to be given to me on completion, and I am going to put them somewhere safe, where you will never find them. Then, we are going to go back to our normal lives, as if tonight never happened.'

Luke looked even more confused now – he obviously thought he'd known what was going on and now had no clue again.

'You're not divorcing me?' He looked suspicious.

'Still not finished.' I shook my head. 'I'm not divorcing you, *yet*. And as long as you abide by some very simple conditions, there will be no need for me ever to.'

I sat up straighter and held up a finger. 'One. You get rid of the secretary. The information to make that happen without a fuss is inside that envelope. She lied on her CV several times – your HR department should do a better job of checking these.'

Luke's eyes widened slightly. He was impressed, despite himself. I'd done my homework and come into this meeting with everything already worked out – more like one of his business associates than his wife.

'Two.' Another finger. 'You never, ever, sleep with someone we know, ever again. I will not be made a fool of, Luke.' He opened his mouth to make another empty promise, maybe he'd be good for a while then slip into his old ways again, hope I'd let my guard down, hope he'd been more discreet. I stopped him. 'I'll just let you know when I'm finished, okay? I understand you, Luke. I know I didn't marry a faithful man – I was an affair to begin with myself and I'm not naive enough to think that men like you will ever change. Well, maybe I was, but I'm not anymore. I can come to terms with you looking elsewhere – better women than me have had to. But I can't cope with our marriage being the after-dinner gossip, the tired old cliché of wealthy businessman fucking his secretary while his poor wife is the only one who doesn't know.' I thought of Rose, and how life must have been for her. Poor Rose. I shuddered. 'And I never, ever, want to be *pitied*,' I said. 'So, darling, what I'm saying, is that if you feel yourself needing to stray, make sure you piss in someone else's garden. A garden far, far away where no one I know will ever find out. No repeat performances, no feelings. And if these little one-off *dalliances?* affect our marriage in any way, I will serve the papers you have signed tonight, take my portion of your ill-gotten gains, and call HMRC myself on the way out.'

Chapter Twenty-Four

Rebecca

I'm sitting in the incident room waiting for Andy to turn up so we can start the briefing when Jimmy sends me a stupid meme that makes me snort despite myself. He's so bloody juvenile sometimes – I don't know how this ended up being a thing. I type back '*you are a*' and insert and aubergine emoji.

Okay, not exactly grown up myself, am I? I grin and pocket my phone, look up to see Tom watching me. He raises his eyebrows.

'Have you got your joke ready?' he asks.

'What?' I say, distracted as my phone buzzes again. Another message from Jimmy. '*You want my*' followed by an aubergine emoji and a question mark.

'Your joke,' Tom says again, and I still don't know what he's on about. 'For when Andy turns up late. You can't use the rolling stone gathering no moss – Rob's here. You asked him if he'd had the training wheels nicked off his trike last time... I think you're running low on late jokes.'

'Nah, I've got loads,' I say, but I'm already typing back a reply to Jimmy and I don't even notice when Andy walks in. I only realise he's there when Tom marches to the front of the room and clears his throat.

'Okay, Rose Whitney doesn't deny being at the cottage the afternoon of the stabbing,' Tom says, picking up a black whiteboard pen and tossing it to Kim. Unlike Derek, Tom is more than happy to conduct his briefings in situ, the plus of this being that no one needs to leave their desks to listen, the incident room is that small. Kim squeezes past him and draws a line from two thirty on our timeline and writes 'Rose Whitney seen at cottage'.

'She says she left before Anna got there at four, but we only have her word for that, no one saw her leave. All we know is that Rose's car wasn't there when the ambulance and police arrived to the emergency call.'

Kim adds 'Rose leaves' in green in a gap between two thirty pm and one forty-six am. In Kim speak, green means unconfirmed information. When we get confirmation of the time Rose actually left, from a witness or CCTV, or a fuel receipt, she'll change the writing to black. Now me, I'd start off with an amazingly logical colour system, then forget to change the colour and end up with a rainbow of unintelligible scrawls, half rubbed off by my left sleeve scraping against the board as I write. This is why Kim will always be a better office manager than I will, despite how many planners, notebooks and pens that push down four different colours I buy.

'If Rose was still there when Anna got there I can see why that would lead to a fight,' Andy says. 'I've heard women don't like it when men invite their exes on holiday with them.'

'Get you, being alright about women,' I remark, and Andy holds up his middle finger at me without even taking his eyes off Tom at the front.

'It gives us a reason for an argument, what it doesn't give us is why Anna refuses to just tell us what they were arguing about. At the moment it's looking like if we charge her she'll plead guilty anyway, so why not just give us the details?'

'Maybe she's not planning on pleading guilty,' I say. 'Maybe she thinks that if she just keeps telling us she's guilty we won't ask her any more questions and then she'll switch to not guilty at her plea hearing.'

'Her fancy lawyer will have told her that we won't stop investigating just because she's confessed,' Tom says, although he doesn't look certain about that. Plenty of cases have been deemed 'open and shut' leading to a shoddy investigation and a not guilty verdict.

'Rose claimed to have an alibi the first time we spoke to her,' I remind them. Kim checks her notes.

'On the phone to unknown male. Shall I follow that up, guv?'

'Yes please.' Tom nods. 'See if you can get a trace on where the phone was when the call was made. If the phone call can be traced to her house then at least we can rule her out as still having been at the cottage. Andy, how are you getting on with CCTV in the area?'

'There are a few Ring doorbells that we've contacted the owners to check, but none of the businesses have it. Crime isn't an issue in the area.'

'Until someone gets stabbed,' Tom retorts. 'Fine. Anything else from the door to door apart from these Toveys?'

'Three sightings of dodgy-looking men of a "different" ethnicity – their words – "casing" houses in the village, turned out to be a couple of guys dropping off charity clothing bags, one report of gunshots that night, probably a bin lid slamming in the wind, and one report of a cat who has been sick more than usual so do I think he's been poisoned?' Andy reels off the list from his notes, keeping a straight face the whole time.

'Excellent,' I said, 'we've rocked up in Midsomer.'

'Are you going to make that joke every time we have a case in the countryside?' Tom asks me, his tone more irritable than amused. My running joke is a running joke – that's the point of it. Tom knows that – so why is he being such prick? I see Kim and Rob share a 'look'. So they've noticed it as well.

'Sorry, guv,' I say, putting an emphasis on the word 'guv'.

Tom looks annoyed but I can't tell if it's at me or himself.

'Okay,' he says, letting out a sigh. Something's irritated him, I don't often see him this rattled. 'Kim is on the ex-wife's alibi, Moss, tie up the Ring doorbell footage. Stone, can you get on to forensics, see what they've got back. Dance, you can come with me to Anna Whitney's workplace. We'll regroup here at say… six?'

Everyone nods and Tom walks out without speaking to me directly. Is there pressure getting to him, or am I getting to him? Either way, fun day ahead for me.

Chapter Twenty-Five

Rose

I used to believe that if you wanted something badly enough, if you worked hard enough, you could get it. I suppose I still think that, but with a caveat; just because you got it, doesn't mean you will keep it. And no, I'm not talking about Luke. I know that people are not possessions, pets or careers, you don't have to preach to me on that.

I worked hard at university, spending every spare moment in the library studying, writing revision guides or in my room at halls reading books like *How to Win Friends and Influence People*. Politics is as much about connecting with people as it is about reading the socio-economic climate, and I wanted to be prepared for both. I think the party where I met Luke was the first one I'd been to that year.

I finished my studies years before Luke did, and thanks to top grades and glowing references from tutors I had offers from no fewer than five work placements, one of them being the ultimate work experience gig – Downing Street. Luke and I were living at an apartment my parents had rented us at this point; he was continuing his course and I was preparing to start work in one of the most famous buildings in Britain.

I'd expected Luke to be thrilled for me. I knew that he was struggling with the demands of his course – he was reaching the stages where he couldn't just charm his way through like he had done his whole life and I knew he didn't think that he was up to it. He was panicking, and I was trying my best to coach him through it, but it hurt that he couldn't look past his own fears and congratulate me. Instead, he froze me out.

The night before my first day, Luke didn't come home from class. I'd cooked his favourite meal for him, put on some cute lingerie, one of his rugby shirts and a pair of satin shorts in the hope that it might cheer him up a little, but when five o'clock came around – lectures finished at four – and then six without him calling or answering his phone I began to worry. Then at seven his phone went off completely, straight to voicemail. I tried calling some of his friends, Don and Richie and David, but none of them had a clue where he'd gone. Donald said Luke had left on time at four and hadn't mentioned having to stop anywhere. I felt frantic. I didn't sleep. Don and I rang around all of the local hospitals, I called his parents, I paced the room until Don told me I was going to wear a hole in the carpet. This was back at a time when Luke staying out all night didn't mean spending the night with another woman, that wasn't even a consideration for me. I was certain he was dead in a ditch somewhere, although Donald assured me that Oxford probably didn't have ditches.

And then, at six am, just as I'd flaked out on the sofa exhausted with worry, I heard the front door open and close.

'Luke?' I shot up, wide awake.

'Hey, babe.' He walked into the front room, dropped his backpack on the floor next to the sofa and dropped a kiss on his head. 'What are you doing up this early?'

I swear my jaw just about hit the floor.

'Up? Up? Luke, I've barely slept! Where the hell have you been?'

Luke frowned. 'I've been with Wes, I told you I was staying at his tonight.'

Now it was my turn to frown. 'No, you didn't. I've been going out of my mind with worry – why didn't you answer your phone?'

'Battery died, you know what these things are like. God, Rose, I'm so sorry, I honestly did tell you but I know you've been so busy with this Downing Street thing tomorrow...'

'Today,' I said, my voice flat. My face burned from the crying I'd spent all night doing, my skin was tight and it ached and I was so, so exhausted.

'What?'

'My first day at Downing Street. It's today.'

Luke looked so horrified that I knew that there was no way he was lying to me – he genuinely thought I'd known he was at his friend's. He bundled me into the shower and made me porridge while I washed and blow-dried my hair, and tried to make my face look less like an extra from *The Evil Dead*.

I was a useless mess that day, of course. I'd pulled all-nighters before (studying, not partying) and lived to tell the tale, but this was different. The adrenaline that had carried me through the night, the worry of not knowing if my boyfriend was dead or alive, that stayed with me all day and I cried in the toilets twice over tiny mistakes that just the day before I would have taken in my stride. And when Luke was seriously ill a week later I took the time off at short notice to look after him, and not long after that we started fighting over the smallest things, and I'd just get so distracted. The placement didn't work out. But it was fine, the permanent spot went to another girl who had been in my class who deserved it just as much. And I needed to find a paying job anyway, I couldn't expect Mum and Dad to pay for everything, and Luke's course was so demanding. I took a job as a course administrator in the university offices, and later on, when Luke qualified and started making good money and we got married I gave up work completely. After all, what was the point in the surgeon's wife filing papers in some office for a pittance?

It all made complete sense, at the time.

Chapter Twenty-Six

Anna

Luke's secretary left without a fuss – and given her generous severance package I didn't blame her. If she'd had designs on being the next Mrs Whitney they had ended swiftly and she'd taken it well. Since then Luke had been on his best behaviour – well, as far as I knew, and that was all that mattered. It felt as though I'd earned his respect with my ruthlessness and my pragmatism, and I was confident that I'd found the key to being married to Luke. He wasn't a man to be tied down, and as long as he hid his transgressions well enough they would go unchallenged. I was determined that I would be the final wife – there would be no need to replace me with a newer model.

-

The night I met Ed we had gone to some upmarket hotel at a charity gala – one of those do's where you have to buy a 'table' rather than a meal, and they stop halfway through to auction things no one wants in order to establish who in the room has the biggest penis. All for those less fortunate, obviously. I swallowed back a yawn and continued to nod along to whatever the vacuous old woman next to me was droning on about – it had got to the point where I actually couldn't have volunteered anything to the conversation even if I'd wanted to – I had literally no idea what she had been saying for at least the previous half an hour.

'I'm so sorry, would you excuse me?' I stood up, not caring about the shocked look that passed across her face, and my legs bumped the table as I pushed out my chair in a hurry to escape. Luke glanced over from his seat opposite me.

'You okay?' he mouthed. I nodded and mouthed back 'loo'. He was back to being engrossed in his conversation before I'd even turned around. His business partner, Donald, raised his eyebrows at me and I raised mine back. I was always incredibly wary around Donald. He never brought his long-suffering wife to these events, and I'd seen him leave with another woman more than once. He was flirty to the point of discomfort, and although the old Anna might have had fun with him with the witty banter and vulgar jokes, that kind of behaviour wasn't appropriate for women in our circles. While other men fell for the 'cool girl' schtick, Luke most definitely wouldn't appreciate me matching his friends shot for shot and dancing Coyote Ugly-style on the bar.

I knew that Donald fancied me. Not least because of the way he watched me across the table when he thought I wasn't looking, or how he leaned in close when we spoke to talk intimately in my ear, quite often letting his eyes stray to places a man shouldn't be looking, especially with his best friend's wife. Donald wasn't totally unfortunate looking but he didn't hold a candle to my younger, better-looking husband and I'm sure he knew it. He had nothing to offer me that I couldn't get at home, and even if he did

I wasn't about to be messing with someone else's mess. Donald was a no-go zone.

I escaped into the corridor and leaned against the wall. The music from the room next to us was loud and young sounding – a wedding or a twenty-first birthday perhaps, and I doubted that the conversation in that room was drier than the Sahara. I imagined going to join in, just dancing the night away where I didn't know anyone and no one knew me, and I felt a bit sad that I knew for certain it would take Luke at least two hours to notice that I hadn't gone back.

I was still leaning my head back against the wall with my eyes closed when a voice said, 'Are you asleep?'

'Busted,' I said without opening my eyes. I sighed and opened just one. Donald Osbourne was looking back at me with a disapproving headteacher look on his face. 'Caught taking a break from it all.'

He pretended to look shocked. 'Don't tell me you weren't enthralled by Mrs Dervish and her tales from the animal shelter?'

Donald had been friends with Luke and Rose back in university, and although I know he had a fondness for Rose, it was with Luke that his true loyalties lay. And that meant accepting his 'bit on the side waitress' as his new wife.

'Oh, is that what she was talking about?' I laughed. 'I did wonder who the hell names their kid Rollo, but with these people you never can tell.'

'I know how you feel,' he said, leaning one arm against the wall next to me. 'I hate these things. But your husband tells me it's not the done thing to ask if you can just write a cheque and not bother attending.'

I laughed, because that's exactly what I'd begged Luke to do earlier that evening, as we'd been lying in bed after a particularly vigorous sex session. I'd been hoping he'd say 'anything for you, darling,' and order us takeout that we could eat in our dressing gowns while watching a cheesy movie before round two. Instead he'd told me that it wasn't the 'done thing' and insisted I wear the emerald green dress without any underwear.

'He's such a bore,' I joked.

Donald grinned. 'You're not a bore though, are you, Anna?'

His voice had a dangerous edge to it – one that made me shift uncomfortably and stand up straight, suddenly alert. I realised that I'd actually never been completely alone with Donald, with no one else around, and the thought of it now made me nervous.

'Oh, I am a *total* bore,' I said, crossing my arms protectively across my chest and trying to keep my voice light and jokey. What do they say, not all men? And yet I've never had a woman strike fear into me with one innocent-sounding sentence. 'Chamomile tea and a crossword kinda gal, me.'

'Oh come on, Anna.' Donald moved closer and ran his fingers down my left arm. His breath smelled of whiskey but he wasn't drunk, wasn't slurring his words, wasn't stumbling. I think I would have felt easier about the situation if he had've been wasted, at least I could put his extreme lack of judgement down to something, but Donald was sober and that made him more of a threat, not less. I stumbled sideways, my heart thumping uncomfortably in my chest – how was I going to get away from this without ruining things between Donald and Luke? I felt a mixture of fear and fury that he was putting me in this position. Donald Osbourne could have any woman in the room, but he was choosing to step right into the fire. 'I have a room upstairs, we could be back down here before Luke even knows we were gone.'

'Come off it, Donald,' I said, still trying to make light of the situation. He'd made flirty comments a million times before but he had never outright propositioned me before. A room upstairs? Had this been planned? It briefly entered my mind that this could be the next level to mine and Luke's little game – perhaps he had set this up with Donald so his partner could 'seduce' me and he could barge in and save the day. A shudder ran through me at the thought of Luke telling Donald about the men I had come on to in front of him, about the nightclubs where no one knew us and I would dance pressed up against some unsuspecting stranger while my husband watched from the shadows.

'You only want me because you can't have me. We both know I'm not going to cheat on Luke,' I told him, my voice firm. If Luke had set this up then he would just have to be disappointed tonight. Donald was far too close to home, Luke couldn't expect to change the rules and just have me run with it.

Donald's fingers gripped the top of my arm and he squeezed tight.

'That's not what Simon Reynolds tells me,' he said, his face inches from mine. Where was everyone? I prayed for someone to walk around the corner as I scanned my memory for the name *Simon Reynolds*. 'Do you want to know what Simon says?' he continued in a sing-song voice. 'Simon says that if Luke hadn't walked in on the pair of you at the Henshaws' party your moist lips would have been around his cock within minutes.'

Oh, *that* Simon Reynolds.

'Have you met Simon Reynolds?' I scoffed. 'If you believe I'm easy enough to screw him, where's your conquest?' I asked, trying to front it out and not let my voice falter. 'There's no challenge, is there?'

'Anna, Anna, Anna,' Donald said, moving so close that his chest was against mine. His leg slipped in between mine, pushing them as far apart as the long tight green dress would allow. 'I've been dreaming about fucking you since the moment we met. If you can give it up for that disgusting turd Reynolds surely letting me have a go wouldn't be too much of a chore. Is it money? Was Simon paying you? I can pay more…'

'What?' I tried to shove Donald away but it was pointless, he had me pinned. A couple walked past, averting their eyes – to them it must look like we were sharing an intimate moment. I could have screamed, but that would have opened a huge can of worms. I wanted to give Donald a chance to get out of this, and I wanted to get the hell out of there. 'Let me go, Donald. *Please*. You're hurting me.'

Donald hesitated, then seemed to come to his senses. He stepped back, looking confused, almost unsure as to how we'd got into that position.

'Anna, I—'

I shoved past my husband's partner and fled from the hotel.

Chapter Twenty-Seven

Rebecca

When is a gym not a gym? When it's a 'club', and costs more than my monthly salary to be a member. The Welti Club is a huge glass-fronted building, with beautiful flagstone paths leading up to an entryway adorned with foliage. Just inside the entryway is a towering water feature, a statue of a woman holding a jar that pours water continuously into the small pool at her feet. On the way in I spot no fewer than three employees tending to bushes, sweeping the path and cleaning the signage, and that's before we even get into the building. The reception area is no less impressive, a face ID entry system which does not recognise a warrant card and, once we've got past security, a lounge area to the left with comfy-looking sofas and water coolers which is occupied by six older women in tennis whites looking pink and shiny. The reception desk is to our right and this is where security steers us to ask the perky redhead behind the counter to speak to the manager.

'Adam is...' She clicks around on the computer for a minute. '...in a new client meeting. He's almost done though, then he's got a general walkaround so he should have no problem seeing you then. Would you like to take a seat upstairs in the hub and I'll send him up?' She hands me a card. 'There's cafe credit for two drinks on there.'

'The hub' turns out to be a posh cafe with four separate areas. There's a quiet space with bookshelves full of classic novels and non-fiction books, charging ports on each table and a coffee machine in the corner. This area is nearly full of people sitting one to a table, headphones in and eyes fixed on laptops. There is one guy at the back talking loudly on a mobile and the others take turns to shoot him filthy looks while he maintains the beautiful indifference gifted to the privileged.

There is a small soft play area with tables spaced further apart, and a couple of sofas and low coffee tables cluttered with baby bottles, changing bags and prams crammed around the edges. Yummy mummies hand out snacks like crack dealers while small children run back and forth from soft play to table and back again. Another section has a huge television screen on the wall with Sky Sports playing, and the fourth is behind a door labelled 'Premium Member Lounge'.

'Jesus, my gym has a vending machine and four lockers,' Tom mutters, looking around in awe. 'This is more of a commune than a gym.'

He's right – it's clear that the Welti Club is more than a place to work out to its members; it's a place to gather, to socialise, to work and to eat. I pick up a menu and study it out of interest. It would rival most of the restaurants I visit. I can imagine Anna Whitney in here after her yoga class drinking green smoothies, smiling and greeting members like old friends.

We use the card given to us by the receptionist to order two coffees and seat ourselves where we can see most of the other tables and the top of the staircase – force of habit.

'I wonder if they do a Blue Light discount,' Tom says, but it's rhetorical because we both know that he would never join a place like this. Tom is a get in, do the job, get out kind of bloke, he's not going to be hanging around drinking matcha lattes and discussing his backswing.

We both stand up instinctively when we see a man heading towards our table. Either Adam the manager knows all of his members by sight or we look the most like Old Bill here. I'm guessing the latter.

Adam is a sight to behold. He is short, and I mean short – five five at the absolute most – and his entire upper body looks as though he has stuck his thumb in his mouth and over-inflated himself, stopping when he got to his hips. His over-indulgence in steroids and arm day has made him look like a character out of Mr Men, a giant upside-down triangle. My dad would have described his walk as 'carrying carpets' and the overall effect is quite ridiculous. I purposely don't look at Tom, who is bound to be desperately trying to rearrange his face into the picture of neutrality.

'Officers?' Adam says, holding out his hand for us both to shake. 'Is there a problem?' He isn't unattractive, I realise, when you aren't preoccupied with his ridiculous head to chest ratio. Which I am going to be for the entire interview. Focus, Rebecca, focus.

Tom takes the lead as is usual. 'We're here regarding an employee of yours, Anna Whitney,' he says. Adam's face remains blank. 'She teaches yoga here?'

I hold up my phone with a picture of Anna on it. Recognition dawns.

'Oh yes, sorry. We have so many instructors come in, it's hard to remember all of their names.'

I try to imagine a world where Matthews doesn't know my name. One can only dream.

'No, she's not been hurt,' Tom is saying, and I realise I have zoned out again. 'She's a suspect in a domestic homicide.'

Adam's eyes widen and I can see all of the PR implications running through his head like a Sky News banner.

'Oh God,' he mutters. 'This is all I need.'

'It isn't exactly the best of news for the victim either,' I say, not even trying to keep the disdain from my voice. Tom gives me 'the look' but Adam doesn't even have the self-awareness to pick up on it anyway.

'What can you tell us about Anna?' Tom asks, but the word 'homicide' has triggered a complete shutdown in our inflated-biceped friend.

'I can't say any more, I'm afraid,' he says, as if he's said anything in the first place. He barely managed to confirm she works here for goodness' sake. 'You'll have to speak to our public relations department.'

'With all respect,' Tom says. 'We are not the public. We're the police, and we would appreciate your co-operation. It's not exactly a difficult question, we're just trying to get as much information as we can to try and put together a picture of Mrs Whitney and her husband.'

'I don't know anything about either of them,' Adam says, going to stand up. 'You'll have to speak to PR. I'm not going to wake up to my face on tomorrow's front page and lose my job.'

Oh for fuck's sake.

'We're not journalists,' Tom snaps, and I cast him a look of surprise. Tom isn't the person to lose his cool. 'We're police officers, and no offence, but you're hardly front page news.'

The insult glides off Mr Big like he's made of Teflon. He pulls out a notepad and writes something on it, tears it off and hands it to Tom. 'That's the number you need to call. Sorry, but it's more than—'

'Your job's worth,' Tom finishes. Adam looks at him blankly, then turns and marches down the stairs.

'What a cunt,' Tom mutters. Wow, he usually saves the C word for reporters and tax inspectors.

'Come on,' I say, getting up myself. 'What a waste of time.'

Back downstairs we are greeted by the redheaded receptionist, only now she has a look of concern on her face.

'Adam has just come marching down here and barked at me not to speak to you about Anna,' she says. 'Is she okay?'

'She's unharmed,' I say quickly before RoboManager can come and kick us out. 'But she's in trouble. Do you have any reason to think she might have attacked her husband? Or anyone else who might have had reason to hurt either of them?'

'I can't see Anna ever hurting Luke,' the receptionist says with a shake of her head. 'Not from anything she's told us about him. He sounds too good to be true. But there is one thing…'

She trails off and glances towards what looks like an office. 'He'll kill me for saying this, but Anna had a falling-out with one of the members here recently. She tried to get her banned from the club, said this woman was stalking her.'

'Do you remember her name?'

She nods. 'Yes, she's in here loads. The manager – not Adam, he's just duty – the proper manager, he said her family was too important to piss off, and unless Anna went to the police and made a formal complaint he wasn't banning Phillipa.'

'Phillipa what?'

'Phillipa Kent. That's the woman Anna fell out with. She said Phillipa was crazy, and that she'd been following her.'

'Did she ever mention Phillipa making any threats against her?'

'No, that was why Phillipa wasn't banned. It was her word against Anna's, and she said that Anna was the crazy one. I don't know any more, sorry.'

'Getting to be a bit of a theme,' Tom mutters as we cross the car park. 'Our murder suspect accusing other women of being mad.'

'Oh, you can't help that,' I say. 'We're all mad here.'

Chapter Twenty-Eight

Anna

I sat down on the wall outside the charity gala, not caring if my expensive dress snagged against the stone and took a few deep breaths. My cheeks still burned in humiliation. I *knew* it had been a bad idea, playing our stupid game at one of his friends' parties. In the clubs of London where no one gave a shit who we were it was fine, but taking such a risk around Luke's contemporaries? Stupid. 'Stupid, stupid,' I muttered. And now Donald and God knew who else thought I was some sort of easy lay? Or worse, a prostitute? Did Donald really think that I'd take his money to let him have sex with me? The idea of it made me want to actually vomit.

I couldn't go back in there now, or ever actually. I'd have to wait until Luke came out to find me, then we would have to move house, move to a practice out of area where nobody knew us. *Damn it!*

'You look like you could use one of these.'

A roll-up appeared under my nose and I looked up, surprised to see someone else there. A man in his early twenties stood in front of me wearing black jeans and a black leather jacket. Not waiting staff, his hair was too long and unkempt. He looked like the lead singer of a band.

'God, you scared me,' I said. 'I didn't see anyone else out here. No, thanks.' I waved the cigarette away with a small smile. 'I just gave up.'

'Sensible. You're here for the big fancy charity party. I saw you with your husband inside. Smart-looking guy. What does he do? Let me guess, a tennis instructor? Or a doctor.'

My cheeks reddened and I felt a sudden irritation, although I wasn't sure whether it was at him insulting my husband or at my husband for being so fucking obvious. Maybe it was at myself for thinking I could play games in a man's world and get away with it.

'He's a cosmetic surgeon,' I muttered, and my irritation grew in proportion with the satisfied grin that spread across his face. 'And what's wrong with that exactly? It's a wonderful profession. He makes people feel better about themselves – he changes lives. How many lives have you changed recently?'

He shrugged, a slow lazy gesture that told me precisely how impressed he was by Luke's life-changing potential. It made me want to slap him.

'Who knows?' he replied. 'Every action has a reaction. How am I to know how many people have decided against taking their own lives because of my music? Music speaks to people on a deeper level than all that Freud bullshit. I don't know why you're getting your knickers in a twist defending him, he looks as though if I called him a stereotype he'd think it was a compliment.'

'Well he's helped women who have had mastectomies regain their confidence and get their lives back. He's done skin grafts for burn victims. I'd say that's pretty fucking important.' My anger was gaining pace now, anger on behalf of a man that a few moments ago I was cursing to hell. 'Besides, if we're talking stereotypes you're hardly breaking the clichés yourself, are you? Leather jacket, tick, roll-up, tick.' I ticked them off my fingers as I went. 'Unkempt, brooding and pouty, tick, tick, tick. Let me guess, you have an old motorbike in the garage that you're restoring for when you fuck off and "find yourself"? No girlfriend because you're too *deep* for the silly groupies that throw themselves at you but I'd bet that your moral compass doesn't lead you far enough away not to screw them? Oh, and did you seriously just say the words "music speaks to people on a deeper level"? Seriously, you look like you've been ripped straight out of a teenage girl's wet dream. If I was lactose intolerant I'd be throwing up from all the cheese.'

He moved away slightly, as though my sudden outburst had pushed him physically backwards, but he was smiling and holding up his hands in defeat.

'Wow, you got me.' He finished the last of his roll-up and threw it on the ground, pushed away from the wall. 'Although in my defence the leather jacket was management's idea, and you are welcome, for all future wet dreams.' He leaned in closer and I inhaled the smell of smoke and body odour, a raw, real smell so far from Luke's soap and expensive aftershave. 'Looks like the only one breaking stereotypes around here is the plastic surgeon's wife,' he murmured, and then he walked away.

Chapter Twenty-Nine

Rebecca

> Can I come over? I'll bring Chinese

Two nights in a row? I think to myself, looking at Jimmy's text. A bit much, to be honest. Not to mention that I don't know what time I'll be finished up here – in an investigation where we're on the clock like this we don't keep normal working hours. Too many hours get wasted that way.

Sorry, working late, I reply, and as an afterthought I send a sad face to show that I'd obviously rather have been at home eating Chinese with him. Truth is, I'd have found an excuse anyway. Two nights in a row gives a bloke the wrong impression. Before I know it he'll be leaving a toothbrush in my bathroom because 'it makes more sense than bringing one' and his dirty socks will be in with my washing. I shudder at the thought of washing Jimmy's socks. No thank you. Jimmy was supposed to be uncomplicated – that's why I've kept him around longer than my usual one-night stands. The problem with blokes and me is that usually the things they're attracted to in me are the things they end up wanting to change. The inside of my head is as messy as my apartment and I have no intention of being 'fixed' by anyone, even someone as pretty as Jimmy. Nice place to visit, but you wouldn't want to live there, if you catch my drift.

The team had agreed to meet back in the briefing room at six, and our trip to Anna's workplace had been cut short by the duty manager's crisis-aversion technique, so Tom and I got back to the station half an hour ahead of time, but Andy was still out. He'd sent a message to warn us he was running late on the Ring doorbell enquiry so at six thirty we are still waiting in the incident room.

'Can we not just start without him?' Rob asks for the third time. 'He might be all night.'

'We're waiting for Andy,' Tom snaps. Rob mouths 'what's his problem?' at me from behind his computer and I give a little shrug. In truth, Tom has hardly spoken to me all day but I'm not massively surprised. This case is gathering some steam in the press now, 'wife of prominent plastic surgeon arrested for attempted murder' playing in a loop on Sky News and BBC, eyes beginning to swivel our way. It's very early days and the media won't expect us to comment yet, but they have the scent of blood. As DI, Tom can feel the mounting pressure more than we can, and we're all painfully aware of how little we have to take to the CPS. All it takes is for Anna to recant her confession and say that intruders threatened her not to talk and we have reasonable doubt.

'Sorry I'm late, guv.' Andy steamrollers in, red faced and out of breath. He looks at me as if waiting for something. Bloody hell – do I really make that many jokes? I hold up my hands in an 'I got nothing' gesture and he sits down.

'Take a minute, Andy, I don't want to have to give you CPR,' Tom says. 'First things first, we have secured a ninety-six for Anna Whitney.'

A small cheer goes up. A ninety-six means that we have ninety-six hours from arrest rather than the usual twenty-four to charge or release Anna. In a murder case it's not difficult to get an extension but there's always a chance that we'll have to release them before we're ready, and that just looks bad.

'Okay. Shall we start with you, Rob?'

Rob clears his throat and is about to speak when the door to the incident room opens. The front desk clerk shoves her head around the frame.

'Sorry to bother you,' she says, a nervous look on her homely face. 'But I've got a gentleman downstairs asking to see you, DS Dance. He's, um… he's wearing a Batman mask.'

A knot of confusion twists in my stomach as I make my way downstairs, accompanied by DCI Kerrigan. I tell him I can go alone – any crank stupid enough to try to hurt me in a police station wearing a Batman mask deserves what's coming to him but Tom insists. We've had our fair share of lunatics in our time and we've learned to be cautious; it's quite sweet how protective he can get over me when he's not giving me shit.

And the sight waiting for me in the front reception does indeed look like the work of a lunatic. A man stands in the front reception, a full Chinese takeaway on the floor in front of him. He is wearing jeans, a tight black T-shirt and, the pièce de résistance, a Batman mask.

'Fucksake,' Tom mutters as he sees who the man in the mask is. I swear to God I die a little inside. This cannot be happening.

'Jimmy,' I hiss as I approach him. 'Take that fucking thing off. You're in a police station – are you mad? You're lucky you didn't get arrested. Who walks into a police station in a fucking Batman mask?'

'Well I thought you didn't want to be seen with me,' Jimmy says, as if this is a perfect explanation for his act of absolute stupidity. He must sense I'm not amused because he takes the mask off and gives me his best grin. 'Oh come on, Becky, I didn't wear the mask in here, did I? I just charmed Linda to tell you I was wearing it when she came and got you.'

'How the fuck do you know the desk clerk's name? Never mind.' I hold up a hand. 'I don't want to know. What is all this food doing on the floor?'

'I brought it for you.' He grins again. 'You said you were going to be working late so I brought you something to eat. I'd already ordered it when you turned me down, if I'm honest.'

When I say nothing, he falters, realising he might not have made the wisest choice. I feel like I've kicked a puppy.

'Thank you,' I say at last. 'But you can't… I can't…'

'Oh Jesus. You really don't want to be seen with me, do you?' Jimmy asks, his face falling. 'I thought that was just a joke.'

Oh my God. If he cries I swear I'm going to have to request a transfer to another station.

'It's not that,' I say quickly. Tom has walked away but he's still standing off to one side, obviously waiting to see what I do. He looks as though he could murder someone, I just don't know if that someone is me or Jimmy. 'I just can't… this is my work, Jimmy.'

'Okay.' Jimmy shrugs but even I can tell he's disappointed. 'I get it. Do you want to take this?' He gestures to the food. 'Share it with the team or whatever. I'll just catch you another night.'

'I'll text you, okay?' I promise. 'Thank you, for the food.'

Jimmy looks like he might lean forward for a kiss, but instead he gives me a salute. He glances at Tom, who is pretending not to be watching.

'Right, no worries. Speak soon.'

And I feel like crap as Jimmy walks away.

'You may as well give me a hand with this and stop pretending you weren't eavesdropping,' I snap at Tom, and gesture to the bags of food on the floor. Tom trudges over and gives me a look.

'What?' I demand. 'Something to say?'

Tom's eyes widen and he shakes his head. That's the thing I like about Tom, he never pulls rank, never reminds me that he's my superior and technically I can't talk to him that way. Well, almost never.

He picks up two of the bags and I take the other two, trailing the smell of fried food throughout the reception and up the stairs. I'll give it to Jimmy, he knows how to put on a spread.

'Wait, did Batman really bring your Chinese?' Rob asks as we return to the incident room and Tom disappears to get cutlery.

'Don't ask, honestly,' I say. 'Who wants a beef chow mein?'

—

I notice that Rob doesn't seem in nearly as much of a rush to get the briefing done once there's takeaway food on the table. I do feel bad handing out the meals that were meant for Jimmy and I to share, but it raises everyone's spirits, so that's a bonus. Everyone except Tom, obviously, who refuses to eat any of it as a mini hunger protest against my choice of bed partner. Which is good because Jimmy only technically ordered enough food for the two of us, although he has two meals and only ever eats half of each one, and I have enough sides to feed a small army. DS Beckford is picking at the chips but Rob and Andy are eating like it's their last meal.

'If everyone's done stuffing their faces,' Tom says, the minute the last prawn cracker has been eaten. 'Me and Rebecca went to speak to the manager at the fancy gym where Anna Whitney teaches yoga. Fucking useless prick. But the girl on—'

'Woman,' I correct. Tom frowns.

'What?' His voice is snappy. He's really pissed off about something. Jimmy? I know he thinks he's a scally but this reaction seems a tad over the top.

'Don't call her a girl,' I say. 'She wasn't twelve. She was a woman.'

He shakes his head, but says, 'The *woman* on the front desk told us that Anna didn't show up to the yoga class she was supposed to be teaching on Friday.'

'What's interesting about that?' Kim asks, looking confused. 'She went to the cottage, we know that.'

'Any change of routine or plans around a crime is interesting,' I tell her. 'You have to determine if it's cause and effect. Did Anna forget to cancel the class for her planned trip to the cottage, or was her showing up at the cottage unplanned? Did she surprise him and he was with another woman? Did she cancel last minute because she knew there was another woman going to the cottage with him?'

'Rose?' Andy asks. I bite my lip, thinking it over.

'Well, Rose *was* at the cottage at one point,' I agree. 'So Anna thinking she might find him there with a woman and then actually arriving to find Rose there would make sense. But the receptionist said something else that was interesting. She said that Anna hadn't been herself recently, and she'd tried to get a woman barred from the gym the month before for stalking her.'

'A stalker?' Andy raises his eyebrows. 'Isn't that something you'd mention if someone had attacked your husband?'

'Well either Mrs Whitney doesn't think the two are related or she doesn't want us to know about her feud with Phillipa Kent,' Tom says. 'But we need to look into every single angle that comes our way here, because there are holes in Anna Whitney's version of events that you could drive a truck through and I don't intend to let her jumped-up lawyer behind the wheel.'

'Do you want me to speak to this Kent girl?' Rob asks. He looks at me and clears his throat. 'Woman?'

Tom shakes his head.

'I've spoken to Matthews, he wants to go there himself. Apparently the Kent family are incredibly important, and incredibly litigious. They had some sort of media scandal a few years ago and they're overly cautious these days. Dance will go with them, for the female touch.'

It smarts a little that Tom is sending me off with the boss without talking to me first. I know he's my superior but he doesn't usually act like it. Is he really punishing me for Jimmy? Or am I being over sensitive?

'Okay, Andy?' Tom asks before I can put my foot in it.

'Nothing, guv,' Andy says. Tom frowns.

'Then why were you so bloody late?'

'Because there was nothing. Literally no sign of Anna Whitney on any of the Ring doorbells that should have caught her driving to the cottage. There are three that I could find that could see the road and her car wasn't on any of them.'

'Does that mean she didn't arrive when she said she did?' I ask. If that's the case, we've got something, well – a sliver of something – to crack open her story.

'No,' Kim says, and we all turn to look at her.

'Bloody hell, Andy, you said that without moving your lips.'

Kim reddens. 'Sorry,' she says, shuffling some papers on her desk and bringing one to the top. 'But I've got this map of the route Anna would have taken. Andy, you were looking at Ring doorbells on this estate, weren't you?'

She points to a road and Andy gets up to have a look.

'Yeah,' he says, pulling out his phone. He pulls up Google Maps. 'That house there' – he points – 'and those two.'

Kim takes out a pen and marks those houses on the map. I see that she's marked the cottage in red, and three access roads leading to the drive, one in red, one in orange and one in green. The houses Andy checked are along the green route.

'If Anna took either of these routes,' Kim points out, 'she would have missed those cameras.'

'And still could have been there at four like she alleges,' I finish.

'But why would she do that?' Rob asks. I'd bet a fiver that as a man he can't comprehend why someone wouldn't just take the quickest route.

'Loads of reasons,' I say. 'Maybe she had an errand to run and it was on this route. Maybe she doesn't like driving certain ways because more cars park on the road or because the flow of traffic is heavier, or because once she almost hit a cyclist there. Maybe she just took a wrong turn and accidentally took the other route. Maybe...'

'Maybe she was avoiding the cameras,' Tom cuts in.

'And maybe she was avoiding the cameras,' I agree.

'But we can't prove any of those things. I'll ask her in her next interview.' Tom makes a note. 'Moving on. Rob, can you tell us about the forensics?'

'Yeah, no problem,' Rob says, pulling out a sheaf of papers. 'We already knew that the murder weapon and the phone had been wiped clean. Well, so had everything else. Door knob, counter tops, barely any useable prints in the whole kitchen.'

'Why bother?' Andy asks. 'If it was Anna, why bother wiping her prints away? We would expect her prints there.'

'Because there was someone else there,' Kim says. 'Someone Anna didn't want the police to know about.'

'If she stabbed Luke, she would be covered in blood,' Tom says. 'It would make a clean-up difficult. And she called 999 straight after the stabbing – Luke was still breathing when the paramedics arrived.'

'So the other person was the one who cleaned up,' I say. 'Anna calls 999 while suspect number two cleans up. Maybe it's not that she's innocent, but someone else was there.'

'If we want to be able to charge Anna with murder, we need to be able to place someone else at the scene with her, not instead of her,' Tom tells us. 'Otherwise her lawyer will argue that Anna only entered the kitchen after the stabbing occurred.'

'What if she did?' I ask. 'What if Luke heard an intruder, went downstairs and got stabbed. Then Anna walked in and called the ambulance.'

'And confessed to murder?' Andy asks. 'Who would she want to protect that badly?'

'Well, it wasn't Rose,' Kim says, holding up her own sheet of paper. 'Rose has an alibi.'

Chapter Thirty

Anna

His name was Ed, and just to complete the cliché, he *was* the lead singer in the band that had been playing at a party in the room next to ours. It hadn't taken long on social media for me to find out who had been at the venue the same night as we were, and from there to find the name of the band and their contact details. I told myself that Luke had been wanting a party for his birthday, and okay, forty-three wasn't a big one but I was a loving, doting wife and besides, who needed an excuse for a party? I didn't even allow myself to entertain the idea that I'd thought about Ed every day since he challenged me outside the party, or acknowledge the sharp pang of disappointment I felt when I found out the number linked to the band's web page belonged to their manager. Of course it did – otherwise who knew what kind of weirdo stalker might get hold of it so easily? The band would love to play my husband's birthday party, he told me, but they were pretty fully booked. Would a Monday night be okay? Luke's birthday was on a Thursday, so it made absolutely no sense to have the party at the beginning of the week, on a work night no less, but I agreed anyway. I told myself I wouldn't get anything better at such short notice; besides, Luke's friends were always out on weeknights.

I sent out invites and found I was right – almost everyone accepted. In fact, Luke was the only one who complained about my choice of evening, at least to my face. I told him that the venue I'd chosen had dictated the evening, and I really didn't want to compromise, I just knew he'd love it. And he was going to – my inner guilt meant that I was pulling out all the stops for the party, a consolation prize for the fact that I was using my husband's birthday as an excuse just to catch a glimpse of another man for reasons I still couldn't fathom.

I had no intention of cheating on Luke, I put that straight with myself. What I was doing was indulging a little teenage style crush, the kind that had you savouring the memory of his blue eyes right up close to you, close enough that you could reach out and press your lips against his and taste the alcohol and cigarette smoke, push your hands into his hair and…

Well, you get the picture. But that's all I ever intended it to be, just an insignificant crush. I never meant what happened next, or the fallout that would follow.

–

I was directing the set-up of the venue when I saw him walk in, followed by the rest of his band and their manager. His eyes widened slightly when he saw me and I knew he recognised me, even dressed down. Did that mean something? It had been weeks, and still he remembered me. Would his vanity convince him that my presence was no coincidence? The band discussed with the hotel manager where to set up. There was no need for the two of us to speak and so we didn't.

In the hotel room upstairs I took a long bath, shaved my legs and other places, and laid out my best underwear.

I don't need a bra, my breasts are small enough and perky enough to do without one, and I supposed when they no longer were, Luke would sort that out for me. I've never ruled out surgery, although there's no way I would ever inject myself with as much of the crap in my face as Rose has.

Luke watched me get ready, blow-drying my hair and putting on my make-up. He often did, entranced by the small ritualistic acts that I moved through. He tried to initiate sex twice but I steered him away – I didn't want to ruin my hair, he'd crumple his suit. Plenty of time for that later, although we both knew we'd be too drunk and tired later to perform. I had chosen a long black satin dress with a split up the side that showed my tanned, toned legs when I walked. It had spaghetti straps and a ruched, low neckline but because my breasts weren't too big or squished together by a bra it didn't show too much flesh. My long blonde hair fell around my shoulders in waves. Luke liked it that way and it had taken a lot of practice for me to perfect.

All night I stayed on the dance floor, feeling as though Ed was singing just to me. *All good singers make you feel like that*, I told myself. *He's far too young for you.* I looked over and saw some of Luke's young female cousins watching Ed and waving, lovestruck looks on their pretty young faces. I saw him smile at one of them and she turned back to her group and started whispering and giggling and I felt sick to my stomach. Oh God, this had been a stupid, impulsive mistake. I felt ridiculous, some grown woman lusting over a man who had only recently left boyhood. I wasn't old enough to be his mother but I was too old to be acting like a teenager. Too old and too married.

Humiliation flooded through me. Had I really planned an entire party, dragged all of these people here, just to see this teenage wet dream? After everything I'd done to ensure Luke didn't make a fool of me, and I'd made a fool of myself. Thank goodness no one knew it.

The party was in full swing but suddenly I didn't feel like swinging. I glanced around for Luke but he was deep in conversation with Katherine Kent and I knew how these things go – they could be there for hours. I knew he wouldn't notice if I went missing so I slipped outside, back to where I'd seen Ed for the first time. I wasn't expecting him to follow – I didn't think he would see me leave any more than Luke would, but unlike my husband, his attention had been on me.

I was sitting on the same wall, in the exact same spot. So I can say that I wasn't waiting for him, and that I didn't think he would follow me, but I'd sat in our spot, so what was I really doing – really?

It took less than ten minutes before I saw him walking over to me. The music had switched to the generic DJ music that bands play while they take a break.

'Enjoying the show?' he asked. I nodded.

'Oh yes, you're very good.'

He raised his beer to indicate the party. 'Good turnout. We play a few weddings here… fancy. I hope your philanthropic plastic surgeon is enjoying himself.'

I pretended to look confused. 'Sorry?'

'Oh, are we going to pretend this is a coincidence? You hiring my band a couple of weeks after we met in this exact hotel?'

'I don't… I…'

He shrugged. 'Okay, sure. Enjoy the rest of the show.'

He flicked his cigarette away and started to walk back inside. I didn't know what to do, I just knew that I didn't want him to leave. I wasn't trying to start an affair, I just wanted one more minute in his company, one more minute of that dopamine high, that adrenaline rush you get when there's someone near who gives you butterflies.

'My favourite film is *Minority Report*,' I blurted out before he'd got more than a few steps. Ed turned around, raised an eyebrow.

'Okay,' he said. 'Is that's what you hired my band to tell me?'

'I teach yoga. I tell people I like reading classic literature but in all honesty I prefer crime novels. I like to walk in the hills and I'd love to have a dog but Luke says it will ruin the house so I go to rehoming shelters and walk with the dogs there. I'm an amazing cook, like *amazing*. I didn't do A levels because my dad committed suicide halfway through my first year. I listen to true crime while I'm driving, and I can recite all the words to every Carrie Underwood song. I am a human being. Not *just* the plastic surgeon's wife.'

Understanding dawned on his face. He nodded and moved towards me, reaching up and pushing a strand of my hair from my face.

'From the moment I saw you I knew you were a lot more than the plastic surgeon's wife.'

'I don't know why I needed you to know that,' I admitted. What I didn't admit was how I'd thought about him at least once a day since I'd first seen him, and how the thought of never seeing him again had made my stomach ache. I didn't tell him that I'd never had a crush quite like it – that when I made love to my husband I closed my eyes and imagined he was the lead singer of a band I'd met only once.

'Because you're not from this world,' he told me. 'And it exhausts you. I see you.'

It had been so long since anyone had really seen me in that way. This world of riches and glamour, it sucked you in and if you weren't careful it could spit you out. It sounds so 'poor little rich girl' even to me, but I was tired of trying to stay one step ahead, tired of keeping up appearances. I wanted something raw and real.

I knew I was playing with fire. The game we played only allowed me to go so far before I summoned my Prince Charming to come and rescue me. I'd never properly cheated on him, but why should the freedom I allowed him only work one way? So when Ed pushed me up against the wall and kissed me, I didn't resist.

Chapter Thirty-One

Interview with Will Harris regarding Rose Whitney's alibi

Interview conducted by DS Kim Beckford

\#

Beckford: Mr Harris, thanks for taking my call.

WH: Not at all, anything I can do to help.

Beckford: I've been given your name with regards to a case I'm looking into – the stabbing of Rose Whitney's ex-husband, Luke.

WH: Wait, am I a suspect? Do I need a lawyer? I've only spoken to Rose a few times…

Beckford: No, Mr Harris, please don't panic. I'm just doing the dogsbody work, following up statements et cetera. Rose Whitney says in her statement that on the night her ex-husband was stabbed, she was on the phone to you late into the night.

WH: Which night was it?

Beckford: Last Saturday.

WH: Um, yes, Saturday? She's right, I was on the phone to her for quite a while.

Beckford: Do you remember what you talked about?

WH: What we'd watched on Netflix recently, music we liked, places we'd visited or would like to visit. Just small talk, some banter.

Beckford: How long have you know Mrs Whitney?

WH: We've been chatting for a couple of months.

Beckford: And how many times have you spoken to Mrs Whitney in that time?

WH: We text one another most days. We speak on the phone a couple of times a week.

Beckford: Would you say the relationship is getting serious?

WH: Not serious enough for me to try to murder her ex for her, if that's what you're thinking.

Beckford: That wasn't what I…

WH: Is that it, for the questions? I'm due back at work.

Beckford: Yes, I think that's it for now, thank you.

Chapter Thirty-Two

Anna

Sex with Ed was nothing like sex with Luke. With Luke the courtship had been slow and steady, flirtatious, then when we had finally made love it was as if everything had been leading up to that very moment. Even when Luke and I had started playing our little games and the sex had got rougher it had been about him dominating me. With Ed it was urgent and fiery, my back grazing against the wall, the thin strap on my black dress snapping. A hand pushing up the satin, probing fingers pulling my underwear to one side and he was inside me, like he couldn't wait one more second to devour me completely. It was about him wanting me, not wanting to control me. 'You are so beautiful,' he murmured in my ear again and again.

When the sex was over, Ed surreptitiously checked his watch and something inside me died. He probably did this five nights a week, had managed to time his orgasm to a set break.

'I've got to get back on stage,' he said, and I nodded, not trusting myself to speak. I wouldn't cry in front of him, this teenage girl's dream. We straightened ourselves up and I braced myself for an awkward goodbye or worse, for him to walk away without another word. Instead, Ed leaned forward and grabbed my hand. 'I need to see you again.'

My heart thumped hard against my chest. I swallowed, knowing that what I said next would change the course of my life completely. To cheat on Luke was bad enough, but an affair? Then I thought about my husband in the hotel room with his young secretary, the nights he went away to 'business conferences', all the putting up and shutting up I'd had to do to keep our marriage from failing, to stop myself from ending up like Rose. 'I can't afford to keep throwing parties,' I said, trying to make light of things. Ed smiled.

'Can I call you?' he asked. I nodded, then he was gone.

I cleaned myself up in the hotel toilets and sprayed myself with a cloud of perfume. Luke was too busy with his guests to even notice I hadn't been around, but once the danger of being caught had passed, the stupidity of what I had just done sank in. Anyone could have walked around that corner and seen us, and then what? My marriage would be over – Luke wouldn't stand being humiliated in that way, divorce settlement or not. He liked to watch me flirt with other men, to stalk me down and claim me as his own, but what I had done was beyond the realms of our little games completely. I had broken the unspoken rules we had set and I already knew from the way my heart was pounding at the thought of Ed that I would break them again, and again.

'There you are!' Luke said, walking straight into the ladies' toilets as if he belonged anywhere he decided to be. 'Where have you been?'

'The strap on my dress snapped,' I said, holding up the limp satin string. I suddenly felt very sad about my dress, even though I knew it was easily replaced. Just like me. 'I came to see if I could fix it but I can't tie it to anything.'

'Oh darling,' Luke said, moving closer to inspect the damage. I hoped the perfume was enough to mask the scent of Ed's aftershave on my skin, and of the sex. 'I'll go and speak to the wait staff, see if they have anything to fix it with.'

'It's fine,' I said quickly. 'I'll pop upstairs and change. I brought a couple of dresses with me.'

We had booked a room in the hotel upstairs and all I wanted to do was bathe and fall into the sumptuous hotel room bed. Instead, I took the quickest of showers and changed my underwear, shoving the ones I had been wearing into a pedal-bin liner and then to the bottom of my suitcase, and pulled on my second choice of dress. This one was red and the colour felt appropriate for what I had become in the last hour – a scarlet woman.

Luke greeted me with a kiss when I returned and I kissed him back, treachery gripping my stomach. Was this how he felt when he strayed? I wondered. Did guilt gnaw at his insides when he kissed me after he'd been with another woman? Or could he easily separate the two, love and lust? Because I was already craving the feel of Ed's urgent lips against mine, his desperate fingers in my hair. I already needed to know when I'd get my next fix, and I didn't think it was like this for Luke, not at all. I looked up at where the band were just preparing to start their second set and couldn't bear to see him standing up there, belonging to everyone in the room. And when they started up with 'Do You Think About Me' by Carrie Underwood I felt like a driver who had lost control of my vehicle. Whichever way I turned the wheel now I was already off the track.

Chapter Thirty-Three

Rebecca

When we pull up outside Phillipa Kent's house I can tell by the look on Matthews's face that this isn't going to be easy. Coming from a working-class background Matthews has a deep-seated dislike for anyone who has more than him which seeps out of him in situations like this. Not for the first time I wish that Tom had been able to come with me to follow up the lead from the gym, but he'd insisted that Matthews had wanted to do this personally and I'm stuck with the boss, feeling like I'm having to hold the teacher's hand on the class trip.

'She isn't a suspect, remember?' I mutter as I slam the car door behind me. 'And she's nineteen. Go easy.'

'I don't know what you're expecting to get out of her anyway,' Matthews retorts, his voice low. 'Daddy is a lawyer – she's another high-class "no comment". Waste of time. Mum's alright though. Met her at some charity gala. Top totty.'

'He's a divorce lawyer,' I counter. 'He's hardly Johnnie Cochran. And no one says totty anymore.'

'Take a few years at university and they all think they're Cochran,' Matthews gripes.

I step up to the door and give a firm knock. When it opens I'm faced, not with nineteen-year-old Phillipa, but an older sister. Long, natural blonde hair falls glossy and straight down her back and large chocolate brown eyes look us up and down in turn. Matthews starts to speak but I take the lead. Take charge, show him I'm capable. I can deal with this woman – he's all bull in a china shop anyway.

'We're here to speak to Phillipa Kent.' I show the woman my badge. 'It's in relation to an incident that happened in the early hours of this morning. My boss, DCI Matthews, spoke to your father.'

'DCI Matthews, a pleasure to see you again.' The woman steps around me to kiss Derek on the cheek and I flush a deep red.

'Mrs Kent, thanks for agreeing to see us.'

She turns to me. 'I'm Katherine, Phillipa's mother,' she says, taking my hand and shaking it delicately. 'Don't look so embarrassed, dear, it's flattering, believe me. Now what's happened, DCI Matthews? I'm sure whatever it is Phillipa doesn't know anything about it, she's never been in trouble before.'

I try not to let the surprise show in my face. Usually you can tell when an older woman has tried to hide her age, the hands and the neck can't be as easily disguised as the face, but this woman genuinely looks like she could be in her late twenties. Maybe the water has anti-ageing properties here, that would explain the price tag. Thanks a bunch, Matthews. He let me charge right into that one.

'Phillipa isn't in any trouble,' Matthews assures her. 'It's just a couple of routine questions. Your husband said it would be fine.'

'Yes, okay, if he says it's fine then it is. My husband is in the drawing room, Phillipa is in her bedroom. Come in.'

She gives a glance at the car and I'm glad we turned up in the unmarked. The amount of times we've gone to take one of the cars out and some cheeky shit going for milk has nicked the keys – somehow I don't think Mrs Kent would appreciate a police car sitting next to the Range Rover on the driveway.

As we follow her inside I look at Matthews and mouth 'her mum?' He grins and mouths back 'drawing room?'

The drawing room turns out to be a regular room, just with a fancier name. The man in the room turns to face us as we enter and from the look on his face I can tell this won't be the easiest of interviews. What I'm not prepared for is how Matthews turns into Prince Charming when faced with the Kents. He never usually lets fancy folk get in the way of his belligerent personality. These people must have teeth.

'Mr Kent?' Matthews walks forward and offers a hand. Phillip Kent – yes, he named his daughter after himself – shakes it but doesn't bother offering his hand to me. 'DCI Matthews. We spoke on the phone.'

He nods but unlike his wife he doesn't start extolling his daughter's virtues. 'Does she need a criminal lawyer?'

It's not as an unusual question as you might think, my barista demands a lawyer before talking to me every morning when I get my coffee. As soon as people find out you're a detective their desire not to be arrested for murder kicks in – even if the worst thing they've done in their life is drive thirty-three in a thirty.

'It's just a few questions to determine the level of Phillipa's involvement at this time – of course if she'd prefer to come to the station with a lawyer she has every right to.'

'I don't need a lawyer.'

The voice comes from behind us and we all turn to see Phillipa Kent standing in the doorway. She is beautiful, in a young, wide-eyed nineteen-year-old way. Her blonde hair is pulled back from her face, she isn't wearing a scrap of make-up and her eyes are red rimmed, as though she has been crying.

'Phillipa?' Matthews steps back and gestures to the uncomfortable yet ornate sofa. 'Do you know why we're here?'

She shakes her head. 'No, but I haven't done anything I'd need a lawyer for, so I can't imagine why I'd need one.'

What is she lying about? That she doesn't know why we're here, or that she hasn't done anything wrong? News broke about the stabbing hours ago, but Luke Whitney has yet to be named as the victim. I have no idea how far the story has been spreading or speculated over on social media though – for all I know the Whitneys' names could be common knowledge by now. These things are getting harder and harder to control.

'If you change your mind at any point, Phillipa, all you have to do is say.'

Phillipa crosses the room and sits confidently on the sofa opposite me. When her mother appears with a tray of tea the cups rattle slightly on the saucers – she's nervous about something, more nervous than her daughter, actually. She puts them down on the table in front of me.

'If you need anything, I'm in the room next door. Are you sure you don't want Daddy in here with you, Pip?'

'I'm fine, Mum, I'm not under caution.' She rolls her eyes at me as her mum leaves the room. 'They are always like this, no offence to you. Could you call me Pippa? Or do you need to be formal?'

'Pippa's great,' I say with an encouraging smile. 'Okay, Pippa, first things first, do you know the name Anna Whitney?'

Pippa nods. 'Um, yes, the name definitely rings a bell. Maybe Insta or something? Is she an influencer?'

'She's a yoga teacher,' I say. Pippa snaps her fingers.

'Right, I think she used to run the class at my gym.'

'And do you get along with her?'

Pippa shrugs. 'I guess. I mean, she doesn't hang around before or after the class to chat to us, I don't exactly know her.' A lie, or at least not the whole truth. Pippa is difficult to get a read on, and I'm not used to that.

'Have you ever met her husband, Luke Whitney?'

Pippa chews her lips, looks thoughtful. 'I don't think so,' she says at last. 'But I think I know what he looks like, so maybe I've seen them together? I can't think where I might have met him though.'

I nod, willing Matthews not to look at me with any tells of his own. His face is like a bloody showreel when he's feeling any emotion whatsoever. The fact is, she's elaborated too much, giving out too much information. It might be because she's nervous – although she's not showing any of the usual signs of nervousness that doesn't mean she's not feeling a little under pressure – two detectives coming to her house and asking for her by name. But it could also be that she's lying. And my money's on the latter.

'What are you upset about?' I ask, changing direction. She starts.

'What? I'm not upset.'

'You've been crying,' I reply. 'There's mascara along the edge of your index finger and all of your make-up has been removed.'

'I poked myself in the eye doing my liner.' Pippa juts out her chin. 'I blinked, my mascara went everywhere, I couldn't be bothered to redo it.'

'If you barely know Anna Whitney, why would she try to get you banned from the gym she works at?'

Pippa frowns. 'She did? No one ever told me that. Why would she do that?'

'She said you were stalking her.'

Pippa's mouth drops open. 'What a bitch.'

'I take it you weren't stalking her?' Matthews asks. Pippa raises her eyebrows and pulls an 'oh please' face.

'Why would I be? She's nuts. She's a random yoga teacher.'

'And you have no idea why she might have said that?'

'She probably mixed me up with someone else. I never even got told she had made a complaint, did I?'

'Right. Do you know anything about an incident that happened last night?'

'With Luke and Anna Whitney?'

'So you do know what happened?'

Pippa eyes Matthews with thinly concealed contempt. 'No,' she says slowly, as if speaking to a small child. 'You asked me what I thought about Anna and if I'd ever met her husband, Luke. It doesn't exactly take a brain surgeon to work out that you're here because of something to do with them. Is she okay? Did he hurt her?'

'Why would you assume *he'd* hurt *her*, Pippa?' I ask, although it's a fair assumption that most people would make.

Pippa shrugs. 'I'd say it's a fair assumption – most people would make it.'

Shit, this girl is cool under pressure. Either that or she can read minds.

'Okay, one last question,' Matthews says, declining to answer Pippa's own question. She doesn't ask again – does she already know what's happened? Why did the receptionist at the gym tell us to speak to her, why this girl? 'Can you just confirm where you've been this weekend? Just so we can put a cross through your name completely.'

'Where did you even get my name?' Pippa asks.

I wander over to the bureau, which is filled with about fifteen framed photographs in different style frames. The Kents on a beach, on a boat, at a wedding. One of the pictures is of three women standing together laughing – well, two women and a young girl. I lean down to take a closer look but Pippa jumps up to snatch the photo up and cradles it protectively.

'The receptionist at the gym told us about the complaint that Anna had made. If there's no merit to it then this will be the last time you see us. If you answer the question.'

'I was here mostly,' she answers, throwing me a glare. 'I popped to the supermarket yesterday morning at eleven, then came back and watched TV in the day room.'

'Which supermarket did you go to?'

Pippa hesitates. 'Waitrose on London Road.'

'Then what, you watched TV all day then went to bed?'

'Yes. Well, I didn't just watch TV, I had a bath, did some beauty stuff, messed around on social media. Wait a sec, Gemma called me about elevenish, I think.'

'Gemma…?'

'Gemma Berkley – just a friend.'

'How long did you talk for?'

'Only about twenty minutes. I went to bed straight after.'

There's no reason for us to think that Pippa even knew Luke Whitney, and no direct evidence other than Anna's complaint to say she had anything against Anna, so there's not much more to ask. We thank Pippa and her parents for their time and I make a mental note to have Kim look into her movements over the weekend when I get back to the station.

Chapter Thirty-Four

Anna

It had been five months since Luke's birthday party and I'd got sloppy, staying too long at Ed's while Luke was at work, racing back with half an hour to get dinner ready, making excuses to go and see his band on a Friday night like some teenage groupie. I should have known that Luke would start to suspect something – he was a serial cheat and if anyone was going to know the signs of someone being unfaithful it would be him. My behaviour was so far out of character from the Anna that Luke knew, and yet I hadn't seen it coming, that night when I got in from the gig late, my hair smelling of tobacco smoke and my head fuzzy from alcohol. I'd expected he would already be asleep, I'd told him I was going to meet an old friend and I might be late and he'd said that he wouldn't wait up.

I kicked off my pumps, almost tripping over my own feet and giggling. Oh no, I was buzzed. Thanks goodness Luke was asleep. I used the main bathroom rather than our ensuite so that I didn't wake him. I took a quick shower to wash the smell of Ed off me, but I couldn't bring myself to brush my teeth, I could still taste him. I towel dried and crept into our pitch black bedroom completely naked, ready to slide into bed next to my husband.

I gingerly peeled back the covers and climbed into bed. Instinctively I reached over to put my hand on Luke but found only an empty space. I sat up, suddenly sober, and felt further. Nothing. Where was Luke? I got up, grabbed my dressing gown from the back of the bedroom door and switched on the light.

Luke was sitting on the end of the bed, fully clothed, staring at the wall.

'Luke?' I said, walking around the bed to stand in front of him. He looked up at me, his face etched with pain. 'What is it?' I asked, thinking that someone must have died, or he was sick. 'Is everything okay? Are you ill?'

'Where have you been?' he asked, his voice flat.

'I told you, I was out with Kelly. We went to see a band.'

'Which band?'

'I… um, I don't remember their name. They weren't that good.'

'Better than when they played at my party?'

I opened my mouth, then closed it again. It was obvious he knew what had been going on and he'd caught me off guard. All the things I should say mashed together in my mind – I should deny it, find out how much he knew, then perhaps I could play it off as a crush rather than an affair. I should turn it back on him, he'd been unfaithful and I'd let him off, did he really think it didn't work both ways? Then I noticed the suitcase beside him and my heart sank. He was kicking me out.

I didn't know what to do. I'd thrown away my marriage, my home, my whole life for a toyboy who probably still sent his washing back to his mum. A singer in a band? What had I been thinking? Lust. Lust and ego, Ed had fed them both. He'd made me feel irresistible, needed, craved, and not in the dominating way Luke did when we played our games, but in a pure, unsullied, *clean* way. But I knew it wasn't enough. I wasn't in love with Ed and it wasn't fair that I'd let him fall in love with me.

'I don't… I can't…'

'Do you love him?'

It was the exact same question I'd asked Luke when I caught him with his secretary, the irony was not lost on me. Because although I wasn't in love with Ed, I did love him, in a way. I felt more for Ed than I'm certain Luke had ever felt for his assistant. I had betrayed him more completely than he had ever done to me.

'No,' I said, because the truth was too messy. Love isn't binary, tick box yes or no.

'Then why?'

I let out a sigh and shook my head. 'I don't know. I'm sorry, Luke. I just enjoyed feeling wanted.'

'And I don't make you feel that way? We had a deal, Anna. You set the terms and I've stuck to them. I haven't been unfaithful to you once since that night in the hotel, not even the casual flings you so graciously authorised.'

That came as a slight shock to me, and instead of making me feel better that my husband had been faithful to me it just made me feel worse. How did it feel more awful to be the cheater than the innocent party?

'I'm sorry, Luke. I understand that you want me to leave…'

Then he did something I hadn't been expecting at all. If you'd told me he would get angry, shout, throw things, even threaten me I might have believed you. And if he'd done that I might have fled, back into the arms of my young lover, and that might have been the end of our story. Instead, he broke down and started to cry.

'Oh God, Luke, I'm so sorry. Please, don't, I made a stupid mistake and I'm so, so sorry.'

I knelt down in front of him and he put his head on my shoulder and sobbed. I held him tight until his sobs subsided and he looked up at me with swollen, puffy eyes.

'Please don't leave me,' he whispered, wiping his face with his arm. 'I'll be better. I'll never even look at another woman, I'll do anything it takes to save this marriage. Please don't leave me.'

I was practically stunned into silence, and Luke took it badly. He put his head in his hands and began to cry again. I stood up.

'Luke, please, I'm not leaving you. I'm just in shock that you're not kicking me out.'

He gave a sniff. 'You're not leaving me for him?'

In that moment I honestly believed that I'd never loved him more. I didn't feel as though the choice had been taken from me, even though just hours before I'd been considering if I might be falling for Ed, if my life with him would be better, or at least simpler. Now I just felt grateful that Luke wasn't throwing me and all of my stuff into the street.

'No, of course not. I love you, and I'm sorry. I'll make it up to you if you think we can make this work.'

He let out a strangled noise and wrapped his arms around my waist, holding on to me as if were he to let go I would disappear in a puff of smoke.

'Of course we can make it work. You just have to promise me you'll never see him again. I don't want to know any details except that it's over.'

I nodded. 'Of course. It's over. I'll tell him tomorrow.'

'No,' Luke said, his voice suddenly so sharp that I was taken aback. 'I'll drive you there and you can tell him now.

I need to know it's done, from this moment on. And I want him to see that you're serious.'

'Luke, I—'

'If you want to make this marriage work, you will tell him tonight and never see or speak to him again. That's my only condition. That way we can move forward with a clean slate, none of us involved with anyone else. No more games. Just us.'

'Okay,' I agreed, my heart racing at the thought of looking Ed in his face and breaking his heart. A part of me thinks that that was the cruellest thing Luke did to me. He wasn't going to let me take the easy way out and break up with Ed over text message, or just ghost him. He was making me face what I'd done and the mess I had caused. It was no less than I deserved, I thought. And the idea of stopping all of the games and returning our marriage back to ground zero, well I thought that was what I wanted. What I needed.

What I didn't know was that he was lying to me even then, even as he sobbed and wailed and begged me not to leave. Even as he drove me to my lover's flat and sat outside as I went in and told Ed it was over Luke had already set in motion the events that would lead to his murder, and I had no idea.

Chapter Thirty-Five

Anna

I stood outside the flat and rang the doorbell. A glance back over my shoulder confirmed that Luke was watching from inside the car and I was glad that it was an intercom buzzer, and that my husband wouldn't have to see the look on Ed's face when I turned up in the middle of the night. He always looked so pleased to see me, whenever I managed to sneak some time away, like a child whose parent had returned from months away, even if we'd only seen one another the day before. It was funny how the cocksure, bad boy singer of the band I thought I'd met that first night had turned out to be a hopeless romantic, although apparently only with me. According to his friends – stoner 'artist' types who hung around the flat discussing books I'd never even heard of while relying on Mummy and Daddy for rent money – I was getting a side of Ed they had never seen before, and before tonight I'd enjoyed the idea that I was the woman who had changed his outlook on love. It had made me feel special. All the while I'd never given him even half of what he deserved. I had been so selfish.

' 'Lo?'

'Ed, it's me, Anna. Can I come up?'

The buzzer squawked an admission and I pushed open the heavy front door and took the stairs – the place was too much of a shithole to ever risk using the lift. Ed was standing in the doorway waiting for me in just a pair of Calvin Kleins, his hair all mussed up as if he'd been dragged from sleep. He smiled when he saw me, that slow, lazy, sexy smile that might have convinced me to stay if my husband hadn't been in the car downstairs like a reluctant chaperone. I guess that's why he didn't want me to go alone the next day.

'Hey, gorgeous, I wasn't expecting to see you again tonight. Hey.' He noticed my expression and immediately looked concerned. 'Are you okay?'

'Not really,' I admitted. I sighed. 'It's Luke. He was waiting up for me when I got home tonight. He knows about us.'

'Shit.' Ed let out a long breath and instinctively stepped forward to hug me. I wanted to let myself be comforted by him but even I knew that would be beyond selfish, to take his comfort and then break his heart. I stepped back and he looked confused.

'Look,' he said, standing to one side. 'I know it feels shit, but the hard bit's done now. Come on, I'll make you a drink then we can get some sleep. Things will look better tomorrow.'

It was in this moment, of course, when I realised exactly what I'd done. I'd allowed this twenty-two-year-old boy to think that there was a future for us, just like every lying, cheating husband does to his poor mistress. Not with my words – I'd never actually promised to leave Luke – but in my actions, in the way I had given myself fully to Ed, our dreamy afternoons in his poky flat eating chocolate-covered strawberries and reheated Indian food, our snatched moments together when Luke was at a 'conference'. But was there seriously a part of him that thought I would want to live like that? I was thirty-two years old, I didn't want to go back to living like a student, trying to rummage for clean underwear in the piles strewn around the flat before going to endless job interviews conducted by people ten years younger than me.

'No, Ed,' I said, leaning over and kissing him on the cheek, lingering too long. His smell, once so new and exciting, now felt familiar and safe. Safer, perhaps, than my husband, because I knew that Ed was completely devoted to me. He never acted as though I should be thankful that he was with me, or that any part of me was less than desirable. But a life with Ed would never be safe. The shine would fade and I would grow resentful of his inability to provide stability, his immaturity and what I had given up to be with him. And eventually he would grow tired of his nagging older woman always telling him to clean up his flat and telling his friends to go home to their own beds.

I still wasn't sure why Luke hadn't thrown me out tonight — I had wondered on the drive over here if he was still worried about the tax fraud I knew he'd been committing, but realistically he must have known deep down that I couldn't use those documents. I'd be cutting my nose off to spite my face — HMRC would take everything and I'd be left with nothing, at least until the whole thing was straightened out, and maybe not even then. I'd come to the conclusion that maybe he just really did love me.

I watched Ed's face crumple as he realised what I was saying, that there was no future for us. It was the first time

I'd realised just how young Ed actually looked. Men did this all the time, dated women twenty or thirty years their junior – Ed was only ten years younger than me, but at that moment he made me feel a hundred. He just looked so breakable. I pictured Luke downstairs in the car, checking his watch. Would he come up here if I took too long? He had sounded like he expected me to announce it was over and just turn around and walk away, but it was so hard to see someone you cared for in pain. How did people put themselves through this time and time again? Had my mother felt this shitty each time my dad found out about one of her numerous affairs? It hadn't ever seemed like it.

'I thought it was me you wanted,' Ed said, reaching out to caress my cheek. 'I know I don't have all the fancy things he has but I love you, Anna.'

This was awful. Horrible. At that moment I would have done anything not to have been that woman, but here I was.

'It's not about the fancy things, Ed,' I said, stepping back to put space between the two of us. 'I don't want to leave my husband. I never said I would. You knew I was married when we met.'

I remembered that moment then, the too-cool lead singer and the plastic surgeon's wife. It had felt like one of those meet cutes from romantic comedies. Except no one was laughing now.

'But—'

'I'm not going to change my mind,' I said, trying to sound as cold as I could. 'I only came to tell you to your face because he made me. I was just going to text you. It was only ever a fling between us anyway, nothing serious.'

Ed's face creased in disgust. 'Fine,' he said, and the word cracked at the end. He cleared his throat. 'Go on down to your husband, he'll be wondering where you are. The pair of you deserve each other.'

He stepped back and closed the door in my face, and that was when I realised that in trying so hard not to become my father, I had succeeded in becoming my mother.

Chapter Thirty-Six

Rebecca

We arrive at the station just before nine am. Kim is already there with Matthews but the other two are nowhere to be seen. I make us all a round of coffees while Matthews updates Tom and Kim on last night's interview with Pippa Kent.

Rob and Andy sidle through the door as if they've been here all morning, bacon sandwiches in hand. Matthews is about to kick off when Rob hands him and Tom a bag each.

'Sausage baguette, red sauce,' Andy says, passing me mine. 'I didn't know what you'd want, Kim, so I just got you bacon bap, no sauce.'

'There's sachets in the bottom drawer,' I tell her. She smiles gratefully but I notice her sliding the bag to the edge of the desk and it stays there.

'Okay, shall we get on with this?' Matthews says with a weary sigh. Kim's hand twitches – she's dying to put it up, but she manages to keep it on the table.

'Kim, why don't you show the DCI what you're putting together with regards to Luke Whitney's movements?' I smile at her and allow myself to feel like a wonderfully generous person. There are plenty of others who would take any opportunity to give a presentation as if they put it all together – I should know, I've had the credit for my hard work snatched away more than once in the past. When I used to work hard, that is.

Kim beams and pulls out a board from the side of her desk where she's printed several maps from Google on A4 paper and stuck them together so they make a huge map of our area of interest. Matthews raises his eyebrows slightly and I feel a bit proud, like my kid has done the best recycling project.

'Here is Luke and Anna's home,' she says, pointing at a pin in the map. 'We got access to his Ring doorbell footage and that shows him leaving the home at ten thirty. Anna doesn't leave until twenty past eleven.'

'Do we know where he went? Not straight to the cottage, unless he stopped on the way.'

Kim points to another area on the map. 'ANPR shows him in this car park twenty minutes later, leaving at eleven fifty-three. I've got a list of stores in the surrounding areas to check CCTV to nail down what he did in that hour.'

'Right, good. Rob, where are we at tracking camera footage en route to the cottage?'

'We've contacted every garage on the route.' Rob holds out a sheaf of paper that looks frankly pathetic next to Kim's grand offering. 'There are four. I've asked for footage working backwards from the time Luke Whitney arrived at the cottage to see if we can confirm the timeline.'

'Work with Kim when the footage comes in – let her do the presentation, eh?' Matthews says, shooting a derisory look at Rob's pitiful sheet of paper as he leaves.

Chapter Thirty-Seven

Anna

What are they doing, while I'm sitting around in this cell staring at the same spot on the ceiling that I've been staring at for what feels like years? How is the investigation going? Are they out there talking to my friends and family? My work colleagues? It strikes me that I don't particularly have a great deal of people in my life, no parents or siblings, my colleagues technically mostly consist of clients and my friends are mostly joint acquaintances. How have I not felt more lonely? I guess I've always enjoyed my own company, since I was a child.

I wonder what Rose has said to them. I bet she couldn't wait to stick the knife in, telling them about how I plotted to steal her perfect life from under her. And why haven't they asked me about Pippa yet?

Pippa. Pippa, Pippa, Pippa.

—

She'd been attending my yoga class for nearly six months when we bumped into her at the golf club. We'd been invited for Sunday lunch with some boring ex-colleagues of Luke's and as we were arriving she was just leaving.

'Anna, hi!' she had gushed, as if we were old friends, when the reality was that she had barely spoken to me in the whole time she'd been taking my class. She arrived, put down her mat, did her yoga, then left. Where the other women would hang around afterwards, or sometimes join me for a coffee in the hub if I was sitting alone, Pippa never engaged. She didn't act in a rude or standoffish way, but the way of someone who has plenty enough friends, thank you, and just uses the club for its original purpose, to work out. She was incredibly beautiful, and often wore little more than a pair of tight shorts and a crop top showing an expanse of young, smooth, tanned flesh and toned muscles. That Sunday afternoon she was wearing a red sundress, white ankle socks and bright white high tops and out of gym wear and with her long blonde hair loose I almost didn't recognise her at all.

'Goodness, sorry, I almost didn't recognise you,' I told her, but she didn't look offended, instead smiling at my husband as if I hadn't even spoken. 'I love your dress. This is my husband, Luke.'

'Thanks, I know I'm just clinging on to the last vestige of summer but it was on sale at Selfridges. Hello, Luke.' She held out her hand for him to shake. 'Have we met somewhere before?'

I saw Luke's eyebrows raise slightly but I couldn't immediately figure out the reason why. I had always been so good at reading Luke, or so I thought, but now I was in no man's land. Did he know Pippa? Had she said that on purpose to tease him, or did she genuinely recognise him from somewhere innocent? She was what, eighteen, nineteen maybe? She would have been around fourteen before Luke and I got together, so if they had slept together it would be since our marriage. Luke may be a womaniser, but he would never, never sleep with a fourteen-year-old girl.

This was *exactly* what I had been trying to avoid when I first gave Luke his ultimatum. Running into women who had one over on me, knowing they had slept with my husband behind my back. Thinking how sad and pathetic I was to be clinging on to a husband who couldn't bring himself to stay faithful, standing in front of me and knowing what my husband looks like naked. I kept my face absolutely neutral, but something about this young, confident woman made me want to claw her face off.

'I don't believe so,' Luke said easily. Everything about him indicated he was telling the truth, but with Luke surety didn't exist. 'Pleasure to meet you.'

Pippa smiled and turned back to me and it was as if the air thinned and the room around us began to move again. The spell was broken; I said goodbye to Pippa and we took our table. Luke's friends hadn't arrived yet and I was glad not to have to wait all through dinner with the unspoken question between us.

'She's pretty,' I said pointedly when we were seated. The words were coated with danger and Luke had the good sense to know it. He didn't ask 'who?' and go red, start to stutter like most men would. He was better at this than most men. He put his menu down and looked me straight in the eye.

'She is,' he said. 'But you are beautiful.'

'Answer the question, Luke.'

He smiled, and instead of charming I just found it arrogant and condescending. 'I've never slept with her, Anna, I swear. I don't remember ever meeting her before, but if she's here now then it's possible she's been at one event or other here in the past. In all honesty though I think she was just trying to cause trouble. She looks the type.'

I could have kept prodding, caused an argument, acted petulant, but we had promised one another after Ed that we would draw a line under anything that had happened in the past and I wasn't going to be the one to break that promise, especially just before Luke's friends joined us.

'Okay,' I said, going back to my menu. 'Thank you.'

He looked vaguely surprised that that was the end of it but after a short pause he picked up his menu again. And in that moment I honestly believed that I had nothing to fear from Pippa Kent.

Do the police even know about her? Or are they just taking my word that I killed my husband and leaving me here to rot?

Has Pippa won?

Chapter Thirty-Eight

Rebecca

'Tell me again what we're doing here?' Tom asks.

'Well *you're* here because Matthews thinks that Phillipa Kent is a dead end and I didn't want to ask him to come with me.'

'Has anyone ever told you your powers of flattery are unparalleled?'

'You get flattered plenty from everyone else. My job is to keep your head size at levels where we can still get you through doorways. Anyway, you'll thank me later. Do you realise what is a ten-minute walk *that way*?'

We are standing outside of Waitrose and I'm pointing to a tall building.

'Offices,' Tom says.

'Behind the offices. The car park Luke Whitney was parked in at eleven am. When Pippa Kent says she was here, in Waitrose.'

'Shit,' Tom mutters. I could have pointed it out sooner – I had spotted that he hadn't made the connection during Kim's presentation, but I had and I had been looking forward to impressing him.

'Morning! I'm Lottie, the manager.' I'd called ahead to let her know we were on our way – no one likes the police just turning up. 'Follow me, we can talk in the office.' She punches a code into the alarm system and unlocks the door. 'Come on through. God, I've assumed you're the police, not a pair of serial killers!' She laughs at her own joke.

Lottie is in her early twenties but speaks to us with the confidence of someone ten years older. Her face is made up and her hair is pulled into a single braid down her back without a stray hair. If you told me Lottie was a new line of android sales assistants designed to replace humans within three years I would believe you without question.

'You assume correctly.' Tom smiles. He is unbelievably useful in every situation where co-operation from the opposite sex is needed, and yes, I'm well aware that if he'd said that about me he'd be accused of sexism. He'd also be accused of lying – I'm not well known for my charm.

'Delivery is in half an hour, but until that comes we can go to the office. It's this way.'

We follow Lottie through to what she calls 'the office' but is basically a store cupboard with a desk. The store's POS – that's point of sale, for anyone who's never worked in a shop, posters, banners, those stand-up cards that sit on tills for half the year and in storage for the other half – is stacked up against one wall, making the space still smaller. A large metal safe sits under the desk with glossy A4 posters stacked up on top.

'Sorry,' she says, without looking in the slightest bit apologetic. 'It's a bit cramped.'

'Don't worry about it. We're here to ask about a girl we believe was in your store Friday afternoon, around eleven am. Were you on shift then?'

'Yes, me and three others,' she says. 'Do you want to see the CCTV?'

'We will do, yes please,' I say. 'But could you tell us if you recognise her first please?'

I hand over the photograph of Pippa Kent that I've printed from her Facebook profile picture.

'Yes, she was here,' Lottie says instantly.

'That was quick,' I say. 'How can you be so sure?'

'Well she's quite, um, noticeable, isn't she? I mean, girls like her tend to stand out.'

Unlike girls like us. She doesn't say it but we both know that's what she's thinking. You could hand someone a picture of Lottie ten minutes after they had served her and they wouldn't recognise her. Same could be said of me, but the difference is that when you hit your mid-thirties you give less of a shit about being 'seen' and generally just feel grateful that they didn't notice the gravy stain on your shirt. Or maybe that's just me.

'And the guy, well, even if I didn't remember her, I'd remember him alright.'

That stops me short and I glance at Tom. 'The guy?'

'Yes, the bloke she was with. Older, very attractive. He might have been like fifteen, twenty years older than her? But he was in really good shape – it didn't look weird until you looked at them closely and saw just what the age difference was.'

'And this guy, could you describe him?'

'I already told you, we have CCTV – I could just show you.'

We wait patiently as she turns on the computer, at least ten years for it to load and another ten for her to log in when we hear the little chime of Windows loading. We're both trying not to look too excited but I know Tom wants to see if it's Luke that Pippa is with as much as I do. The timing works – he could have quite easily been with her buying ingredients for the stew he will later share with his wife and still make it to the cottage before Anna arrived.

'Okay, what time did you say?'

'If you could just start it at ten fifty and let it run,' Tom requests. We are looking at a screen split into three, one third showing the front doorway of the store, a third on the back door that leads into the office where the safe is kept, and where we sit right now, and the last third on the shop floor. At exactly eleven am we see Pippa approach the front doors of the store completely alone and stand with her phone in her hand, looking into the distance. The quality isn't amazing but both of us notice when she lifts her head and smiles. She's seen someone.

Luke Whitney moves into the shot, leans down and kisses Pippa Kent on the lips in full view of the CCTV. He takes her hand, as it looks like he's done plenty of times before, and they walk together into the store.

'I guess that's who you're looking for?' Lottie says, pausing the CCTV and rewinding. 'Do you want me to get a print-off of that still?'

I wonder for a fleeting moment if she's related to Kim back at the station. 'Yes, that would be perfect, thank you.'

She clicks a few times and the printer behind Tom begins to whirr. Lottie presses 'play' and the CCTV footage begins again.

Pippa and Luke walk hand in hand around the supermarket, looking very much like any other couple doing a shop. I still find it strange every time I watch footage of someone who is missing, or deceased. Seeing them going about their lives knowing that less than twenty-four hours later they will be dead. Luke certainly didn't look like he had a care in the world wandering around Waitrose yesterday afternoon with one of his wife's students. Does

Anna know about their affair? Is this footage the reason Luke Whitney is lying in the morgue?

We watch for ten more minutes as they wander around, Luke grabbing the occasional item and dropping it into the basket. *The ingredients for the stew*, I think. *He's shopping with his mistress for ingredients so that his wife can cook him a stew.* I'd bloody stab him if I was Anna.

Eventually they pay for the items and walk out, still holding hands. They don't seem particularly bothered about being seen. Is that what happened? Did someone see them and call Anna, warn her what her husband was doing behind her back?

Is that what Rose was doing at the house? Did she know about Pippa? Did she threaten to tell Anna? But if that was the case, why wasn't Luke stabbed until one am? Hours after both Rose and Anna had seen Luke, plenty of time for them to start a row.

'Could you email this to us please?' I ask Lottie before she can suggest it herself. 'From the moment this woman arrives until they walk out. Did they go left out of here, or right?'

'Looked like left,' Lottie says, rewinding a few minutes. She's right, they leave the shop and turn left. I make a mental note to check outside and note any other cameras that might have caught where they went after they exited the shop.

'You've been really helpful, thanks,' Tom says. Lottie nods, not particularly flattered by the compliment. 'I'd really appreciate a copy of their receipt, if you can identify it by the time stamp?'

'No problem,' she replies. 'And I'll ask any of the staff if they can remember these two, anything about their demeanour or their conversation.'

'Um, brilliant, thanks.' I nod at Tom, desperate to get out of here before she starts giving me a list of things I should be working on.

Chapter Thirty-Nine

Pippa

I know that Anna thinks Luke picked me for some kind of revenge on her, but she couldn't be more wrong. Luke Whitney was firmly on my radar a long time before Anna even came into his life, and she still doesn't know it.

We were already screwing the day I bumped into them at the golf club – meeting the two of them at the golf club was the only time that things didn't go exactly according to my plan, but at least he didn't see me with my parents I suppose. The absolute last thing I wanted was for Luke to see them.

Anna knew better than to think she could hold on to Luke by changing herself to be a cardboard cut-out of what men wanted women to be. Good for her. But the fact that she'd messed up and been screwing some pretty young thing made my job a lot easier. They'd promised to draw a line under it, start over, blah blah blah, but with Luke it was all about power and possession. He couldn't stand the idea of that twenty-something-year-old man satisfying his wife, it ate him alive. So he started an affair with a woman even younger. Pride comes before a fall, didn't anyone ever tell him that? But an affair wasn't enough – he had to leave her for me, and for that I was going to have to make sure Luke was besotted with me.

I'd spent almost two years at this point, just watching them whenever I could. I turned down parties and dates, while other girls my age were going to the pub, holding the hands of older boys to get into nightclubs, sneaking their parents' alcohol and topping vodka bottles up with water so Mummy and Daddy didn't notice, I was sitting in the rain opposite restaurants so I could get a glimpse of them arriving and leaving, poring over Anna's Instagram and TikTok yoga and wellness videos, practising mimicking her speech and the way she pushed her hair from her face. This woman had stolen Luke from his wife and I was like a detective trying to find the smoking gun that would lead me to how.

I thought about them so much it was like they were a part of my real life. I knew when Luke got a promotion and when Anna was sick (she cancelled her classes and ordered Hello Fresh). I daydreamed in class about all of the ways I wanted to ruin his life. I flitted between a few different scenarios. Some would have him so in love with me that he ended his life rather than live without me in it — would he slit his wrists in the bathtub, the way Laura had? Or perhaps he would jump from a bridge, or in front of a train, the latter being too quick for my liking but I'd live with it. I passed my exams, but badly, and I know Mummy and Daddy thought it was because of what had happened and I suppose in a way it was, but I didn't think about that anywhere near as much anymore. Now I look at it I see that I was letting my obsession seep in like water, filling up the hole grief had left. The only future I had to focus on was Luke's, and how I intended to shape it.

Despite my crummy grades I got into sixth form, but nothing else changed. I just had fewer hours in education and more free time to pop to the coffee shop where I knew Luke went for his morning latte, or – and this was a big one – sign up for Anna's yoga class. The idea of being so close to her, having her speak directly to me, was so terrifying that I cancelled twice before getting up the nerve to attend, thinking that she would recognise me instantly from one of the million places that I'd seen her. It's so weird, the feeling that you can know someone so well and yet they have no idea you even exist. Maybe it's the same way that people feel like they know radio presenters and podcasters; they are so present in your daily life that you almost forget that they've never met you before. But Anna clearly hadn't seen me following her anywhere, she just came in and set down her yoga mat as if I wasn't a bomb about to blow up her entire life.

Then the time came to actually engineer a meeting between Luke and I. I'd spent so much time watching his movements whenever I wasn't in college, but still, meet cutes are not as easy to engineer as they appear in the movies. It's pretty difficult to get someone to accidentally spill their coffee on you, or catch you when you trip. It's not natural to bang into someone.

Eventually it was a good old coincidence that brought us together. I had been waiting outside Whitney and Osbourne for him to emerge, when it had started to rain. My umbrella had broken on me and the Uber I'd ordered hadn't shown. I was cold and getting soaked through and I'd forgotten completely about stalking Luke and was in the depths of self-pity when a voice said, 'Is everything okay?'

For all of my attempts to engineer the perfect meet-up, here I was, washed up and looking terrible, standing in front of the man himself with my eyes full of tears.

'I'm fine, thank you,' I said, my heart racing. I turned away, hoping he would just leave and not look too closely at my face. When I did manage to engineer the perfect meeting down the line I didn't want him to remember me and think I was stalking him.

'It's just, you don't look okay,' he pressed. 'You look a bit upset.'

'I just don't like the rain,' I said. He let out a laugh and I was forced to turn to look at him rather than staring in the other direction like an idiot.

'Me neither. And your umbrella has failed you, I see.' He nodded at the broken contraption in my hands. 'Why don't you come inside and I'll make you a hot drink and order you a cab?'

'Okay, thank you,' I said, hoping that my make-up wasn't streaked all over my face. I followed him back to the practice where a woman was just locking up.

'Oh, sorry, Mr Whitney, I didn't realise you were coming back.'

'Don't worry, Nora, we're just going inside to wait for this lady's taxi. I'll lock up when we leave.'

Inside Luke got me a towel and went to put the kettle on. I towel dried my hair, mussing it up for good measure, and wiped my face – incredibly my expensive make-up had stayed nearly perfect and I hadn't been wearing much to begin with. Ironically, Luke Whitney preferred the natural look and I had spent two years perfecting it.

'Here you go.' He walked back into the reception area and handed me the cup of coffee I'd asked for. I'd taken off my coat and I noticed that his eyes never once flickered from my face. He held my gaze a second too long. He was one cool customer.

'So you're a cosmetic surgeon?' I asked, trying to sound casual. The truth was, as confident as I could be with boys my own age, I was quickly realising that I was out of my depth with Luke Whitney. It was tempting to lay it on thick but I had a feeling that the things that would work on much younger men weren't going to cut it with Luke.

'For my sins,' he said.

I started to make a comment about wanting my breasts enlarged, to draw his attention to my already ample chest, but I stopped myself. I had to be smart, that's what I'd told myself all along. Not some airhead that he meets at every charity event.

'My father wanted me to go into medicine,' I said instead. 'But I faint at the first sight of blood. How disappointing for him.'

Luke laughed. 'So what did you do instead?'

I groaned. 'Finance. I know, boring, but I couldn't stand the idea of wasting my life being something vapid like a yoga instructor.' *Sorry, Anna.* 'At least with finance I know how to manage my money for when I make millions with my real passion.'

'Which is?' Luke asked. His eyes were locked onto mine and I could tell he was trying his best to keep them there. I hadn't dressed to bump into him so I was just wearing a plain white T-shirt with a little pocket on the breast and a pair of jeans.

'Breeding dwarf rabbits.'

Luke burst into laughter and I dropped my serious face and grinned. 'What? What are you laughing at? I'm serious!'

'Are you really?'

'No, of course not.' I started laughing and handed him my half-drunk coffee. Our fingers touched on the mug –

intentionally. *Oh yes*. 'Thanks for the coffee, but I really need to get an Uber sorted and go. I have this date tonight.'

'Lucky guy,' Luke said, and I blushed for real. I already knew I was going to have to be careful around him, more careful than Laura had been, or I might forget the reason I was doing this.

'Lucky me, actually,' I lied. 'He's an incredibly eligible bachelor. Or so my mother keeps telling me.' I rolled my eyes. 'The way she acts you'd think I was some thirty-five-year-old spinster. Thank you so much for the coffee.'

'Will I see you again?' Luke blurted out as I turned to leave. I gave his left hand a pointed look. 'Sorry,' he said instantly. 'I don't know why I said that. It's not appropriate.'

'How about I call you in fifteen years when I need some work done,' I joked.

'Here.' He grabbed a card from his secretary's desk and handed it to me. 'Just in case your umbrella breaks again.'

Chapter Forty

Rebecca

My phone rings and it's a number I don't know. When I answer it a semi-familiar voice says, 'Have you heard? Jimmy's been arrested. Cops took him in this morning.'

'Oh for fuck's sake,' I mutter, realising it's Gina, Jimmy's aunty. Her voice is only familiar because she's cut my hair a few times – Jimmy and I don't exactly attend one another's family events. Hell, I don't even attend my own family events. 'What for?'

'Possession with intent to supply. You know Jimmy.' Her voice is pleading. 'He only shifts a bit of weed. He's no harm to anyone.'

'I can't help him with this, Gina.' My voice is firmer than my resolution. I picture Jimmy in a prison cell. He's too good looking for prison, he's always said so and it's true. He's no thug, just a minor league scally, and I feel a pang of pain at the thought of him being locked up.

'Becky, *please*.'

'If I've told him once, I've told him a million times. I can't pull favours if he gets in trouble. It's not like the TV, Gina, we can't just lose a bit of paper and get him off.'

'You'll go and see him though, won't you? Make sure he's okay?'

Oh yeah, Gina, I'll just pop down to the cells and tuck my bit on the side in, take him some milk and cookies and read him a bedtime story. Of course I don't say this, I say, 'I'll try,' and end the call.

How has Jimmy gone and got himself caught? It doesn't really make sense that he'd be on our radar, he's a small fry weed dealer, not some big time coke pusher. Unless…

The answer hits me as I see DI Kerrigan exit the incident room and take a left.

'Tom!' I shout, and he swings around. He must see the fury on my face because he frowns and takes a step backwards.

'Is everything okay?' he asks.

'No, everything is not okay,' I snap back, fury flooding my face red. 'Did you have Jimmy arrested because I'm sleeping with him?'

Tom steps back again and his frown turns to a glare, and in that moment I know it's true. And Tom knows I know, because he gets angry.

'What?' he asks. 'Do you honestly think I'd do something like that?'

I open my mouth then close it again, completely unsure of what to say. We both know he's lying to me but if he's going to deny it then I have to choose whether to call him out or not, and perhaps ruin our friendship. Or has he already done that? God, what a mess.

'Did you then?' I settle for asking. His face darkens.

'I'm major investigations, not *petty crimes*.' He spits the last two words out to make it perfectly clear what he thinks of my choice of bed-partner.

'Really?' I ask, my voice full of contempt. 'Because what you've just done seems pretty petty to me.' He opens his mouth to speak but I cut him off with an accusing jab of my finger. 'You know Jimmy only supplies to his mates.'

Tom's eyes widen. 'Have you heard yourself? Making excuses for a scummy drug dealer because, what... because you fancy him? You *love* him?'

'Don't be ridiculous,' I reply, but my voice falters. I don't love Jimmy. *Do I?*

Tom must have seen the confusion cross my face because he scowls, makes a disgusted noise in his throat and turns to walk away from me. I want to call him back but I wouldn't know what to say, and whatever I say it is bound to be wrong.

—

We have Anna Whitney moved into the interview room for a fourth time, keenly aware that we'll be charging her with her husband's murder very soon, unless I can convince her to tell us what really happened in that cottage. When we enter she's sitting on the grey Formica chair, staring ahead at a crack in the plaster on the wall.

'We just have a couple more questions for you, Mrs Whitney.'

The lawyer mutters something to Anna but her face remains as blank as it had been when we first brought her in. When neither of them speak Tom reaches over to the tape recorder and presses record.

'Were you aware, Mrs Whitney, that Luke was having an affair?'

For the first time since we entered the room Anna turns to look at me, shaking her head. I can't make out from her face whether she's lying or not, which throws me. She just looks exhausted and beaten. I feel like we could have told her Luke had murdered sixteen schoolchildren and she'd have kept that same emotionless expression.

'It's not true,' she says with a sigh. 'Whoever told you that is mistaken. It's an easy mistake to make, our relationship is…' She hesitates, searching for the words. 'Well, I suppose you could say it's complicated. But Luke would never cheat on me. Not without… it's just not true.'

Not without what? I want to ask, but Tom is already speaking.

'We have CCTV footage of the two of them together.'

It's almost as though the news of her husband's affair causes Anna more distress than the certain knowledge that she's going to be charged with murder. She looks broken.

'Do you know the name Phillipa Kent?' Tom asks. His voice is sharp and he hasn't looked at me the entire time we've been in here. Anna and her fancy lawyer wouldn't notice, because Matthews has done the previous interviews, but usually Tom and I bounce off one another when we're in the flow of an interview. Right now I'm letting him do all the questioning and I have no desire to help him whatsoever.

'Yes.'

'Can you tell us who she is?'

She gives a weary sigh. 'If you've spoken to her you know who she is.'

'We'd like to hear it from you.'

Anna shakes her head as if she can' quite believe it. 'Phillipa used to be in my yoga class.'

I can't believe he would have Jimmy arrested to try and keep him away from me. That is the pettiest bullshit I've ever— shit, I've missed the last few questions.

'You'd have to ask her,' Anna says. Probably in answer to why Pippa had stopped going to Anna's yoga class.

'Did you know that she knew your husband?'

'No.' Anna's cheeks redden. 'We met her once at the golf club and she seemed to recognise him but he said he didn't recognise her.'

'And did you know her parents were friends of Luke's? Phillip and Katherine Kent?'

Anna shakes her head. 'No. To tell you the truth I barely remember the first names of the women in my yoga class, I wouldn't have taken much notice of hers, let alone wonder if she was related to two acquaintances of ours.'

It occurs to me, as it has on every occasion that we've interviewed her, that Anna is an incredibly good liar. I can tell that she's not being entirely truthful half of the time but she has me up against the ropes the other half.

'The woman on reception told us you'd tried to get Pippa thrown out of the gym. You said she was following you. This was just a few weeks ago.'

Anna frowns. 'That's not true. Maybe I asked to have her taken off the class list because she had missed some? That's how that works though, that's not unusual. It frees up space for people who will attend. Nothing more to it.'

'Did you ever talk to her in class at all? Before, maybe, or after?'

'No. Oh wait.' She looks as if she has suddenly remembered something, then deflates. 'I remember her saying to one of the other women in the class something about men being confusing, about how they say one thing but do another. One time she came to class looking as though she'd been crying quite a bit. She was upset with Luke, wasn't she? Men who say one thing and do another. Was he… did he tell her he was going to leave me for her?'

'You'd have to ask her that I'm afraid.' I try to keep my voice as neutral as possible but Tom cuts across me.

'Well you certainly can't ask *him*, can you? Shall we get back to the reason we're all here?' He's getting annoyed, and I don't know if it's because the woman sitting across the table from us has all the answers we need, and she's refusing to give them up, or because I'd spoken and reminded him I still exist. 'Did you stab your husband because you found out about his affair with Phillipa?'

'No.' Anna looks at me almost pleadingly. 'Please, I'm telling you. Phillipa Kent has nothing to do with this. Please, just leave her out of it.'

Chapter Forty-One

Pippa

Luke was furious after the meeting at the golf club. Even after I'd insisted that it was a complete coincidence that I'd been there at the same time as them – which for once it was – he still didn't believe me. Ironic, I suppose, that I'd been stalking him for thirty-six months and the one time I get caught is the only time I wasn't actually stalking him.

'What am I supposed to think,' he yelled, 'when I find out that you've been taking my wife's classes for months? How long, Pippa? Before we met?'

I screwed up my face and pretended to be confused. Obviously Anna hadn't told him exactly how long I'd been taking the class, thank goodness, because there was no way he would believe that it was a coincidence that his mistress was one of a dozen women who his wife taught yoga to.

'Of course not before we met! What would the chances of that even be? I took a class after we met because I wanted to see her. I know.' I held up my hands and tried to look chastened. 'It was stupid and immature and I only meant it to be one time, but the gym automatically signed me up for the class for three months and instead of cancelling it I went along a second time. Then I actually really enjoyed the bloody class, didn't I?'

Luke was shaking his head, unable to believe I had been so stupid. Well, if it was a choice between believing I was a stupid little girl and a conniving, manipulating stalker, well colour me a teenager in love. As long as he didn't find out who my parents were. If that happened the jig was up for me and God knows how he would react.

'You have to leave the class,' he said, rounding on me. It was my turn to look at him as if he was stupid.

'Seriously? Quit the day after I bump into you at the golf club? You said she was already suspicious, you don't think that's going to look even worse?'

'Worse than "have we met before?"' He mimicked me in a high-pitched voice. 'Seriously, Pippa? Of course she was going to ask questions.'

'Only because she doesn't trust you,' I snapped, hearing the irony. 'Look,' I said, sighing and trying to push down my impatience. 'I've said I'm sorry for asking if we'd met, but I promise I did not bump into you on purpose. Now did you book a six-hundred-pound-a-night room just to yell at me? Because if you did you could have done this somewhere much cheaper.'

He scowled, but he didn't carry on telling me off. I took that as permission to reach behind myself and unclip my bra, slip one shoulder off and pull it through the sleeve of my T-shirt, dangling it in front of him. He raised one eyebrow and tried to carry on looking furious but I could see he was weakening. Over my T-shirt I rubbed my nipples, then stepped forward to take his hands and replace mine with them. He didn't resist, like I knew he wouldn't, and his thumbs began to rub at the hard nubs, then his mouth covered mine and the meeting with his wife, and me basically stalking her, was all but forgotten.

Perhaps, looking back, I was far too sure of myself in the way that attractive teenagers often are. I was drunk on the power I had only just discovered I could wield and I let myself believe that because I gave myself to him sexually, because he wanted me there and then, because I could make him forget his wife for a few hours, maybe even a day, that meant I had control over him. I never had any control over Luke Whitney, and I was stupid to ever think that I did. I soon found out that I had made a huge mistake.

Chapter Forty-Two

Rebecca

It's three pm when Kim calls me over to her computer, her tone hushed and her face worried. Matthews was apoplectic when he found out about the Waitrose footage and has been like a bear with a sore head ever since. Not surprising, Pippa played a blinder last night and has left him looking a bit of a prat. Luckily for him it was just in front of Tom and I that he'd dropped the ball, and luckier still that we'd chosen to follow it up ourselves, basically lifting the DCI out of the hot water.

'Make sure someone checks her alibi,' he snapped when we told him what we'd seen on the footage. 'Get her phone records and see if her parents can absolutely guarantee she was in the house all evening and never left.' Then he marched out and we haven't seen him since.

'Rebecca? Can I show you something?'

'What have you got?' I ask, walking over to her desk and peering over her shoulder. She's looking at a photograph of a car, looks like it was taken from a speed camera. 'Is that Anna Whitney's car? When's it from?'

'Friday night. She was doing forty-six in a forty. It's along the route we've surmised that Anna would be taking to get to the cottage.'

'Okay, great work, Kim.' I turn to walk away, irritated I made the fourteen-step trip between desks to confirm something we already knew.

'Wait, sorry.' I turn back and Kim is pointing to the time at the bottom of the screen. 'That's not what I called you over for. I called you over because this photo was taken at one eighteen am, Saturday morning really. Twelve minutes before Anna called the emergency services to say her husband had been stabbed.'

'What?' I let the information sink in. Anna's story all along has been that she was at the cottage from four pm Friday evening. If she didn't arrive until one o'clock in the morning, that means her whole account of the evening is a lie.

'Have you double checked this?' I ask Kim, searching the photo. It shows a light coloured Audi TT, the same car Anna drives, and a blonde woman behind the wheel.

'I've checked and triple checked it. The registration matches, and that's her driving it. It's her car, for absolute certain.'

'I don't suppose anyone touched the hood when they arrived?'

Kim shrugged. 'There's no note of it, but it's unlikely. There was a potentially fatal stabbing on the scene – I can't see anyone checking when the car was last driven.'

'No, me neither,' I grunt. 'Right, better call the DCI – congratulations, DS Beckford, you've just given our number-one suspect an alibi.'

—

By the time that the DCI arrives the whole team are congregated around Kim's laptop and she's recounting the story about how she discovered Anna's reg in the system – like it isn't as simple as typing a combination of seven numbers and letters into a computer. I wouldn't mind so much but Rob was tasked with confirming Anna Whitney's timeline of events after this morning's briefing at nine bloody am. Running her car through the system should have been the first thing he did. Now DS Beckford has stepped in to save the day. I'm pleased for her, obviously, but a little irritated that she's wearing the star pupil badge so often lately.

'Right.' Matthews points at Tom. 'Tell me what's going on. And not the "Anna Whitney has an alibi" version – the version where you tell me she could have made it from the location of that speed camera to the cottage in time to stab her husband.'

Tom screws up his nose. 'I'm going to let Rebecca tell you. She's the one who's spent the last half an hour looking for every conceivable way it could have been done.'

What he means is *I'm going to let Rebecca tell you that it couldn't have been done.* Because it couldn't. I take a deep breath and vow to drop Tom Kerrigan in deep sloppy shit every chance I can. I get to be the bearer of the worst news possible.

'The cottage is a twenty-minute journey from the camera *at least*,' I say. Matthews looks like he might explode. 'That's the fastest it could have been done – and only if she broke the speed limit by ten miles an hour on every road. Which we know she didn't because there's one more speed camera en route and she didn't activate that one.'

I pick up a whiteboard pen and start scrawling:

1.18 – Anna's car activates speed camera

1.30 – Control receive a call from the cottage to say Luke Whitney has been stabbed

1.42–1.45 – Most likely time Anna Whitney arrived at cottage

1.46 – Emergency services turn up at cottage

'This,' I say, pointing at *most likely time Anna Whitney arrived at cottage*, 'is based on the shortest possible route – which, by the way, is not the most obvious route and involves some country lanes which would be an absolute bitch to navigate in the dark at that time of night. We didn't think she'd made this route because Andy checked Ring doorbell footage from three thirty onwards but didn't go as far as one am because we were under the impression Anna was there at four pm.'

'Right.' Matthews rubs a hand over his face. 'So the absolute earliest Anna Whitney might have walked into the cottage is twelve minutes *after* the call was made to emergency services.'

'Which means there's no way she made that call,' Kim finishes.

'There's one way to clear it up,' I suggest. 'Has anyone listened to the 999 recording?'

'I've got the transcript here.' Kim shuffles through some papers in front of her.

'I've read it.' I try not to sound impatient, she's doing her best and I was new and eager once. 'I mean has anyone *listened* to it, to check it's really Anna Whitney's voice?'

Heads shake around the room. DCI Matthews goes a deep shade of pink and I can see he's about to kick off so I add quickly, 'Not that anyone would, usually. Before this new evidence we had no reason to suspect Anna wasn't the one who made the call.' *Besides the lack of fingerprint evidence on the phone*, I think. 'But it's me and Tom running this investigation, so if anyone should have thought to have the recording analysed it should have been us. And obviously we've got a budget to consider. Do you think we could get an analyst authorised now though, guv?'

Matthews nods impatiently and snaps his fingers.

'Yes, yes, just bloody get it done. I want to know before we go back in there whether it was Anna Whitney who made that call. And if she didn't, she was in that cottage either at the same time or within minutes of the person who stabbed her husband. So if she isn't our main suspect she's our star witness. How her fortunes seem to have improved in just one day.'

Chapter Forty-Three

Rebecca

'Okay.' Anna looks at the photo of her car taken from the speed camera, along with the route planner I've printed off and placed in front of her, with three different routes highlighted. I'm pointing at the timeline of events – it's all there in black and white for her to see. Practically impossible for her version of events to be true. 'I didn't arrive at the cottage at four o'clock. I arrived in the middle of the night. But I could still be the one who stabbed Luke. I just did it as soon as I arrived, not like I said.'

'We thought you might say that.' Tom places a tape recorder in front of her, leans over and presses play.

'Ambulance, please. And police, I think.'

The voice that fills the room is breathless, frantic-sounding even. Anna's expression hardens. Patrick Tate looks at her.

'Ambulance service.'

'Hi, um, hello, it's my husband, he's been stabbed, please come quickly!'

'Okay, love, try to keep calm. Where has he been stabbed?'

'Please, send someone quickly!'

'What's the address, please?'

The voice gives the address. 'Please, be quick, there's so much blood.'

'Can you get something to stop the bleeding, maybe a towel or something and just hold it on the wound—'

'Please hurry, I think he's going to die!'

There's a banging as the phone is dropped. I lean over and press 'pause' on the tape.

'Is that you, Anna? On that call?'

She doesn't know what to say. Probably because – and we've listened to it a dozen times, alongside the recordings of our interviews – we are all certain it isn't her. The expert we use in cases like this (usually to prove someone *is* making the call, not isn't) can't get back to us for another three days and we're running out of time to interview Anna with a charge so DCI Matthews instructed us to take a chance. Put it to her that we know it isn't her on the recording and see how she reacts. As it turns out, she doesn't know how to react.

'It, I… I mean, I…'

'It's a simple question, Mrs Whitney, either it is you or it isn't. You've already told us that you stabbed Luke, then you called 999. So the answer to my question should be quite easy, really. I should tell you, before you answer, that we have experts in voice analysis who consult with our team.' I'm not lying – we do have experts who consult with our team. They just haven't consulted with our team yet.

Anna sighs and puts her head in her hands, her elbows resting on the table.

'Well then you know, don't you? You know that's not me.' Tears spill down her cheeks and she looks at her lawyer and mouths, 'I'm sorry.'

'Who is it then, Anna? Don't you think it's about time you told us the truth? What really happened?'

Anna's lawyer requests a break, which Tom refuses. We're so close to finding out the truth, we don't need her calming down and reverting to 'no comment', or worse, pretending that she's the one who stabbed Luke.

'Come on, Anna,' he cajoles. 'Surely you don't want everyone thinking you stabbed Luke when you didn't. Your friends, family, your work colleagues. Just tell us the truth. It's easier than trying to keep up this lie.'

'I wasn't supposed to be going to the cottage,' Anna says quietly. She sniffs. 'Then I found out that Luke was taking Pippa. He had said he was going to the cottage for the weekend, just for a bit of a break, but I saw a message from her about how much she was looking forward to it.'

'You must have already known about the affair,' I say, pretending to come to this conclusion for the first time. 'Is that why you tried to get her thrown out of your gym?'

'I suspected,' Anna admits. 'Luke and I, well, I've said before that the relationship was complicated. I believed, well, I still believe, that Luke was sleeping with Pippa to get back at me for a perceived indiscretion. We'd bumped into her at our golf club and he'd seen me get jealous about her. I think he targeted her because he knew that I felt insecure about her. She was young, beautiful, she was the perfect choice, I suppose. Other than Rose, I can't think of anyone I'd feel worse about Luke sleeping with. I've seen her in little more than her underwear, she's physically perfect.'

'So you think Luke wanted you to find out about the affair? To hurt you?'

'I absolutely know that he wanted me to find out. Luke was clever, so clever that if he wanted to cheat on me without me finding out I'd never ever know about it. Besides, he was the one who made the promise that he'd never cheat on me again. Before Ed we'd had a deal, he was allowed to indulge in extra-marital activities as long as it was with someone who would never get back to me, someone who would never humiliate me. But I found out about him and Pippa so easily... he wanted me to know because of what I did with Ed. He was trying to get back at me.'

'I take it that this Ed was the "perceived indiscretion".'

'He was.'

'We'll take Ed's details in a minute. Was Pippa still at the cottage when you got there?'

'No.'

'But you assumed it was her who had stabbed him?'

'Yes.'

'Then why did you confess? Why did you take the blame for her?'

Anna looks at me, her eyes almost pleading with me to understand. 'Because it was my fault she got caught up in this mess. She's just nineteen, Detective. And my husband screwed her to get back at me. He didn't give a shit about the impact it would have on her life, or how she would feel when he cast her aside. He chose her because he wanted to punish me for what I'd done. He wanted to humiliate me, to replace me with the younger version of me, someone who would cause me the most pain. As much as I dislike Phillipa Kent for sleeping with a married man, none of this was her fault, and I couldn't see her life ruined.'

'For the tape,' DCI Matthews says, looking at me as if he's furious that I was right all along. 'Are you telling us that you didn't stab your husband?'

Anna puts her face in her hands and nods.

'For the tape, Mrs Whitney.'

'Yes,' she says through her fingers. 'For the record I'm saying I didn't stab my husband.'

Chapter Forty-Four

Pippa

'You're what?' Luke froze, one arm half in his shirtsleeve, the rest of him still naked, his flaccid, post-coital cock hanging limply between his legs.

'I'm pregnant,' I repeated, although I knew from his face that he'd heard me. He looked like he'd just contracted my morning sickness. 'It's yours,' I added, just in case he hadn't grasped that part.

Luke sat down on the edge of the bed with a thump and rubbed a hand over his face. 'How far?'

Even though I'd practised this so many times, I was unprepared for how daunting it would be. My mouth was dry and my heart thumped uncomfortably. In my mind he had always been instantly delighted, but in reality he just looked dumbfounded. Of course, it was going to take some getting used to, but once we worked things out he would be happier than he'd ever been. Just like I'd planned.

When I first started watching Luke Whitney, I'd been fully prepared to ruin his life – I just hadn't decided how. Then we'd met IRL, and I'd seduced him almost as easily as expected. He was male, and his wife had had an affair with a younger guy, a cooler guy. He needed to repair his ego and I had been the perfect way to do just that.

'About eight weeks, maybe nine,' I answered. 'I haven't been to the doctor's yet. I thought maybe we could go together?'

Luke looked aghast. 'Have you told anyone else about this?'

I shook my head. 'No one. Just you.'

He let out a relieved sigh. 'Okay, that's good. It'll be okay. I can fix this. I'll make you an appointment at the clinic, it's very early days, it'll just be a couple of pills. Then it will all be back to normal.'

'I don't...' I frowned and reached down for the sixty-pound hotel dressing gown I'd discarded at the side of the bed. I'd noticed the sign when I first let myself in – we had arrived separately of course, we always did – that informed guests that robes were available to purchase for sixty pounds, which was posh people's way of warning you that if you stole the dressing gowns your room would be charged for it. After today I would definitely be stealing the dressing gown. Let Luke fucking Whitney pay for it.

'Pills? Like, abortion pills?' He flinched at the word 'abortion', but that was what he meant. Luke was asking me to kill my baby. He was saying that he wasn't going to leave his wife, not for me or for the tiny life he had created inside me. This wasn't how this was supposed to go.

He looked at me now with what looked like – God, was that pity? Oh Jesus. Could humiliation make you physically sick? I shook my head, trying to put everything in order. What had I been thinking? That he'd look at me any differently than the slut of a secretary he'd fired after one night in a hotel? Had I believed him when he said he loved me, despite everything I knew about him?

Every plan I had made to ruin Luke Whitney's life was crumbling around me.

'Pippa, sweetheart.' Luke reached out and touched my knee but already I could see the distance between us widening into a gulf. *He* was already checking out on *me*. I was losing him. 'I told you when this… *thing* between us started that it wouldn't ever be more than a physical *thing*…'

I swear to God if he calls this a 'thing' one more time I'm going to cave his head in with his hundred-pound bottle of piss-tasting champagne.

'You said you understood. You said you weren't one of those silly little girls who expected a man to leave his wife because she shook her—'

'I'm not,' I hissed between clenched teeth. I remembered the conversation well, me putting on my sultriest voice and telling him that I was young, desirable and that I could have any man I wanted. *And I want you*, I'd said, running a finger down the side of his face. *But not forever. I'm not one of those silly little girls who expects you to leave your wife because I shake my tight little ass at you. You love your wife, I get that. But you also can't stop thinking about how I'd taste.*

'I just thought we were happy, that we were having a good time. I love you, Luke, I thought you felt the same.'

I tried not to let my voice sound whiny on that last line but obviously I failed because I saw the fear in his eyes.

'I love spending time with you too, Pip, but it's not that easy for me. I'm married.'

'You left your first wife for Anna,' I snapped. 'What was so different about that?'

'I didn't love Rose. I love Anna.'

'More than you love me?'

Luke sighed. I had been so, so wrong. I'd waited until I was so sure that Luke was obsessed with me before playing my trump card. We were seeing more of each other than ever, he was leaving work early to meet me, lying to Anna more than he ever had. He was with me more and more when he could have been with her. And now he was pretending he didn't love me? That he would be able to just dismiss me and my baby with a scribble on a cheque.

'We can't just run away and have a child together. You knew that! I didn't lead you on or make you any false promises.' It was Luke's turn to sound whiny now. 'This isn't fair on me.'

I could have laughed if I wasn't so horrified.

'Fair on *you*? You're asking me to abort our child and you want *me* to be fair on *you*?'

'I'm not asking you to abort *your* baby,' Luke said, getting up off the bed and grabbing his clothes from the floor. He stalked towards the bathroom, calling over his shoulder. 'I'm telling you to.'

Chapter Forty-Five

Rebecca

Pippa Kent sits in the interview room, a sullen look on her red, blotchy face. She looks a mess, her hair is unwashed and her sleeves are sodden from wiping away snot and tears. Not surprising, her married lover is dead and she has been lying to the police. It's a lot to take for a nineteen-year-old.

'We have footage of the two of you at Waitrose together on Friday morning.'

The news doesn't surprise or concern Phillipa Kent. On the contrary, she knows exactly why she's been brought here and she's lawyered up. She stares at the table in silence.

'Is that a question?' her father's lawyer asks.

'No, but this is.' Matthews throws him a glare. 'Why did you lie to my officers yesterday when asked if you knew Luke Whitney?'

'Because the point of a secret affair is that you keep it secret.' Pippa sniffs. 'Luke wouldn't want his wife knowing about us and I didn't want to upset him.'

'Did you already know Luke was dead at the time of our chat yesterday?'

'No.'

'You'd been crying,' I point out.

'I told you, I'd poked my eye with my mascara.'

'And you didn't think a police interview makes it completely necessary to tell the truth?' Matthews asks.

'I've already said I'm sorry for not being completely honest about my relationship with Luke,' she says, her voice taking on a whiny edge. 'I didn't know what the questions were about. I still don't. If Luke was attacked at the cottage I don't know how I can help you.'

'Did you know Luke was going to his cottage after he left you Friday afternoon?'

'No.'

'Were you supposed to be going with him? Why did you cancel, were you ill?'

'Actually, I was,' Pippa says. 'I'd been throwing up the previous day. But I was still going to go. Then Luke phoned me at seven am to say that Anna had told him she was going to the cottage but would I meet him in town.'

'He didn't say why?'

She shakes her head.

'For the tape?'

'No, he didn't say why. I thought he was going to take me somewhere, but he just asked me to meet him at Waitrose.'

'And that was it? Just a romantic date to Waitrose?'

'I was confused too, you'd have to ask him why.'

'Doesn't it seem a bit strange that Anna would suddenly cancel her plans to go to the cottage with Luke? Do you think she knew about your affair?'

'No, if she knew about me and Luke, she'd have said something, wouldn't she? Unless she found out that night, when she was at the cottage, but she'd already cancelled her plans before then… God, I don't know, do I? That's your job, I suppose, to put it all together.'

She's right, more's the pity.

'Right, so as far as you are aware, Anna Whitney had no knowledge of your affair with her husband. How long had the affair been going on?' Matthews asks. Pippa looks down at the table.

'Four months. We met about six or seven months ago but the first time we… the first time anything happened was four months ago. We met outside his office, it was pouring with rain and I didn't have an umbrella. He invited me in and let me dry off, and he gave me his number.'

'Did Luke Whitney know how old you were when he met you?'

'I don't know,' she replies. 'He knew I was studying finance at college, I don't look ten years older than I am, so I presume he knew my rough age, but if you're asking if he ever asked me how old I was then no. I'm over the age of consent, we weren't doing anything illegal.'

No, just bloody disgusting, I think, remembering that Luke Whitney was forty-three years old – actually old enough to have a nineteen-year-old daughter himself.

'Do you have any proof of your whereabouts Friday evening? You told us before that you were home all evening – is that still your recollection?'

'Yes, because it's true,' Pippa says. 'As for proof, we have a Ring camera on the front door, I suppose I'll be on that coming in. Oh – and I Ubered some donuts at elevenish – that will be on the door cam too I guess, and the delivery guy might remember me.'

Luke was stabbed at one thirty am. The holiday cottage is less than an hour's drive – still just about time for Pippa to order her donuts then get to the cottage…

'Oh, then Gemma called me at *three in the morning*. Stupid cow woke me up to tell me about some French dude she'd got off with at a party.'

I can almost feel Tom crumple beside me.

'She called on your mobile?'

'She Zoomed me on her laptop. Free wifi at the place she's staying with her parents. I must have looked like a zombie and there's her and this French dude staring at me in my Hello Kitty PJs. Just ask her, I'm sure you can confirm it pretty easily.'

Chapter Forty-Six

Anna

I didn't react well to finding out about Pippa, I'll admit that. I hit the anger stage with a vengeance, going through the house destroying anything I could get my hands on that Luke even slightly cared about with all the restraint of a wild alley-cat. Suits with missing buttons and torn lapels fell in crumpled heaps atop scarred leather shoes and ties cut in half with kitchen scissors. The bone statue of that couple embracing – the one we bought on our honeymoon in Mexico – snapped clean in half. Lucky really, that his car wasn't on the drive, otherwise God only knows what mess it would have ended up in.

How could he? How fucking could he?

And when I was done and exhausted I threw myself on our bed, sobbing hysterically until an image of my husband fucking Phillipa Kent on that very bed, her nubile nineteen-year-old body writhing around in our clean white sheets, forced its way into my head and I barely made it to the bathroom before throwing up, yellow vomit splashing the sides of the enamel bath, clumps settling in the plug hole. I sat, suddenly freezing cold and shaking with fury, my back pressed against the cold tiles and my fists in my hair, and surveyed the shattered remains of our life around me. My chest was heaving from the effort of tears and rage and the smell of aftershave and expensive moisturisers stuck in the back of my throat when it hit me. What the fuck was going to happen now? When he got home and saw the mess, what was he going to say? He was going to ask why I'd lost my mind, destroyed hundreds, maybe thousands of pounds' worth of things. And I'd have to tell him that I knew he'd been fucking one of my students, and that would be that. Once that sort of thing had been said, well you can't unsay it. And maybe he'd beg my forgiveness, possibly. Or maybe he'd pack a bag and walk out without looking back, the way he did to Rose when he met me. Was that what I'd given my life up for? To end up in a sobbing heap on the bathroom floor, just like those who had come before me? I caught a glimpse of Luke's razor on the floor. No, I was stronger than that. It wasn't me who would suffer for this.

He promised me. After Ed he swore that things would change, he swore to me that it was just me and him. And now he wasn't just sleeping with a girl less than half his age but one of our friend's daughters. *Our friends' daughter.*

I needed to buy myself some time. To think, to plan. Luke wasn't in love with Pippa, she was just something new and exciting. This was the mistake his other women had made – to react without thinking, without knowing him and staying two steps ahead. Pippa hadn't spent years and years knowing Luke inside and out, she was none of the things I'd worked so hard to become. She was just a tight teenage ass with tits still where God put them.

Was this his revenge, at last, for Ed?

What was I going to do?

But I knew what I needed to do. I needed to clean up this mess, replace the things I could before Luke saw them and get the time I needed to figure out my next move. I moved through the rooms almost as feverishly as I'd destroyed them, tidying up, fixing the things that could be fixed, making a list of those that would need replacing. I had hours – one trip into town would cover most of the things – anything I couldn't get today I would pretend was misplaced until I could.

The whole lot came out of my account – he would never need to know.

By the time he arrived home I was exhausted, physically and emotionally. I'd only been home an hour, decanting all the bags and boxes, taking them to the bin at the end of the street rather than risk leaving them in ours. I'd made fingerprints in moisturisers and tipped out enough aftershave that he couldn't tell it was all brand new, then ordered a meal from Luke's favourite takeaway. I was just finishing my make-up when he walked in.

'Smells amazing,' Luke remarked as he walked into the kitchen and wrapped his arm around my waist, placed a kiss on my cheek. 'Have you had a good day?'

It was too much. Tears flooded my eyes again, spilling down my cheeks until I couldn't breathe from the heaving sobs.

'Anna, what's wrong, sweetheart?' Luke pulled me in close and I had to think fast or risk everything.

'I was doing some cleaning and…'

'Well there's your problem.' He put me at arm's length and smiled. 'It's just a shock to the system,' he said. 'You know how you hate to clean.'

'It's not funny! I was dusting and it just fell, I couldn't stop it.' I pulled him by the hand over to the dining table where I had laid out the statue from our honeymoon. When I looked at it again my earlier rage resurfaced, the images of destroying everything he saw as a symbol of himself. What he had done to me, the same way he had done to the others. How stupid I had been for thinking I might be different, that I might be clever enough to change him. When Luke saw the statue he put a hand on my shoulder.

'Oh sweetheart, it's okay, we can get it fixed. A bit of glue and it'll be good as new.'

I cried again then, quietly this time. Luke thought it was relief. It wasn't. I was crying because I knew that there wasn't a glue strong enough to fix what had been broken that day.

Chapter Forty-Seven

Rebecca

'So Phillipa, Rose and Anna all have alibis for the time of the stabbing?' DCI Matthews asks again from the front of the briefing room. I can't tell if Tom is relieved or furious that Matthews has taken charge of the investigation once more, his face has retained the same grim look it's had for days.

'I just got confirmation from Gemma Berkley that she was on a Zoom call at three am to Pippa, and Pippa was in her room. I've emailed the customer support team at Zoom with my details for them to get back to me to back the claim up but for now I think we should assume that she's telling the truth. There's a record of the Uber Eats and the delivery guy remembers her answering the door at eleven oh eight pm. And her mum emailed over the link to the front doorbell footage and the passcode.'

Kim reels all of this off so fast my head starts to ache. This woman definitely has more hours in the day than Beyoncé.

'And Rose was on the phone to her Tinder match,' I add. 'He's confirmed that they were talking for about an hour between twelve and one, and her mobile phone records confirm she was at home when that call took place.'

'So the only person we know for sure was in that cottage is Luke Whitney,' Kim muses.

'And whoever has a size ten feet,' Andy reminds us.

'Oh.' Kim gets to her feet abruptly. 'I completely forgot to say with all this alibi excitement. Postmortem came back half an hour ago. It's all as expected, except the footprints are a dead end. Luke's feet were a size ten.'

'No,' I say, tapping the photograph of the wellies pinned to the board. 'Luke's feet were twelve.'

'Not according to the postmortem.' Kim hands a sheet of paper to DCI Matthews and he shoves it at Tom to read.

'She's right,' he says with a frown. 'Size ten. He must have bought his wellies a couple of sizes bigger, for thick socks.'

'But the footprint wasn't made by the wellies,' I argue. 'It was made by a shoe. And if it was Luke's shoe that would explain the lack of evidence of any other size ten male in the cottage but it wouldn't explain where… unless…' A thought occurs to me that changes everything we've thought about the case so far. 'We have to go back to the cottage.'

Chapter Forty-Eight

Rose

I was scrolling on my laptop, reading about the latest political scandal to hit the Conservative party, when my doorbell rang that morning. I was expecting a parcel, I was not expecting a pretty young woman of around nineteen looking like she was about to throw up on my door mat. I don't remember now what I first thought she was there for – I probably thought she'd just got the wrong address – but she definitely didn't have my parcel and she didn't say a word, just stood there looking at me.

'Can I help you?' I said after a couple of seconds' silence.

'I don't know,' she said, and she shook her head and swallowed hard. She looked as if she was going to cry. She also looked scared.

'Are you in some kind of danger?' I asked, looking past her up the street. There didn't seem to be anyone around, no one was following her.

'No, nothing like that.' She shook her head again. 'I'm here about Luke. Luke Whitney.'

The breath felt like it left my body. And that was when I looked at her, really looked at her. I'd seen her before, only much younger than she was now.

'Oh my God,' I said. My hand flew to my mouth and I took a step back. 'I know who you are. You're Laura's sister.'

—

'What on earth were you thinking?' I asked her for what seemed like the third time. Pippa shook her head, silent tears running down her cheeks.

'I wasn't thinking,' she whispered. 'I don't know why I did it, I didn't plan to… I just wanted to see who they were, what he was like. I never had a plan…'

She looked like she was going to be sick.

'What is wrong with me?' she asked. 'I was thinking about how I was going to ruin his life and I've ended up ruining mine.'

I'd pulled Pippa Kent into the house the minute I recognised who she was, and she'd told me the whole crazy story. How she'd tracked down Luke and Anna after her sister had died by suicide and spent hours watching them, following their every move. As terrible as it sounded, I actually understood that kind of obsession. You don't fall headfirst into that kind of behaviour, you edge towards it, slowly at first – you just look them up on social media, go and see what their house looks like, take a look at their workplace… then boom, you're in the hole and you don't even know how you got there.

Now Pippa was sitting opposite me cradling the cup of tea I'd given her and still the tears rolled down her cheeks like a leak she couldn't plug.

'And he's going to do exactly to me what he did to Laura, cast me aside without a backward glance. I haven't ruined his life, I've given him a few months of great sex with a girl young enough to be his daughter.' She laughs without humour as bile rises in my throat at the thought of this girl having great sex with the man I love. 'I've made him a legend, for fuck's sake.'

She looked even younger than her nineteen years when she said this, and even in her pitiful state, feeling sorry for herself as her life burned down around her, I still felt a pang of jealousy. I'd give anything for just one more night with Luke. The way it used to be, before Laura, before Anna... just him and me lying naked in bed on a Sunday morning in a post-coital haze of love. This girl had kissed him, tasted him, and now she was carrying his baby – a little piece of him forever.

A piece he doesn't want anything to do with, I had to remind myself. *A piece of him that he has told her to kill.*

I paced backwards and forwards wearing grooves in the plush living room carpet. I had to be very careful what I said next – this girl was young and impressionable and clearly in a vulnerable state.

'Have you told your parents?'

Pippa raised her eyebrows. 'God no. My father knows Luke – he'd bloody kill him.'

'Well, at least you'd get your revenge,' I said, my tone more flippant than the situation warranted. Pippa's mouth dropped open.

'I'm not serious,' I said quickly. Good Lord, this was a mess. I should have told her to leave, Luke's business was none of mine anymore, I needed to move on from him and the chaos that followed him. First Laura, then Anna... now this?

I sighed, suddenly feeling exhausted. 'If you decide to keep the baby, you will have to tell them eventually,' I said. 'It's not the kind of thing you can keep a secret.'

'Let me worry about that,' Pippa said. She lifted her chin and I could see underneath that pain and confusion a sliver of the woman who had stalked my ex-husband in order to ruin his life.

'Why did you come here, Pippa? How did you even know how to find me?'

'You don't stalk a man and his wife for years without knowing where his ex-wife lives, Rose. I came to you because you're the one person who knows what it's like to be used and cast aside by Luke. Well, apart from my sister, and she's not here for me to talk to. Because of him. That man has taken everything from both of us, and he's just going to move on and take everything from someone else if we don't stop him.'

'Anna,' I said, thinking aloud. Pippa frowned.

'What about her?'

'She's the one he will take everything from next. Think about it, Pippa – he left me for Anna, but that hasn't stopped him cheating on her more than once. He can't help himself, he'll never stop. If we tell her about you she'll see that, she'll have to realise that she's losing him too. We have to warn her. Then we'll use her to make him pay for what he's done to us all.'

Chapter Forty-Nine

Pippa

My sister, Laura, was nine when I was born, and by the time I was old enough to idolise someone, it was her. My first memories of her she was a teenager, the most sophisticated and wisest person in the universe. She would let me sit on the end of her bed or she sat at her dressing table following make-up tutorials in *Bella* magazine. I must have been six or seven, and she talked to me about grown-up stuff, boys she liked and how much she hated the other girls in her class. She was my first ever best friend.

When I was eleven and starting secondary school, Laura took me to her hairdresser's and had my hair cut, coloured and blown out. Our mother was always far too busy but she was happy to provide her debit card, and Laura and I took full advantage.

When I was twelve and crushing on a boy in the year above it was Laura who helped me write witty comments on his Insta stories and took me to see the films he liked so I understood the references. We dated for six months and he told me I like, totally got him, you know? Which I didn't at all, but Laura did. She knew so much more about boys than I did.

When I broke my leg at the start of the summer holidays that year my twenty-one-year-old sister set up a 'den' in the garden, complete with projector and screen, pillows and blankets and spent almost every day keeping me company, or ferrying my school friends back and forth from our house to make sure I didn't miss out.

When I was thirteen, Laura met Luke Whitney.

I was happy for her at first. He was older, she said – although she never mentioned that he was married, of course. She would come home from dates with him and sit on the end of my bed sharing the chocolates he had given her and telling me about the fancy vegan restaurants he had taken her to because he knew how important her veganism was to her. Everyone else just made fun of her for it. He was a plastic surgeon, she told me, and he knew our parents. I should have known something was up because she made me swear I wouldn't tell them about him, but if he was that successful and charming and wonderful why wouldn't she want them to know she was with him? I suppose I assumed it was the age gap, but there is eleven years between Mum and Dad so I should have known. I should have known and I should have told them anyway. What was the worst that could have happened? Laura would have been mad at me but that would have been nothing compared to what actually happened. But I was so young and I didn't know then what love could do to you the way I know now.

By the time I was fourteen, Laura had almost stopped coming over completely. Fine, I'd always known that one day she would get a life of her own, and I wasn't exactly unpopular. I had grown into my too-large eyes and inherited my mother's beautiful porcelain skin. People wanted to be around me and so I barely noticed that Laura didn't have time for me anymore. That was mistake number two.

She showed up at home one night, her face blotchy and pink, and she looked so thin, thinner than I'd ever seen her. It didn't suit her. At first I thought she was ill and she hadn't wanted to tell us, but it became clear pretty quickly that she hadn't been eating or sleeping. His wife had found out about them – she'd never even told me he was married – and he'd called things off. Apparently the wife was pregnant and he couldn't leave her. Laura didn't believe for one second that she was telling the truth, she thought that Rose Whitney was lying to hold on to Luke, but when she'd said that he'd called her crazy. In all honesty, she *did* look crazy. Or crazed, I should say. Utterly and completely crazed.

I begged her to move back in with us, but she wanted to stay in her flat in case he changed his mind. Even at fifteen years old I knew that he wouldn't change his mind. Even if he took Laura back for a while, carried on their affair off and on, I knew that if he was going to leave his wife for my sister he would have already done it.

That was why I was so surprised a few years later when I tracked down Luke Whitney and he was already remarried. If he'd been willing to leave Rose, in the end, why not for my sister? She was beautiful, clever, funny, kind. What did Anna have that Laura didn't? I became obsessed with trying to find out. I followed her everywhere, watched her every movement outside of her home until I knew more about Luke Whitney's wife than he did. Sure, she was attractive – natural beauty, where Rose had fought so hard against mother nature that she no longer even slightly resembled the woman he had married – and she had a way of making everyone she encountered smile, a well-timed double entendre, a little flirt with the

Waitrose cashier, but nothing that made her stand out above my wonderful sister.

Not until the night of the Henshaw party. I'd gone with Mummy and Daddy, knowing that Luke and Anna were on the guest list, and I made barely any effort to look older or sophisticated because I didn't want Luke or Anna paying me the slightest bit of attention. Anna would be more likely to spot me following her if she recognised my face and I had become almost dependent on seeing her, on watching her, learning her ways and mimicking her hair, the way she dressed, her easy way with men. At the party I avoided being introduced to them, stayed on the other side of the room whenever Anna was speaking to anyone. She didn't even glance my way. Good, I didn't want her to see me as a threat; I didn't want her to see me at all.

Luke and Anna looked stunning together. Her long blonde hair was wrapped up in an effortlessly chic style, soft tendrils framing her face, and her large blue eyes and rosebud lips had been accentuated by subtle but perfect make-up. Luke's charm was undeniable, he had thick dark hair, a handsome face and a muscular build apparent even in his designer suit. Women practically swooned when he spoke to them, even my mother, which made me almost physically sick to watch. She had no idea that the man she was fawning over was responsible for the death of her eldest daughter. But I did.

Luke had been talking for some time with a huge-breasted woman with a braying laugh when I saw him look at his phone and smile. I watched him excuse himself and leave the room, waited a few minutes and excused myself, telling my mother I needed the bathroom. I was on the upstairs landing when I heard raised voices. I stopped to listen; a man was apologising, hard, then he just came flying out of the room, his nose covered in blood. Luke slammed the door behind him but by the noises that were coming from that room I knew that Luke and Anna were fucking. Luke had stormed upstairs, assaulted a man and was screwing his wife's brains out. I didn't exactly understand what their little game was right there and then, but I vowed that I was going to. For Laura.

Chapter Fifty

Rebecca

'Can't we put the blues on?' I ask from the back seat of the unmarked police car. We're winging our way back to the crime scene based on my hunch and I just want to be there already. My bladder aches with a nervous wee – an unfortunate trait for a police officer because there are quite a few situations that make me nervous and usually very few opportunities to go for a wee.

'No.' Matthews's taut reply comes from the front. He says he thinks this is a crock of shit, but he wouldn't have made the trip with us personally if he wasn't curious.

We're going to the Whitneys' holiday cottage to look for Luke's missing shoes. Matthews thought I was nuts when I told the team that I thought they could be the key to solving this whole case, but the more I think about it the more I know they have to be important. The only footwear found at the holiday cottage were Luke's size twelve wellingtons. But there's no way he drove two hours and turned up in the wellies, he would have changed into them to go for his walk. So where is the footwear he drove to the cottage in? No other shoes were entered into evidence and I specifically asked Jack to make sure any men's shoes found were logged, which means the SOCOs never found them. In the video of Luke at the supermarket he's wearing black shoes, and it has suddenly become of utmost importance that I locate them.

Far from the hustle and bustle of last time we were here, the cottage is completely deserted. After forensics finished there was no need to keep an officer on site, so the scene is considered released – which will be unfortunate if we do find anything else here, but life isn't always as flawless as on TV. Ideally – for the perfect crime drama – we'd have an officer situated here night and day, so that the missed evidence was still perfectly within the chain of custody, but here we are.

Matthews parks up and I'm out of the car before the others have released their seatbelts.

'Suit up!' Matthews calls to me, and I groan, catching the bag he throws to me with a forensics suit and gloves in. Both my legs go in one hole in the rush and I almost topple on my face, but Tom catches my arm to steady me. We do that awkward look thing and he grins, the first grin I've seen from him in days. Since he found out about Jimmy. Has that really been why he's been in such a foul mood? Because I'm sleeping with someone? Jimmy in particular, or just anyone? I've always thought we'd both been relieved when we didn't end up having a drunken one-night stand, but maybe I've been as clueless about my relationship with Tom as I have been with this whole case.

'We've got everything backwards,' I say, and he looks confused. 'Luke Whitney, Anna Whitney. We need to find those shoes.'

'Oh,' Tom says, helping me get my leg into the right hole. 'Come on then, let's find them.'

Tom and Derek take the upstairs, and Kim searches downstairs, which I'm secretly glad of because I know

Luke's shoes aren't in the house at all, and I want to be the one to find them. I want that little thrill a detective gets when they spot the missing link. Our SOCO team is good, if the shoes were in the house they would have found them – which means they are outside somewhere. I make my way around to the back of the cottage, expensive golden gravel crunching under my feet, and unlatch the shiny black iron gate that leads to the well-manicured back garden.

The rubbish was already searched, so I know they aren't in there. But if my suspicion is correct, they won't be too far away. I pull out the recycling bins and glance behind them – nothing. That's when I see it – a small drop of blood on the flagstones, to the far left of the back door. Forensics wouldn't have had much reason to be looking over there – there's no escape route that way so any intruder or accomplice would come out of the back door and head right. You'd only go left if, perhaps, you were hiding something.

I drop a marker next to the blood, photograph it and swab. I'm in a rush to find the shoes but not so much that I've forgotten how to do my job. No one is in danger – quite the contrary, if my theory is correct. I find two more blood droplets and repeat the procedure.

I look everywhere in the beautiful, perfectly manicured garden as the light fades as fast as my hopes. They can't be far – not if my theory is true. I look over the wall into the field but it's difficult enough for me to peer over, let alone—

'Rebecca?' Kim's uncertain voice comes from behind me and my heart sinks. I was wrong about them being outside – she's found them.

'Have you got them?' I ask, turning around to face her. She's standing by the back door with her phone in her hand and shakes her head.

'No,' she says, and it sounds like she's trying not to be heard by anyone else. 'And this is going to sound really silly so I'd prefer to just say it to you, if that's okay?'

'Of course,' I say, trying not to sound impatient. If she wants boy advice now is not the time and I am really not the person.

'I just looked out of the kitchen window while I was searching,' she says, 'and I noticed this.'

She holds up a photo on Instagram, the poster is @RoseW. The picture is of the back garden of the holiday cottage with #happyplace.

'Explain to me like I'm five,' I say, getting irritable. Kim points to a small rose bush at the start of the flower beds in the garden then holds out the photo again.

'That bush isn't in this picture.'

I'm about to say 'So?' when I see the date on the photo. The picture was uploaded Saturday afternoon, hours before the murder.

Holy shit.

'You think there's something under there?' I ask, piecing it together in my mind. The hole is quickly dug before the stabbing. The shoes are thrown in to make it look like there was another man at the scene, and the bush is put in on top.

'If it's a new planting it shouldn't be hard to—' Kim starts but I'm already reaching into the bush, ignoring thorns that scratch my fingers, pulling the bush up. It comes away freely, the roots not yet taken hold. I toss the bush to the side and look into the hole at the black bin bag partially covered in soil.

'Sir!' I shout. 'Sir, I think we've got something!'

As the more senior officer, Matthews photographs and processes the area. Tom, Kim and I watch impatiently until he retrieves a black bin bag from the dirt. I lean over, heart racing, knowing this could be a big fat nothing burger but thinking it really, really isn't. The bag is heavy, heavy enough for it to be shoes. It snags on its way up, there's a bit of resistance, then it gives. Matthews opens it up and lifts out two blood-soaked tea towels, and a black, size ten pair of men's shoes.

—

DCI Matthews is already on the phone to forensics to tell them to get down here and do another sweep of the back garden. He's furious that this was missed the first time, but I can barely hear anything he's saying above the pounding of blood in my ears. Could this really mean what I think it means?

'Okay,' Matthews says, hanging up the phone. 'They're on their way. Is there anything else I should tell them to look for in particular?'

'Blood trails on the floor,' I say. 'In particular we need a diagram of the pattern of blood spatter versus blood droplets, size, shape and whether they look like cast-off.'

'You think you know what happened.' It's a statement, not a question. Tom knows me well enough by now to know when I'm onto something – I think it has to do with how my voice goes all squeaky and I talk too fast.

'I think I might have a theory,' I admit, knowing that the journey home is going to consist of me making notes and Tom demanding to know what I'm thinking.

Back at the incident room we wait impatiently while Kim pulls the evidence and parts of the case log that I need.

'Luke Whitney's phone,' she says, handing me the plastic evidence bag. I slip on gloves and slit open the seal, turn on the phone and pray it has charge left in it. The Apple logo appears and the whole team gather round me while I punch in Luke's passcode. The tech team have already downloaded thousands of photos and messages that we're making our way through, but that's not what I'm looking for. I scroll through his apps, but the one I want isn't there. I open his voice recordings – nothing.

'What are you looking for?' Rob asks.

'I thought there would be some kind of voice changing app on here,' I admit. 'Maybe he deleted it?'

'Try the App Store,' Kim suggests. 'Under recent purchases.'

I navigate to the store and check Luke's account. There it is, exactly where Kim suggested.

'Don't restore the purchase,' Tom warns me. 'We'll have to have tech do that.'

'When they do, I'm pretty sure they will find our 999 call on there,' I say, sliding the phone back into the bag, adding a new evidence seal and signing and dating it.

'Okay, Dance,' Matthews says with a sigh. 'Run us through what you're thinking.'

'I'm thinking that the crime scene looked staged because it was,' I say. 'By Luke Whitney.'

Chapter Fifty-One

Rose

I saw them together. He didn't think I knew about them, he thought they'd been so clever, but I knew everything he did. The way some bosses micro-manage the lives of their staff because they can't be trusted with their jobs, Luke couldn't be trusted with our life. He held my continuing happiness in his fingertips and I was certain he was a dropper. As it turned out, I was right. Luke was like a child with a sibling's toy, once he has won the battle he doesn't want it anymore. There's always something new and shiny for him to reach out for and he's never had to face a consequence in his life. My father used to say that Luke was the kind of man who could fall in the ocean and come out dry, and it wasn't a compliment.

I knew he was with her that night, and I knew what he did to her.

The rain was lashing against the blackness of the windowpanes and I'd taken myself up to our bedroom with a mug of tea and a book while I waited for him to finish writing up the day's notes. It was such a beautiful sound that I'd been reluctant to turn on the TV the way I usually would, otherwise I never would have heard him on the phone, his voice deep and husky, the way I'm sure he had spoken to me once upon a time, asking her where she wanted to meet. I'd known he was seeing her for a while but this was the first time I'd heard it arranged so blatantly, in my house while I was just a couple of walls away, and this was the first time I'd been curious. As quickly and quietly as I could manage with my heart pounding a tattoo into my chest I'd thrown on a vest top and leggings, rolling them up so they couldn't be seen under my huge dressing gown. When Luke came into the bedroom to tell me an emergency had come up I'd pulled the neck in around me and told him I was feeling ill anyway, I was going to get an early night. Drive safely, I said, adding, *and not too fast* silently to myself. I heard him call her back to tell her he was on his way. It had been easy, I hadn't asked any questions. And I heard him say the words 'I love you too, Laura.'

And when he'd got home I'd broken the 'news' that I was pregnant.

Chapter Fifty-Two

Rebecca

'By Luke?' DCI Matthews repeats, with the incredulous look I knew he was going to use. 'Our murder victim?'

'Hear me out,' I say. 'I know it doesn't sound like it makes sense…'

'I think it makes perfect sense,' Kim says. 'Luke got Rose to post that picture on her Instagram of the cottage, knowing that when Anna saw it she would come to the cottage to catch them. He sent Rose home when he saw Anna leave on their fancy doorbell camera. When he knew she was close he stabbed himself and made the phone call to set her up.'

'You're honestly saying that Luke Whitney died by suicide?'

'No,' I reply quickly. 'Well, not on purpose. I don't think for a second he expected to die. I think he planned to frame his wife for attempted murder. Maybe she had something on him that made divorcing her impossible, or maybe he just wanted her to really suffer for her affair.'

'As a surgeon I'm sure he thought he knew how to stab himself to avoid damage,' Kim says. 'He probably even used numbing cream or a local anaesthetic. Then he cleaned himself up and hid the tea towels and his shoes, hoping that the shoe print we found would insinuate another man had been there. If he'd lived he probably would have told us that he walked in on Anna and her lover at the cottage.'

As glad as I am that Kim is on board with my theory, I don't like her butting in and treading on my Poirot moment. Still, it's nice to have back-up for a change. Matthews, however, has gone slightly puce.

'What went wrong? How did he end up dead?'

'Maybe he went too deep? Got overconfident, rushed it. Something obviously went seriously wrong.'

'Why did Anna confess then?' Andy asks.

'For exactly the reason she told us. She thought that Pippa had stabbed Luke and she felt guilty. I don't think she has any idea that Luke tried to set her up for murder. His death was an accident.'

'Accidental death,' Matthews says. He looks like he's perking up slightly. 'Okay,' he says slowly. 'If the forensics fit I'm happy to drop the charges against Anna Whitney on the basis that Luke Whitney's death was an accident. Looks like you were right, Dance. Anna Whitney was innocent.'

Chapter Fifty-Three

Present

The clouds hung overhead, dishwater grey and pregnant with rain. As the people at the periphery of Luke's life dispersed from his graveside, scattering into their expensive cars to go and drink overpriced champagne in toast to a man none of them really knew, the only three women who knew him at all remained standing over the hole in the ground.

'A lovely service,' Rose noted, her voice low and her lips moving as little as possible. From her vantage point on the slight hill to the left DS Rebecca Dance probably wouldn't be able to make out a word that was said, but there was no way any of them were going to blow it at this point.

'Wasn't it?' Anna smiled. 'Luke hated funerals. He said the only person they would really matter to was too dead to see it. That people should show each other how they felt about one another more in life and they wouldn't feel the need for this overblown act of guilt at the end.'

'Well, he always was a pompous asshole,' Rose replied. The girl to her left let out a choked sob and slid a hand over the slight swell of a baby bump.

'I'm sorry, I... my driver is waiting.' Phillipa Kent turned and walked steadily away, like a drunk who was trying too hard to prove they were sober.

'We're going to have to keep an eye on her,' Rose said, turning her head so that DS Dance would have no view of her words. 'She's the weak link here, Anna. I think she actually loved him.'

'Of course she did,' Anna murmured. 'Which is why I've taken some precautions.'

Rose raised her perfect eyebrows. She had gone back to her dark hair and it suited her, Anna thought. 'Like what?'

'When Phillipa gets home she'll find Luke's watch in the footwell of her car. Covered in his blood. There's no way of her knowing what else I might have planted, or where. If she ever speaks to Dance, or any of the rest of the team for that matter, she'll find that there are several other pieces of evidence linking her to the crime.'

Rose smiled. 'I always knew you were clever,' she said. 'Can I assume there will be some equally damning evidence somewhere in my own home?'

'You can be as sure of that as I can be that you've taken your own precautions, Rose,' Anna said, her voice measured. 'We've both been Luke Whitney's wife, remember?'

'Yes,' Rose murmured, leaning close enough to Anna's ear that no listening device in the world could pick up what she was saying. 'But only one of us stabbed him to death.'

Chapter Fifty-Four

Anna

He could have convinced me not to do it. Even though I knew he'd been with Pippa that afternoon, and that he was buying her something expensive because he thought she'd aborted their baby and he needed to keep her sweet. Even though I now knew he had been with her *before* he'd found out about Ed, when he'd made me end things with my lover and promised it would be just the two of us from then on, before we'd seen her in the golf club when he'd sworn to me that he'd never met her before. I still might have forgiven him if he'd come clean and begged me to take him back, even knowing that Pippa had lied about the abortion and that my husband's baby was still growing inside her. I might have been weakened, had it not been for that photograph.

The house feels so empty without him. I'll sell up, of course, now that Luke's 'plan' has been revealed and our names have been cleared. I'll move away, start somewhere new as the widow of the man who tried to frame his wife for murder. And even the other two women involved in the plan will never know that Luke's death was anything more than a tragic mistake.

It had been Rose's idea – of course it had. For all the derision I felt towards her it turns out she was actually the cleverest of all of us. Of course, Luke wasn't supposed to die in her version, Rose loved him too much to suggest we kill him, but her idea of vengeance was definitely one best served cold. We were going to make it look like Luke was framing me for attempted murder. She made it sound so simple; stage the scene the day before, cut him shallow, then when he claimed I'd stabbed him, I would claim that I'd walked in and found him bleeding. My version of events would work better with Rose being seen in my car on the CCTV. Luke would be arrested. He'd lose everything, his friends, his career, maybe not his freedom – he'd probably get away with a suspended sentence – but I'd be forgiven for taking him to the cleaners in the divorce court, after all he tried to frame me for murder. And Luke would finally know how it felt to lose.

The day of the murder – because that's how it ended up of course – I arrived at the cottage at four pm just like I'd told the police, and left my coat in the car for Rose to wear. I closed the kitchen blinds, which offered the only view of my car from the kitchen, so that Luke wouldn't see that it was missing. While Rose was spending her evening driving back and forth in my car, speeding past the Gatso with only her blonde hair showing in order to establish my alibi, Pippa was sitting on Rose's bed chatting to some guy she'd been grooming on Tinder to provide Rose's alibi. Then she was going to go home and Zoom her friend Gemma to establish that she couldn't have been anywhere near the cottage. We had it all worked out.

I was the weak link. Pippa only had to make small talk with some old letch, Rose just had to drive a certain route in my car at a certain speed. I had to stab my husband.

I put the stew on with the ingredients Luke had bought from Waitrose. DS Dance was right, he wouldn't have had any clue what to get without my list, only I didn't mention the list because I wanted them to believe I'd surprised him, make it look like he'd been going to meet Pippa and I'd dropped in last minute. We'd mulled around for a bit, watched *Shutter Island* and had a few drinks. The film was just finishing when Luke began to rub my shoulders.

My body went rigid. After so many years with the same man I knew what this was – it was Luke's precursor to sex. Evidently he didn't see why me being there instead of Pippa had to change his plans for a dirty weekend away, we were completely interchangeable to him. As he leaned down to kiss my neck I still felt my resolve weaken. Things had been so great between us, it felt completely unfair that I had to give this up. Luke hadn't wanted Pippa to have the baby, so maybe that meant he wasn't going to leave me for her. He gave a small moan into my collarbone and I tipped my head back to give him better access to my neck. He shifted around so that he was facing me and he reached down to lift up my skirt. As he bent over I caught a flash of white sticking out of his back pocket.

'What's that?' I asked, shuffling backwards so that I was sitting up properly again. I needn't have asked though, I knew what it was I'd seen.

'What?' Luke asked, looking behind him to see what I was getting at.

'In your back pocket. What is it?'

He reached around to his back pocket looking genuinely curious, and pulled out a square photograph. Or to be more specific, a scan photo.

When had the little bitch done that? And why? Was she trying to tell him that she hadn't really aborted his baby? Or perhaps he already knew and they were setting me up. Maybe they were planning that I'd really go down for stabbing him? Maybe I was the one Rose was planning revenge on, and she'd used poor hapless Pippa to get it. Well fuck them.

Luke looked at the scan photo and his eyes widened. If I didn't know him better I could have sworn he was honestly shocked, but that was the problem with Luke, I did know him better. And I knew that meant he couldn't be trusted.

'What is it, Luke?' I asked. I was genuinely interested in hearing if he would tell me the truth or not, although the minute I saw what he had pulled from his pocket I knew that the evening would not be going ahead exactly to plan. I had been deceived, maybe just by Pippa or maybe by Rose too. I could no longer trust anyone but myself.

'I don't know where I've picked this up,' he said, tossing it onto the table. 'Probably the hospital.'

'You haven't been to the hospital today,' I said. His face reddened.

'Last time I wore these trousers then. Look, baby, it's late, shall we just go on up to bed?'

'Not feeling so frisky anymore?' I asked, my tone icy. 'Or are you just wanting rid of me so you can call Phillipa and ask her why your baby is still alive when she promised you she was going to get rid of it?'

He paled, but said nothing.

'Well?' I pushed. 'What lie are you going to tell next? Let me guess, it meant nothing, *she* meant nothing. Just another of our little games that you *forgot to tell me we were playing*, is that right?'

'Anna, I'm so sorry,' he sighed. 'I've told her it's over, this must be her way of getting back at me. It's only been six months, I think she did this to try and make me leave you. I think she's obsessed with you, you know, she only started taking your classes because you were my wife…'

'Liar,' I spat. 'Pippa started taking my classes twelve months ago.'

Luke frowned. 'What? Anna, I swear—'

'Save it,' I snapped, standing up and walking into the kitchen. I poured myself a glass of wine, hand shaking. I had no idea what was going on anymore. Had she really told him she'd got rid of the baby? And how long had they been together? He said six months, but she'd been in my yoga class for twelve. None of it was adding up, and I knew that the best idea would be just to ditch the plan altogether and just pack my things and leave, but then nothing would change, Luke would probably run off to be with his younger woman and me? I'd become Rose. Or worse… my father.

The broken bottle was on the counter top where I'd placed it ready earlier, concealed by a tea towel. Luke came towards me and I took a step back.

'Go away,' I warned him. 'Don't try and talk your way out of this one, Luke Whitney, you and your lies and your games. She came to see me, you know? Pippa.' I spat the name out and Luke looked stunned. 'Oh yes, didn't know that, did you? Her and Rose, quite the little pair now. Your long line of women scorned. Pippa hasn't killed your baby like you told her to. It's alive, and now everything is going to come out!'

I was shouting now, my voice raised hysterically, waving my hands like a mad woman. Luke grabbed my arm and tried to pull me towards him, maybe to calm me down or… what else? What was his plan, him and Pippa? Were they going to frame me… or kill me? Maybe I had unwittingly set the stage for my own murder.

I suppose you could say I wasn't thinking clearly, or perhaps I was thinking clearly for the first time in a long time, but as he yanked me towards him my fingers reached out to find the broken bottle. They closed around the neck and I pushed it forward – more just as a warning than to actually hurt him, but it sank into his stomach and almost instantly a red stain began to spread out from the wound.

Luke's eyes widened in shock. The blood was coming thick and fast. He held out his hand to me and muttered one word: 'Ambulance.'

There was *so much* blood. It pumped through my fingers, warm and slick as I pressed down on the gaping wound in his stomach, trying to undo what had already been set in motion. But it was too late, he was going to die. I wondered who I would be now, without my love for him, and without my hatred of him, both tethering me to life like an anchor. I still had a choice. I could keep the bottle in place, stem the blood flow, call for an ambulance – I could probably still save his life. Then a picture of me being taken away in handcuffs as Luke and Pippa walked off hand in hand, his other hand on her growing baby bump, formed in my mind, Rose smirking in court as I was sentenced to life in prison for attempted murder, and I pulled the bottle from his stomach, sealing his fate.

He did this to us, I forced myself to think, before I could allow myself to feel any regret. Regret was useless now, it wouldn't save his life, or mine. *It was his choices that led us here, not mine.*

A sound gurgled in his throat, like he was choking on his own saliva. Oh God, I couldn't bear it if he spat blood at me. This was too raw, too much.

'Luke?' I leaned in close to hear him speak. 'What is it?'

The flagstone floor was cold and hard underneath my knees. I had loved this floor. I'd loved everything about the holiday cottage in the Cotswolds, from the country style kitchen with its navy Farrow and Ball cupboards and thick oak worktops, to the black AGA that we'd used to dry our socks after muddy walks in the hills, and the copper pans that hung from the ceiling. It had all been so perfectly styled, like everything in Luke's life – from the outside. Even the indoor plants were fake, although they looked real until you got very, very close and realised they didn't smell, didn't rip if you crumpled them between your fingers.

'What is it?' I stroked his forehead and leaned in closer. 'Luke?'

His lips were next to my ear now and I expected to hear him say that he would always love me, no matter what I had done. I knew that he loved me, despite all that we had been through. He was mine and I was his, he had promised me that in the hills surrounding this very house more than once. There was only me, he'd said. Only me who'd mattered, anyway. But he'd been lying then like he lied every time, to all of us. He'd told all of us the same. One after the other we had been wound into his web of deceit. One of us had had to break the spell.

My silent tears rolled into his dark hair. *What have I done?*

'Game.' Luke's voice was hoarse, barely above a whisper. He coughed, a spray of blood hitting my cheek. 'Game over.'

Yes, it was almost over, but not quite. As his eyes closed I laid his head down on the cold floor. I had work to do.

Grabbing two of the tea towels I covered them in Luke's blood, trailing it to the sink and back, letting small droplets fly, trying to remember all of the steps I had to take to make it look as if Luke had staged this scene. I shoved the towels and Luke's shoes into bin bags and stuffed them into the shallow hole Rose had dug outside yesterday. Then I went back in and poured the wine we'd opened down the sink and cleaned my fingerprints off the Budweiser bottle. What was next?

I started to panic, heat rising in my cheeks. I had to work quicker than this, and yet I felt like I was forgetting something. My heart thumped uncomfortably, but I knew it was just because the time was near when I would have to play the recording I'd stored in Luke's iCloud Drive summoning the police and ambulance to the cottage, hanging up before they could ask me any questions that I'd have to use my real voice for. I'd used the house phone as Rose had instructed. Everything would point to him trying to frame me and me walking in at the last minute. When the police arrived I would admit to stabbing Luke and I would be arrested. And this whole plan would hinge on the police seeing through the staged crime scene and finding my alibi. Of course if they didn't then Rose would call in a sighting of 'me' driving too fast towards the cottage… unless she decided to double cross me. And she could, of course. Any of us could turn on the other in an instant. It was something I'd considered many times since, whether I might eventually have to kill the other two women involved, my partners in crime. Because three can keep a secret, if two of them are dead.

Chapter Fifty-Five

Present

She waited until everyone had left the grounds of the crematorium and it was completely empty before making her way over to the other grave. She twisted the ring – the one Luke Whitney had given to Laura Kent – from her right hand and slipped it off.

'I did it, sweetheart,' she said, lifting the small urn from next to the golden plaque on the wall. She slipped the ring inside, hearing the clink as it hit the bottom of the urn, then replaced the flowers inside. 'Just like I promised.'

It had been too long since she was last here – with the investigation it would have been too risky. It still was risky, but she hadn't been able to resist visiting one last time. Weeds and grass clung to the headstone practically obscuring the words *Laura Jessica Kent*.

'*We* did it.' The voice came from behind her, making her jump.

'Jesus.' She turned to see Pippa was walking towards her. 'I thought you'd gone.'

'I had the driver wait around the corner. I wanted to say thank you. I couldn't have got away with all this without your help.'

'I just steered them in the direction we needed them to go. At least now she can rest.'

'I hope so.'

The woman held out her hand. 'Do you have it?'

Pippa pulled the photo out of her bag, the last photograph of Laura and her friends, and the thing that had almost given the entire game away the day DS Dance had been to her house and picked it up to look at it. Pippa handed it to DS Kim Beckford. 'I wish we didn't have to burn it. She looks so happy.'

'She was happy,' Kim said, running her finger over the photograph, lingering on the spot where she and Laura stood in the middle of the group, arms around one another, huge smiles on their faces. 'Until she met him, she was so happy, Pip, try to remember that. She was the best person I knew.'

'Thank you again,' Pippa whispered, tears forming in her eyes. 'For everything. I don't know how I would have done any of this without you. I know what you've risked.'

'The other two have no idea?' Kim asked. 'They still think it was because of the baby?'

'Rose has figured out who I was,' Pippa said. 'She'd looked Laura up a few years ago and she saw the resemblance as soon as I turned up. She has no idea who you are though, I promise.'

'I need it to stay that way, Pip. If anyone finds out I know you and I didn't disclose it I won't just lose my job, the whole case will be reopened. We could both go to prison.'

Pippa made the sign of the cross over her heart. 'I'll never tell a soul, I promise. You were the best friend she had, Kim. I'll never forget that. I don't know how to repay you.'

Kim lifted a hand and smoothed a stray hair away from Pippa's face. She looked so much like Laura that it was hard sometimes for Kim to even look at her without her heart breaking. Laura hadn't just been the best person Kim had ever known, she had been the yin to her yang, like a soulmate without the sex. But that was before Luke Whitney had taken her away from them all. Oh, she knew that Laura had made the decision to take her life by herself, but her confidence, her spark, everything she was had been chipped away by that man and even then it wasn't enough. He had left her heartbroken and unable to see a way out. When Pippa had gone to her and asked for her help at first she'd told her to stop whatever she was planning and forget Luke Whitney ever existed. But when the opportunity of a transfer had come up closer to Laura's little sister, Kim had taken it, just to keep an eye on her, the way Laura would have wanted. Only she'd dropped the ball, believed Pippa when she said she'd called things off with Luke, and Pippa had found herself pregnant and desperate. And Kim knew that there was only one way to stop Luke Whitney from ruining another woman's life, and another, and another. She had made a promise on Laura's grave that she would look after Pippa, but now she had done as much as she could do.

Kim took a lighter from her pocket and held it to the corner of the photograph, letting the flame take hold and spread before dropping it to the floor. The photograph curled and disintegrated into ash, eventually burning itself out.

'You need to forget you ever knew me,' DS Beckford said, her eyes filling with tears. 'That's how you repay me. You can never contact me again, Pippa, I'm so sorry.'

Pippa nodded. 'Don't worry, I understand,' she said, picking her handbag up off the floor. 'If that's the price I have to pay, so be it. At least he's gone now. It's over.'

Acknowledgements

I'm going to do these backwards this time because after ten or eleven books writing acknowledgements gets a bit samey. So first, THANK YOU to my husband, Ash, for putting up with me for so long, and for recognising when a deadline must be looming and hiding the breakables.

To my kids, Connor and Finlay. It will never cease to amaze me how many towels you can use in a week. Thanks in advance for the very nice retirement village you will be paying for me and your dad to live in. Joke's on you.

To Gail, thanks for being Finn's spare mum and for being an amazing friend. To Sarah, Lorna, Jo, Laura and Andy, who are always there when I need you, along with my mum and dad, mother-in-law, and my ever-patient aunty Jo who gets more of my irate phone calls than any person should have to deal with. And Kat Diamond, Susi Holliday and Lucy Dawson, for people who maim and murder daily you're really very nice and I'm very lucky to have you all.

To everyone at Canelo, starting with Alicia Pountney and Louise Cullen, who together are an absolute dream team (and Alicia you will check this for me, right?). To Hannah Bond, Miranda Ward, Becca Allen and the rest of the team, thank you so very much.

To my readers, without whom this job would be a hobby. Your messages of support mean the absolute world to me and remind me how lucky I am to be able to make shit up for a living and get paid for it. I really do appreciate it. And to the independent bookshops, especially Booka and The Berwyn Bookshop, who support so many authors. We love you for it.

So last, to my long-suffering agent, Laetitia Rutherford. Ten years of putting up with my ridiculous questions and my shiny new idea syndrome. Lucky for you I mostly know what you would say in reply to my emails now so I send them to myself and save you the bother of telling me to just focus on the book I'm actually contracted to write.

Also at Watson, Little, thank you Ciara McEllin, whose emails are my favourite ever and Annie Ku (sorry both about the tax forms, I'm never actually going to get quicker at those) and Rachel Richardson, who makes sure my books get to readers all around the world.

If I've missed anyone, the error is, as always, Alicia Pountney's.